GEORGE BUTLER

GEORGE BUTLER

A

NOVEL

C.B. LESTON

Library of Congress Control Number:		2013917773
ISBN:	Hardcover	978-1-4931-0814-5
	Softcover	978-1-4931-0813-8
	Ebook	978-1-4931-0815-2

Rev. date: 09/28/2013

To order additional copies of this book, contact:
Xlibris LLC
0-800-056-3182
www.xlibrispublishing.co.uk
Orders@xlibrispublishing.co.uk
306998

Contents

CHAPTER 1

Stargazing

When George Butler was ten, his parents gave him for his birthday a quarter-scale working model of a tractor identical in all but size to those used in their building company. It came complete with a full set of attachments and a petrol engine enabling him to drive around the extensive gardens of his home to his heart's content.

Specially made to order, this was no ordinary present, even for parents as wealthy as the Butlers. But they were purchasing peace of mind. Anything to divert George from his dangerous desire to drive a site tractor was worth the money. And had they known just how long George would hang on to the tractor, they would have thought it good value at any price.

Hardly a day passed, rain or shine, without the tractor being taken from its shed and revved into action. 'He may not be good at books', George's parents would tell their visitors, 'but he has his skills.' Modesty forbade them from going any further, but they had also noticed that the tractor brought out something else in George.

Determined as he was to spend as much time as he could at the wheel, when friends came round to try their skills, he was unstinting in his generosity in handing over the controls. Precisely what this might lead to eluded them, but it encouraged their hopes that he might be developing leadership qualities.

But that was not what was in George's mind. One day, he innocently thought, they will invite me to drive their tractors. His life was a good life and so he assumed, life must be for all his friends. And not just for now but forever.

At fifty, George still had the tractor, complete with its shed, although he was not quite sure why. It was great fun to give driving lessons to the children of friends who came to visit. No child ever went away disappointed with its day.

But at heart, he suspected that he kept the tractor as a memento of how kind life had been to him. The Lord had certainly given him his share of the good things. Was the Lord now about to take them away?

He stood on the driveway of the Old Hall gazing at the stars whilst trying to recall the forgotten art of prayer. The most he could manage was, 'Lord help us.'

Remembering his childhood faith, George knew that he had not always been so inhibited. There were no uncertainties then as to whether or not there were angels in the heavens and demons in the underworld and a fatherly god keeping watch over all he had created. Alas, those days of innocence had been lost in the bewilderments of teenage years and a gradual slide to the mental comfort of being agnostic. The older he had become, the more content he was to leave the search for the meaning of life to others.

But what he needed now was a miracle, some helping hand to make his last desperate attempt to escape from the city a success. So many things could go wrong. So many lives could be ruined or even lost. Was he leading his wife and friends to homelessness and starvation? Was he leading them into criminal activity for which, if caught, there might be no mercy? He feared the worst, but they must not know it. They had put their trust in him. But was he up to it?

Overshadowing everything else in George's mind was recognition that it was his error of judgment, which had landed them all in their present dire predicament. Together, worried about the future, they had put in years of prudent planning for a lifestyle change should one become necessary. Yet when their worst fears were realised and the time to move came, it had been his decision as leader of the group to delay their departure. Just one day too many, and this was the outcome.

George took a few steps down the driveway and then, with his head lifted up to the sky, began a slow perambulation around the four stolen ambulances that occupied most of the roadway within the estate's small group of houses. Gleaming in the starlight, they looked more like giant props on a stage set than part of the realities of everyday life.

But there were no floodlights for this stage, there was only starlight. The city lights had gone, and in their place had come the stars. Such bright stars, bringing back long forgotten memories of childhood and of evenings spent gazing in wonderment at the scale and mysteries of it all.

That was when they lived in the countryside. How simple life had been then. And what a price had been paid for life in the city.

Suddenly, it was beginning to come back to him. He could remember Sunday mornings, sitting on the hard, wooden church bench, his parents on either side. He could remember the prayer, not all of it, just bits of it. 'Give us this day our daily bread.' He could remember trying to work it out. Why were they praying to the Lord for their daily bread? It came from the bakers! And it was good bread! So much mystery! But nothing to bother about; next Sunday would come soon enough.

Strange, thought George, it slipped my mind and I never sought out the answer. Even now I still don't know the answer. Yet it must mean something, different things perhaps, to different people. Not much point in praying for bread if you live on fruits in the jungle. Not much point in relying on the Lord when hunger and poverty is all you have got and all you are ever going to get.

Perhaps it's all about hope. Hope that somehow, somewhere, someone will give you that which you need to survive. Not bread necessarily, just something. That would be his prayer.

The Lord wouldn't mind that he didn't really believe in him, not many people did in this modern world. It was all so perplexing now that the astronomers measured the scale of the universe in millions of light years and claimed to know of millions of stars. Even the Lord would have been hard pressed to create a universe so gigantic in seven days.

And so George prayed. What more could he do? He had no control over the events that were destroying his life's work and his life's dreams. It was beginning to look as though no one had control. Nor was he responsible for the nation's downfall. And it was a certainty that those who were responsible were never going to admit it.

Yet the events were not precipitated by wild forces of nature or by the unavoidable and unforeseeable perils of life's existence. These events had been prophesied and debated. They were the inevitable result of decisions made and actions taken.

Yes, someone was responsible. But it was too late now for playing the blame game. Time was running out, and tonight was to be his last night at the Old Hall. Tomorrow morning, they must leave come what may. He wouldn't mention the ambulances in his prayer. The less said about them, the better.

And whilst the stargazing, while George was praying outside his house in the city, far away in the countryside province of Bowland an elderly retired couple were praying for him, gazing at the same stars and wondering what had become of him. Where was he, where were the others, and were the others still with him? He should have been here days ago. Things were not looking good.

Nothing was looking good for anyone. But none of John and Mary's prayers were for themselves. Their ship of state had sunk, but they at least had reached dry land. Others were still in the water. They were the ones in need of prayers.

Of course, it would be nice to have electricity, live phones, and television again, but they could live without them. It would be nice to know that their future was secure with money in the bank and regular pension incomes, but they would learn to manage without them. Yes, there would be hardships, they knew that, but in their quiet and peaceful valley, they had safety. That counted for a lot, more than a lot. Perhaps that was everything.

No point then in self-pity. Prayers for themselves would have deserved rejection. The Lord had better things to do looking after those in real need.

And behind it all, there was the nagging feeling of guilt. What part had they played in all this? They had joined the partying like all the rest. They should have known better. In the end, someone was going to have to pay for the life they had all enjoyed. Was it bad luck, or just desserts, that it happened to be their generation?

On the upper balconies of a plush five-star hotel high in the mountains above Lake Geneva, there were other stargazers, men in sharp suits taking a break from the all-night emergency discussions that had brought them together. Throughout the day, they had flown into Geneva from all over the world in a succession of lavishly equipped private jets.

The world's media was not on hand to film and photograph their arrival, and the world's media would know nothing of their departure. Their wealth ensured that they were spirited in and spirited out of airports and cities throughout the world in absolute secrecy. These were the men who owned and controlled the trillions of dollars lodged safe in offshore tax havens, away from the hands of financial authorities, regulators, and tax collectors.

They were not in Geneva to pray. They were there to try to resolve a dilemma of their own making, the dilemma of assuming responsibilities, which needed more than money to be deliverable. Entirely unintentionally, they had stepped into the Lord's shoes. People were now praying to them for their daily bread. Their financial wizardry in transferring to themselves the wealth of nations was backfiring. The warning signs that they were killing off the geese that laid the golden eggs were all around. Self-interest had driven them to experiment with philanthropy, but they were beginning to learn that money was not everything.

CHAPTER 2

The Old Hall

George's grandfather, a builder of some repute, had acquired the Old Hall, dilapidated and unoccupied, in the purchase of farming land on the then outskirts of the city. Like his father before him, he was an avid purchaser of land. It was not that he wanted to farm it. He had no desire to spend his life behind a plough and even less desire to rise before dawn to milk cows and feed pigs. He was simply motivated by the logic of the old adage, 'Buy land, the Lord has stopped making it.'

He was never in a hurry to build, and all but a modest amount of his land was tenanted. He was happy just to see his family's name in the title deeds, content in the knowledge that whatever became of the land, eventually it would always be worth more than what it cost to buy.

For him, the right time to build would come when it would come, and for much of the land he had inherited or purchased, that time never came in his lifetime. But as the city spread ever outwards, becoming a sprawling metropolis, attracting people from all over the world, the wisdom of the family's land purchases became more and more apparent, year after year.

When George's father, Robert, took over as head of the family business in his mid-forties, he grasped the opportunities for expansion created by rapidly expanding city suburbs with relish. Within a generation, Butler & Son, 'Family Builders' became Butler Developments Limited 'House Builders for the Nation'.

But still, the Old Hall stood empty in its five acres of neglected gardens and woodlands, its broken windows and crumbling roof attracting nothing but the pigeons and the bats. Only its high brick perimeter wall and stout entrance gates saved it from suffering even worse fate at the hands of scavengers and vandals. Internally, little was left to show that once it had been the stately home of a colliery owner who, anxious to make his mark in society, had turned a large working farm into a gentleman's estate, building on it a ten-bedroom mansion and landscaping the grounds with trees, lawns, and ponds to a standard that which received commendation from all gifted the pleasure of strolling the grounds.

For two generations, the mansion served its purpose as a prosperous businessman's residence, but then, as the coal seams dwindled and fortunes declined, bit by bit the land was sold off to adjacent farmers eventually leaving only the deteriorating mansion and two hundred acres or so of farmland. When that came up for sale as a job lot, it was snapped up by Robert's acquisitive father as another useful addition to the Butlers' burgeoning land bank.

As the years went by, thousands of houses were built by the Butlers on the once-productive farmland of the colliery owner's estate, creating a new city suburb. Most of the housing was intended for the city's rapidly expanding middle classes, but some avenues of fine detached houses for the wealthy were built on the more attractive parts of the land. In recognition of the historic name of the land, the suburb was called, somewhat ironically considering its changed usage, Glebe Pastures.

Much of this urban development took place under Robert's management of the company, and it was to Robert that all questions on the future of the Old Hall were directed. But even advancement of the housing estates towards the very boundaries of the Old Hall did not produce any firm answers from him. Nor did anything halt the hall's decay.

To many, this apparent neglect of the building and neglect of its obvious development potential seemed a mystery. But Robert was no fool, and it was not lost on Robert that this was a very desirable plot gradually inching its way towards what would eventually become regarded as being close proximity to the city centre.

Robert had never been tempted by the thought of making the Old Hall his family home. He was a man of the country, a shooting man, a racing man, and a man with the wealth and good fortune to live life as a country squire. And this he did with admirable style but without a shred of the pomposity that normally went with the role.

He purchased and renovated an old country manor house and, over the years, turned the neglected gardens into a national treasure, open to the public for charitable purposes. On his untimely death and that of his wife in an aeroplane crash when returning from their holiday home in Switzerland, the house and gardens became a hospice for sick children, a bequest that touched the nation.

But, although not interested in renovating and living at the Old Hall, Robert was never disposed to sell it. He toyed with various ideas for turning it into a hotel, a nursing home, a conference centre, and even as the office headquarters for Butler Developments. And any of these might have come to fruition but for his apparent reluctance to become involved in tedious debate with local officials on resolving the various planning restrictions which had become attached to the property. Years later, it occurred to George that his father might always have had it in mind that the future of the Old Hall should be for him to decide when eventually he took over the business.

George was not an academic child, but as the only child in a wealthy family, his obvious preference for sports over studies was accepted by his parents without concern. One day, he would take over the family business and educational achievement would not be the key to the managing director's door.

And George, blessed by the advantage that his unusually large size gave him over others of his age, was good at sports, very good. Without effort, the captaincy of this team, and that team, came to him. And without fail, he repaid the honours with his enthusiasm for teamwork and his aptitude for improving his skills. The possibility of successful life as a professional sportsman was evident from his mid-teens but George was not tempted. Life in the building trade had been in the family's blood for generations, and it was very much in his.

When George revealed in his final year at school that he had set his sights on obtaining a degree in business studies, his parents gave him full support, notwithstanding their hidden concerns that, given his amiable nature, George might easily be led down the wrong path at university. They arranged private tuition for his entrance examinations and went to the expense of buying an apartment close to the university for him in the belief that halls of residence were drug-fuelled sinks of iniquity.

They need not have worried. George cruised through his exams and settled down to his degree studies with the same enthusiasm that he had always shown for sports.

To his parents this was something of a surprise. But in reality, it was no more than blossoming of character. George was determined that, whatever he did, he would do it well. And he had the good sense to realise that this meant concentrating on the goals that mattered to him. He knew that to retain his place as a first team rugby player, to retain his reputation as a scratch golfer, and to get a good degree, little time could be given to leading a wild life of any sort.

There was one other steadying influence in his life. In his final year at university, George fell in love. Frances, the object of his besotted attention, was another third-year undergraduate, an arts student with a string of admirers wholly in keeping with her looks. Unbeknown at first to George, these concealed a steely single-minded personality.

She knew what she wanted in life, and she had been keeping her eye on George for the best part of a year. He was big, handsome, reputedly rich, and a charmer with all the confidence his background bestowed. A big pussycat was how her female friends described him. And they were not far from being right, although that was not how opponents on the rugby field described him.

Yes, she could fall in love with George, and she did. Three years later, they were married. They settled into one of the grander houses built in the city by the Butlers, made many friends, and as George's predestined rise in his family's business progressed, Frances steadily developed her own career as a publishing executive.

When, in his late twenties, George was appointed commercial director of Butler Developments, he was attracted to the Old Hall like a moth to a flame. Situated off the Avenue, a road of fine houses built by the Butlers and regarded by many as the city's premier address, it was approached by an impressive private tree-lined driveway. Set part way down the driveway but well back from the Avenue, a pair of magnificent, wrought iron gates stood between stately pillars in the high brick wall which encompassed the estate. Stone faced, and of classical design, the Old Hall had the potential to be a very attractive residence for any man of means and social standing.

And unlike his father and his grandfather, George was not unhappy with city life. He liked the countryside, he liked country pursuits, but taking all things into account, he liked the city better. It had more amenities, more of a social buzz, and more opportunities to meet people and make friends. A quieter country life could wait until retirement.

George enjoyed doing what his father, Robert, had little interest in doing, battling with the planning authorities. As Robert saw it, he and his father before him had worked tirelessly to provide the housing developments the city needed. They had done the city proud and deserved better than bureaucratic obstruction of the proposals they put forward for development of the Old Hall site.

So it was left for George to take things forward. And for him, with his charm and persuasion, his contacts and his reputation, it was not difficult to get his own way. 'You want to restore the Old Hall to its former glory and to build within the grounds five, upmarket detached houses suitable for city professionals? Well, why not; that sounds like a very good proposal. We wish you every success Mr Butler.'

CHAPTER 3

The Residents

George took his time with the project. The next five years were spent on meticulous restoration work, which, he persuaded his father, was good for the company in bringing back into the business traditional skills and craftsmanship and in creating a new historic buildings renovation division.

Throughout that time, he was also gradually working towards obtaining his father's consent to transfer the ownership of the Old Hall Estate from the company and into his own name. Construction of the new houses advanced in pace with the restoration. George had no intention of selling the houses before he took occupation of the Old Hall, and the relentless price inflation of the time was a strong disincentive to putting anything on the market. The longer one delayed the sale, the greater the return.

All this suited George very well. It gave him time to discretely circulate news of the development without rushing into sale contracts. And George wanted not only time to build but time to choose his purchasers. His expectation was that business friends, golf club, and rugby club friends would provide a pool of prospective hopefuls. He was not disappointed. None of the houses ever came on to the open market, and George assembled in the estate a little colony of friends with himself as chieftain.

The Williams family got plot 1. Neil, still in his thirties, but already a prosperous lawyer with his own expanding practice, had been a childhood friend. They went to primary school together, to grammar school together, and then on to university together. George saw Neil as an academic version of himself, a hard worker, ambitious in everything but always with the dreams of a sporting enthusiast. Neil could not match George's golfing skills or his exploits on the rugby field, but he had the edge at snooker.

But competition between George and Neil, such as it was, never came in the way of what seemed certain to be a lifelong friendship. There was no outward envy on either side, although secretly George envied the obvious joy Neil and his wife, Jean, had in their twin girls.

He and Frances seemed destined to miss out on parenthood. They had tried everything and failed. They had contemplated adoption, but after days and nights of nervous discussions, they had put off the final steps. Gradually, they became settled into their own busy lives; he with business and sports, Frances with her time-consuming career, her tennis, bridge, and the horses she kept at paddocks on the outskirts of the city.

The house on plot 2 went to Robin and Janet Harvey, a quiet couple in their mid-sixties. Robin, a retired bank manager, was a golfing stalwart, proud of his rise to captaincy of the golf club and his high standing as a man never known to turn down any proffered chairmanship, remunerated or otherwise. When George, as a teenager, had taken an interest in the game, it was Robin who had taken him under his wing and steered his progress to top of the club rankings.

Janet owned and ran a small consultancy business. She and Frances had a lot of common interests and professional links. When consigned to the role of golf widows, they liked nothing more than setting off together for shopping trips and culture events. Like George and Frances, the Harveys were also childless, but they gave the impression that this was by choice. With their busy lifestyles and multitude of recreational interests, it was difficult to envisage how they could have coped with children.

The Rigby family took plot 3. They were sociable, cheerful, and extremely active in their recreational interests. Bill, the father, had inherited a haulage business on his own father's early death, and everything about Bill suggested that he intended to live life to the full just in case he suffered the some misfortune.

Although small in stature, Bill, like his father before him, was addicted to rugby. His size had confined him to midfield positions as a player, but his ability for quick-thinking manoeuvres had made him a top-class player. It was not until he reached his forties and decided to settle down and get married that he turned to refereeing instead of playing.

Bill was in his mid-twenties when the precocious fifteen stone, 15-year-old giant George, came on the scene. George, determined to learn the game's skills at the speed he was growing, astutely enrolled Bill as one of his tutors. This was done without formality and without so much as a request or by-your-leave. It just happened or seemed to just happen. Looking back, Bill often marvelled at how easily he had been drawn into the role. Nevertheless, the two became very good friends, and George was delighted to have him as a neighbour on the Old Hall Estate.

Bill and his wife, Carol, fifteen years his junior, had three children, all bright, rumbustious, and self-confident. Bringing them up was more than enough as a full-time task, and Carol had never wished to be anything other than a happy housewife. Before meeting Bill, she had worked as a secretary, but looking after a home and children was her obvious destiny in life.

It took Frances a little time to establish a close friendship with Carol; their personalities could not have been more different, but once established, they got on surprisingly well together. More than once, Frances confided to George that the energy the Rigbys brought to the estate was one of its great attractions.

Peter and Anne Robinson were the youngest couple to move into the estate. They bought the house on plot 4. Both in their late twenties, they ran a prosperous dental practice, which they had fortuitously acquired from its retiring owner. Their family plans were at an early stage, on ice until their careers and business plans were more fully developed.

Anne was one of Frances' first cousins, and their family ties had always been close. Their mothers were twin sisters of the sort who seemed ever to remain joined together offspring. The two daughters were moving in the same direction.

The oldest couple to move into the estate, John and Mary Rainford, also had family connections with the Butlers. John was George's uncle on his mother's side. When John informed his old friend Robert Butler that he was nearing retirement from his career in the army and that he was looking for a nice house in the city where he hoped to make contacts for directorships and the like, Robert ensured that he was put on the shortlist of potential purchasers.

John had been fortunate that throughout his career, Mary had followed him around, filling all spare time she had by writing romantic novels. Some of these had provided more financial return than she had ever contemplated, and it was only with her money that their move to the Old Hall Estate had been possible.

John and Mary settled in well with the younger families on the estate. They had led interesting lives, they knew lots of people, and they brought with them the relaxed participation in communal living ingrained in those who have spent much of their lives in the comfort of a well-managed officer's mess.

They had only one child, their son, Graham. Married with two young children, he lived with his wife, Rebecca, on the far side of the city. It would not have offended John and Mary in the least to be described as doting grandparents; they would have taken it as an accolade. Few weekends passed without a trip across the city or a family lunch at the estate.

For fifteen years, life at the estate had been as good as anything George could have dreamed of. Fifteen years! Fifteen years, thought George, as he slowed to a halt on his perambulation around the ambulances. Was that how long they had all been together? He could not get this out of his mind. What good times they had been—dinner parties, garden parties, sporting outings, and sometimes holidays.

His plans for the little estate could not have worked better. He had established a small community of his dreams, and throughout those fifteen years, they had stayed together until six months ago when Neil sold his practice and moved to Canada with his family. That had knocked a hole in George's heart; the suddenness, the finality of things, and the aching thought that Neil was doing the right thing, getting out when the going was still good.

If only they had all taken Neil's lead. If only all had gone except Frances and himself. That might not have been so bad. But they had not. The rest had stayed, putting faith in a plan he had devised and putting faith in his judgment as to when it should be activated. And now the burden of responsibility was crushing him. He should have led them out when there was still time. One day's delay, and it had come to this.

So many lives in his hands. And so many risks in tomorrow's journey. A miracle was needed. But was the Lord listening? And what of John and Mary? How were they coping, alone and away from home, looking after the remote property in Bowland on which all their fallback hopes had rested?

CHAPTER 4

The Farm

George need not have worried about John and Mary. They were as shell-shocked as the rest of the nation at what had happened, but they had made it to a safe haven. And to them, it was not remote. Much of their time in the three years since they bought the holiday cottage at the farm had been spent there. It had become a well-used second home. And with the village of Lostock only a mile away and the half hour trip to St Jude seeming shorter each time, they made it, the early feelings of being a bit cut off had long since been forgotten.

The last week had been a nightmare for them, as it had for everyone else. But quite unexpectedly, they now felt more at home than ever before. They had become part of a village community. John had enrolled in the 'home guard' as he liked to call it and was already in charge of organising duty rosters for the newly installed barrier on the village street.

Mary had been recruited to serve on the newly constituted village committee for fruit and vegetable management. They were even beginning to wonder whether they would welcome the restoration of television and telephone services. And yet, without some form of telephone link, how would they ever find out what had happened to George and the other residents of the Old Hall Estate.

It was four days since George had called to say that they were all on their way. Log fires, food, and drinks had been prepared in the farmhouse to welcome their arrival. But no one had arrived, and no word of their whereabouts had reached them.

After two sleepless nights, John had set off in his car with the intention of driving all the way back to the city if that had to be done to find them. He got no further than the toll booth on the estuary bridge at Stourmouth. Only five days earlier, he had crossed without incident on the way to the farm, but now guards and armed troops stood at the barriers.

John explained the nature of his journey. He was going to the city to look for lost friends. The soldiers were polite but blunt. All routes in and out of the city were closed, all traffic on main roads around the city was controlled; he was wasting valuable petrol on a fruitless journey. He should go back to St Jude.

John was not disposed to argue. If he was having difficulty getting out of Bowland, what sort of chance would he have of getting back in?

As he drove back to the farm, John tried to make sense of what was going on. The army appeared to be in control of the country, but no strutting general had appeared on television to declare his leadership of the nation. No columns of trucks and tanks were rolling through the countryside towards the capital. And he knew from experience that the army had neither the means nor the motivation to take over the government. After a lifetime of service as a dedicated officer, he was as well placed as anyone to know that.

So if it wasn't a military takeover, what was it? The army was certainly doing a good job in Buckland. Within days of the power going off and the panic setting in, they had restored calm, visiting every town and village, setting up local guards and committees, distributing ration books, and providing reassurance that normal life would soon be resumed. They had been courteous, helpful, and well organised. Without their presence, who knows what would have happened?

But there was no getting away from it. They must have had a pre-prepared plan. Perhaps the power and telephone cut-offs were all part of that plan, part of a black-out to keep people in the dark until some drama, yet to be revealed, took place. How very strange to think that Borovia's little army could be involved in such a plan. But who was pulling the strings? John was no nearer to the answers when he got back to the farm.

Mary took his news of the day better than he had expected. She had been preparing herself for some really bad news, so no news was something of an improvement. They were still talking over the events of the day when Graham and Rebecca with the grandchildren came round to join them for the evening meal. It was becoming a regular routine.

Much as Graham and Rebecca were relieved to be out of the city, and much as they regarded living in George's spare holiday cottage as living in luxury, they were still in a state of shock at their enforced move. But just to be sitting round a table with John and Mary, all of them together, was better than any medicine.

It was not easy though to pretend that all was normal. And for Graham and Rebecca, it was desperately difficult. They had been working so hard to achieve the hopes and dreams they shared for the future of the family: the move to a bigger house, the purchase of a holiday home in the sun, university places for the children. What had become of those? Everything was ruined, and they might never even get back to their own home again.

Despondency was disguised as best it could, but it was always just below the surface. John and Mary knew it, the children knew it, but keeping a stiff upper lip was not always easy. And so another evening had to be passed with artificially upbeat conversation about new schools, new places to visit, and new friends to be made.

When dinner was over and John and Mary were alone again, they left the cottage for their now-familiar evening stroll around the farm. The peace was so complete that to talk would have been unthinkable. But they had a lot to think about, the family, George, the others, and the strange phenomena of not having even a shred of certainty about what the next day would bring. And so they strolled and stood, stood and strolled, saying nothing whilst gazing at the valley's wondrous display of glittering stars. Each knew what the other was thinking. Each knew that the other was praying. When the gin and tonics they were carrying were finished, they went back inside the cottage to sit with recharged glasses and reminisce.

They thought back over the old times and how quickly things had changed. Dinner parties to disaster in fifteen years. No longer would there be the knock on the door and the invitation to the Old Hall gardens for an impromptu evening partying on champagne brought home by George in the boot of his Range Rover. No longer would there be the splendid dinners laid on by Frances in the grandeur of the Hall's magnificent dining room. No longer would they all set off in style from the Old Hall in a hired motor coach for a day at the races in the Butler's private box. But they had all seen it coming.

The once cheerful dinner chatter about holidays abroad, second homes, and the increasing value of their investments gave way, as the years passed, to worried concerns on the deteriorating job prospects for the younger generations, the rising costs of nursing home care for the elderly, and the gloomy deterioration of the nation's finances. The stability of years past was slipping away, and all they could do was watch it happen.

And yet they had all wondered, did they really believe that the impending doom they so earnestly discussed was actually going to happen? No, things were too comfortable for that. Life was going on as normal, and there was still plenty of money around. Getting a table at a good city-centre restaurant was still as difficult as ever. Driving anything less than a top-of-the-range imported car was taken as a sign of poverty. The wealth of the nation was on show for everyone to see.

If change was going to come, it would not come suddenly. It would be a slow process, carefully controlled by the authorities. The politicians would see to that. They were the ones in charge, and they were confident that the nation was simply going through a temporary downturn, a slip on the road to ever-increasing living standards. Recovery was on its way, or would be, as soon as growth was restored.

But still, the niggling doubts had remained. Why was the nation living on borrowed money? The whole of the Western world seemed to be living on borrowed money. Could it be that the politicians were simply buying votes on borrowed money? Could it be that the affluence of the western world was on the wane and that for years, it had been nothing more than the sham of the bankrupt spendthrift? Who would know what was reality, and when would they know? How close were they to the edge of the precipice, and how much time would they have to adjust to some new economic reality? Should they trust the optimists who said that everything would turn out all right or the pessimists who said they should prepare for the worst? In the end they, had backed both horses. They'd looked over the edge, hadn't liked what they had seen, but concluded it was out of their hands. They would carry on as usual, but they would put in place a fallback plan. They had George to thank for that.

One evening, still well remembered by John and Mary three years after the event, the conversation at dinner had taken a particularly sombre tone. They had been discussing why it was that governments of wealthy nations such as theirs needed to borrow and what would happen if no one wanted to lend. Would they be able to pay for the imported food needed to feed their own overcrowded country, and would they be able to pay for the imported fuel and power supplies they all relied upon?

Then someone had asked, 'What would happen to the people who only have state pensions or welfare benefits if the government runs out of money, would they starve?'

Silence had descended. There was much shuffling of napkins and fiddling with cutlery whilst everyone, heads down, conjured up something to say that would not reveal the unspeakable thought that perhaps they might starve.

George had retrieved the situation. 'It will never come to that no matter how bad things get. But it makes you think. Just supposing that one day we all wake up to find that we have no power, no fuel, and nothing like enough food to feed the nation. Where would you rather be, in the city or in the countryside? I know which I would prefer. Perhaps the time has come to go beyond simply talking about our worries. Perhaps we should have a fallback plan.'

'What about emigrating', Neil had suggested, 'before we all go down with the ship.'

They had stayed late that evening. They talked long and hard about the possibilities and difficulties of emigrating and the less drastic option of buying properties abroad to use as bolt-holes. Some were quite taken by the idea of starting a new life abroad, but for most, emigration was a step too far. The idea of second homes abroad attracted more support.

They were well embroiled in the pros and cons of foreign property purchases when George, who for once had been unusually quiet, entered the conversation. 'We could have a bolt—hole here in our own country, a sort of self-sufficient rural retreat, somewhere safe where we can look after ourselves if everything really does fall apart. Between us,

I'm sure we could raise the funds to buy something. Let's ponder on the possibilities and talk about this again in a few weeks.'

They had all left the Old Hall that night with minds reeling. Was it really necessary to prepare for the worst? Was the nation really on the road to ruin? Why not just sit it out and wait to see what happens?

But still, a few weeks later at their next get-together, they had slipped easily into discussion on the merits of doing something rather than doing nothing and the possibilities that might be open to them. And so it went on for some months.

It was pure chance that eventually led to purchase of the farm at Lostock, although Mary was more than pleased with her part in finding somewhere that was of immediate attraction and obviously worthy of further study. Situated in a small valley in the south-west province of Bowland but only ten miles from the attractive fishing and sailing port of St. Jude, the farm met all the requirements of a dream bolt-hole, land, isolation, a fine, old farmhouse, and a set of six, well-built holiday cottages.

She and John had spent a pleasant week at one of the cottages, and on learning from the owner's wife that the entire property was likely to be put up for sale, she had taken it upon herself to suggest that she knew a prospective purchaser who could act very speedily. John, although surprised at Mary's initiative, had not been displeased, and it was agreed that he would discreetly pass the details on to George to see how he responded.

'Thanks for that,' George had said. 'But don't mention it to the others just yet. I'd like to have a look myself before flying any kites. But I must say that it sounds interesting. I'll have a word with Frances to see if she fancies a trip to Bowland this weekend. Here's hoping this farm is all you say it is.'

On his return, George had wasted no time in going round for a chat with John and Mary. 'What a find! I've spoken to the owners, and we have the makings of a deal if we can act quickly. But I guess that moving at too much speed may cause a bit of an upset with some of the residents unless we play it carefully. No one will want to feel rushed or pressurized. What I suggest is that we put together a few facts and figures, backed up by some of the camera shots I've taken, and some preliminary figures on how a purchase might be financed. We could form a company or we could go for separate purchases. I'll invite everyone to a special dinner, and we'll see how it goes. Now to make sure that no one is taken by surprise, it would be best if, before the dinner, you could do the rounds and let everyone know what we will be talking about.'

That dinner, they recalled, had been a turning point in many of their lives. All except Neil and Jean were excitedly enthusiastic in principle about purchase of the farm. Neil and Jean had wanted more time to consider the possibility of emigrating. In the end, they had decided that a new life in Canada was best for them. And from their later letters, they seemed to be happy there, even if some of their letters hinted of sadness at the loss of the close neighbourly friendship they had once enjoyed.

After the fateful dinner, George, satisfied that he had sufficient support to justify negotiations on the purchase price of the farm, had worked tirelessly with the farm owners and the estate's residents to devise a purchase plan that could be rapidly implemented. Not everyone had George's financial resources or his readily available funds. But without them, nothing would have been achieved. In the end, George had bought the land, the farmhouse, and two of the cottages. The Harveys, the Rigbys, and the Robinsons had each bought one cottage, and so had they.

For them, the purchase had proved a blessing. They had spent more and more time at the cottage, walking, gardening, getting to know the villagers. And Mary had started to write again. For the other families at the Old Hall, the demands of work and children's schooling limited their visits to weekends and holidays. But, Mary and John reflected, it was always best when they were altogether a bit like one happy family.

Sadly, that had only lasted for three years before they were all jolted back to the reality of why they had bought the farm and cottages in the first place. The long struggling economy of the nation had fallen into a state of collapse, with strikes, riots, successive currency devaluations, and unstoppable inflation. Within months, all the dire forecasts of total financial disaster came to be realized.

They had been at the Old Hall Estate as the riots and looting moved towards a crescendo. The police, suffering the same day-to-day hardships as the rest of the population, were losing heart, confidence, and control. George had called a crisis meeting at the Hall. 'We need to secure the farm. Is anyone free to go down?'

They had been the willing volunteers to leave that day. Everything they needed was already at the cottage.

'Keep in touch hour by hour if things get worse', George had said, 'and put the heating on.'

CHAPTER 5

Meltdown

For the first hour of their journey, very little was said between John and Mary. They sped down the quiet motorway each locked in the silence of troubled minds. This was no ordinary trip to the countryside. It was not a trip for small talk and planning outings. It was not a trip they would want to remember. They were fleeing out of fear, and they had no desire to talk about their fears. And then it occurred to them, not only were they the first to flee, but in their anxiety, they had forgotten to tell Graham that they were fleeing.

Driving on down to the farm was not an option. How could they ring Graham from the safety of the farm to ask if he and his family were feeling safe in the city? What sort of parents would that make them? Without saying a word, they both arrived at the same conclusion. There was nothing for it but to stop and think. They turned into the first service area and sat silently for a while to gather their thoughts before discussing what to do.

As they sat there in the car turning over the possibilities for rectifying the situation, it suddenly dawned on them that they had never confided in Graham the true reasons for their purchase of the cottage. They had passed off the purchases of the farm and the cottages as no more than prudent investments made on the advice of George and Frances. And for Graham and his family, happy to spend holiday time sharing their cottage at the farm, that had been the only explanation ever required. All they wanted to know was that, one day, in the course of time, the cottage would be theirs. Why spoil that with the uncomfortable truth of the original reason for the purchase.

But even if the truth had to come out now, they still questioned, as they sat worrying in the car, how much of the truth could be told. Should they say that they were just off to the farm for a few days, and with things being difficult in the city, would they like to join them? Or should they say, we think it's time to get out of the city, and we think you should come with us? The trouble was that they themselves were not sure what they were doing. Within a week, they might be back at the Old Hall Estate having a drink with the others to celebrate the return of life's normality. Then again, they might not.

Mary had eventually thought of a plausible way out of the dilemma. It involved ringing Frances to see if she and George would be agreeable to letting Graham and his family have the use of their spare cottage. If they said yes, then that could be offered up as the excuse for the sudden invitation to the farm. The rest could come later, whatever the rest might be.

Frances and George both welcomed the idea of Graham and his family joining them at the farm, and both were more than happy to know that the spare cottage would be put to good use. So, in better spirits, they had driven to the next junction, turned round back up the motorway to the ring road, and then followed it around to Eastcote suburbs north of the city centre.

The reception they received when they reached Graham's modest detached home immediately put to rest the problem of explaining the nature of their visit. Never had they been greeted with a warmer welcome. Their very presence obviously generated a much needed feeling of reassurance and support.

The whole of Graham's family were clearly at wits' end with worry. They hadn't left the house for days. The children were at home because the schools were closed, the schools were closed because all the teachers were at home, and Graham and Rebecca were at home because they did not think it safe to leave the children alone at home.

The suggestion that they should all head off together to the farm at Lostock for a short while was accepted with rapture. Cases and bags were packed at lightning speed. Within minutes, they were all at the door, and Graham was loading his car.

They made good speed to the farm, and Graham and his family were soon settled into George's spare cottage. With the evening gathering in, Mary wasted no time in cooking up supper for all, and together again around the dining table, it was almost like being on holiday.

Those had been good times, times they would want to remember. The times they had chatted for hours after the children had been put to bed, going over the day's events and their planned excursions for the following days. But that particular evening, they were all exhausted from the stress of their sudden relocation. Everyone was ready for an early night.

After supper, when Graham and family were back in the Butler's cottage, it was time for John and Mary to relax with a drink and watch a bit of television. That fateful moment remained with them, and would remain with them, for years.

The nation's currency, the crown, had collapsed on the international markets. It was all but worthless against other currencies. What that meant for the value of the crown as the domestic currency, no one seemed to know. Expert after expert came on screen to confirm in despairing tones that the effect on the prices of imported goods would be catastrophic and that essential food, power, and fuel imports could no longer be guaranteed. When asked whether crowns in the bank, crowns in savings accounts, and crowns in pay packets would retain their value or whether they also would be worthless, no meaningful answers could be obtained.

Throughout the evening, the emergency programmes continued. Politicians came and went, saying little but stay calm, don't panic, modest belt tightening will be necessary, but if we all pull together, we'll come out stronger than ever in the end. Church leaders came on screen to blame society's ills, the reckless pursuit of wealth, and the immorality of burdening future generations with huge debts built up to sustain unearned affluence. Doctors in hospitals, managers of nursing homes, and community leaders were interviewed, bringing to the screen the full horrors of the uncertainty that had descended on the nation. It was all still going on when George rang.

'John, have you seen the news? It looks like complete disaster. There's something I would like you to do for me. There's a safe in the farmhouse, hidden behind the headrest in the main bedroom. The combination number is 5-8-7-6; make a note of it. You'll see when you open the safe a fair amount of money in various currencies. Head for the shops in St Jude tomorrow and buy up all the provisions you can. Try to spend the crowns first, but you'll have seen on the news that shopkeepers are already demanding dollars. And see what you can do to stock up with petrol and diesel. Sorry to land this on you John, but do the same for yourself. Use my money if you have to. If what we are hearing on the television is right, cheques and card purchases seem to be finished.'

John had confirmed that he was happy to oblige, but if the mission was to succeed, he would have to be very careful. Displaying evidence of possession of large quantities of cash might attract unwanted attention. He would be keeping a careful look out to ensure that he was not being followed since the last thing they needed was a break-in at the farm.

Being seen with an overloaded car would not do either. It might be necessary to make a number of trips. It might even be sensible to go further afield than St Jude. Perhaps to Stourmouth, which had many more shops and which might well be less risky if anyone was minded to follow him. But he would do what he could, and he would report back tomorrow.

When the call was over, John discussed with Mary the concerns he had about scouring the area for purchasable supplies. They both agreed that it had to be done. Not just for Frances and George, but for themselves and Graham's family.

Fortunately, they had brought with them from the Old Hall all their cash savings, most of which was in dollars. They had felt uncomfortable when first they started storing dollars instead of crowns, but for years, that had been the advice of financial advisers and newspaper columnists, and everyone else seemed to be doing it. It was just as well that they had joined the crowd, or was it? How much effect had it all had in bringing down the crown? Very little they hoped, but it was too late now to worry about that. The potential consequences of the crown's collapse were getting too close for comfort.

Mary had been keen to join and assist John with the shopping, but John would not hear a word of it. If using dollars was to become illegal as had been suggested in some of the television reports, he did not want Mary to be involved. Perhaps, they concluded, it was best that she stayed at the farm to help Graham and the family settle in.

Tomorrow could be a long day's shopping. And, anyway, it would not be a day for selecting this or that, it would be a day for taking whatever was available and fighting one's way through the crowds to the front of the queues.

The next morning's television brought more bad news. The riots and looting in the city were intensifying. The government had sat all night to bring in new laws freezing currency transfers, limiting cash withdrawals from banks, and making it a criminal offence for dollars to be taken in return for goods and services.

Their worst fears were being realised, and correctly as things were to work out, they realised that the nightmare had only just started. Their imaginations ran riot in contemplating what might happen next and how it would all end. They had planned for the future, but was there a future? What a colossal price they were all going to have to pay for their nation's feckless past.

John set out on his shopping expedition with trepidation and a heavy heart. He headed first for Stourmouth thirty miles away. It was much bigger than St Jude, and all the better for that for what he had in mind. He passed two petrol stations displaying 'Out of Fuel' signs before it dawned on him that it might be worthwhile to check whether that was really the case.

He was right in his thinking. At the next petrol station, a quiet discussion with the manager revealed that 'Out of Fuel' meant that there was only fuel for dollar purchasers. He filled his tank, bought and filled a few jerry cans, and went on his way.

Any hopes he had of one-stop food shopping at the supermarkets on the outskirts of the town were soon dashed. The car parks were so full that he could only park on the grass verges. Inside the store, the shelves were clearing rapidly. The aisles were packed, and the tills blocked as staff argued with shoppers intent on ignoring the advice given to them on entering the store that bulk purchases were not permitted.

He headed for the smaller shops in the town centre. Bit by bit, and by deft display of crowns in one hand and dollars in the other, he filled his car and, deep in thought, drove back to the farm. He disliked what he was doing and disliked even more the act of doing it. But, needs must, he persuaded himself. One more day and the shops will be cleaned out anyway. Head down, keep going, and what will be, will be.

After unloading the car, John rang George and recounted the day's events. 'Stick with it for another day or so,' George had suggested. 'Back here, things are no better. You'll see it all on the television.

'I'm calling a residents' meeting tonight. Top of the agenda will be our food reserves. We must do everything we can to ensure that, when we make a run for the farm, we've stacked up as much as we can get our hands on. So tomorrow morning, we'll be out in force to see what we can get.

'I'll warn everyone about the trouble you've had at the supermarkets, but they'll not be too surprised. Everyone here who has been out has had the same problems. Absolute chaos, they're all calling it. Some found themselves queuing at check-outs for over an hour. We can't afford to waste any more time like that. So we'll be going to smaller stores. And, hopefully, they'll be more likely to prefer dollar purchasers.

'But I can foresee problems getting safely away from some of corner shops in the city with bags full of goodies if we can't park the cars nearby. Still, we must give it a try, even if we have to work in groups. Have a nice evening, John, and give our love to Mary. I'll ring you in the morning.'

Mary had stood by anxiously listening to the call. 'Is everything all right up there? George sounded a bit stressed.'

'Oh yes', said John, 'George has things under control. He's going to ring us in the morning. By the way, after dinner tonight and when the youngsters have gone to bed, I think we need to have a chat with Graham and Rebecca. I'm going to need some help tomorrow on another provisions run.

I didn't do too badly today on my own but the atmosphere out there is getting a bit testing. Everyone's on edge and on the lookout. It's not far short of panic in some places. It's all happened so quickly, and people are frightened. You can see it in their faces. I'd rather not take anything for granted tomorrow, so it will be best if Graham and I work as a pair if he's up for it.'

'Would you like me to come?'

'No, you stay here with Rebecca and the children. There's plenty for you to do preparing for the arrival of George and the rest of them. Don't let all this get you down. Things will work out, you'll see. And we couldn't be in a safer place.'

'I know', said Mary, 'that's how I feel. Just imagine what it must be like in the city at a time like this. Wondering where your next meal is coming from and wondering if it's safe to go out and get it. We're very lucky to be here John. I just wish that the others were here with us.

But you know, even if all these troubles were not going on, I would still like it here. I won't mind if we have to live off the land, grow our own vegetables, keep a pig, and plant a small orchard. I'm already looking forward to getting some poultry. Farmer Brown came round this afternoon while you were out, and he's promised me some ducks and chickens. He says he's quite happy to continue running this farm from his place if that suits George.

And I've volunteered us all as extra farmhands if we are needed to help in stepping up production. The children will like that. By the way, I do wish we could keep the children away from the television, it must be frightening them.'

The television that evening was more than enough to frighten the children. It terrified the adults. Coverage was entirely given over to filming riots and looting in the city centre, interspersed with plaintive pleas from politicians for calm and interviews with shocked citizens who were anything but calm. There were reports on the crowds assembling outside the banks and graphic scenes of vehicles heading out of the city and queues forming at the city's seaport and at the airport.

The next day, still stunned by the continuing reports of mayhem in the city, John and Graham set off to acquire whatever provisions they could, by whatever means. Nearly everything was closed. In desperation, but with some measure of success, they took to knocking on the doors of closed corner shops and village stores blatantly offering to purchase in dollars.

Worn out by hours of badgering and bargaining, they returned wearily to the farm. In total, over the two days, they had collected enough food for themselves and George and Frances to last about a month, perhaps a little more with extreme economy. But if the other three families still with George and Frances turned up without supplies, they were going to be in trouble.

The expected call came through from George. 'John, what a day! What an awful day! We're all back now, and we didn't do too badly, but we won't be going out again before we leave. Gangs of rioters and looters are everywhere, and hardly a policeman is to be seen. I think they are giving up the fight. They're probably staying at home to look after their own families. The mood here at the Old Hall is that we should all set off for the farm tonight, but I've suggested that we leave it until tomorrow, giving us time to board up the properties. Anyway, we'll see you tomorrow evening. And how are things with you? Is everything okay?'

'Not bad, George, but we've cleaned out the shops and any further expeditions may do more harm than good. We don't have rioters and looters just yet, but some of the looks we are getting in the rougher parts of the towns are anything but friendly, and some are close to menacing. Time to tighten up security and batten down the hatches I think. See you tomorrow.'

Although they were not to know it at the time, the events of the night and the following day destroyed all hope of any such early get-together. Throughout the night, the television channels showed continuous coverage of rampant mobs torching the city hall and the parliament buildings, with the fire and rescue services being driven back by hails of bricks and other missiles.

A helicopter was seen flying from the grounds of the presidential palace. Fleets of ministerial cars and ambassadors' limousines, flanked by security guards, could be seen fleeing from the central leafy squares towards the city airport closely followed by streams of private cars desperate to keep in touch. By morning, little but smouldering ruins and clouds of smoke remained of the edifices, which for centuries, had stood as evidence of the nation's orderly government.

John and Mary had sat up all night transfixed by the televised horror. No thought of going to bed had crossed their minds. The nightmares before them on the screen had to be endured. Sleep was impossible. They had to know how it would end.

But the end was not in sight. Worse was yet to come. The rioting and looting was spreading throughout the commercial and shopping centres of the city with smoke and flames pouring from the high-rise office blocks and handsome department stores. In the mid-afternoon, one by one, all the television channels went blank. And in the late evening, the lights began to flicker, and the fridges ceased to hum.

As darkness and silence descended upon the valley, their thoughts went back to the Old Hall Estate and the once happy band of residents. Where were they now? George had rung to say they were on their way hours ago. It was getting late, too late. If only the phones were still working, they could get some peace of mind. Another sleepless night awaited them.

CHAPTER 6

The Tanks

Like John and Mary and the rest of the nation, George had stayed up throughout that fateful night. His forebodings had been realised in an orgy of violence far beyond anything he had ever contemplated. Yes, he and his friends had foreseen troubles ahead, and yes, they had planned for the future. But what point now was there in their Arcadian vision of retreat to a simpler life? Could heaven exist as a suburb of hell?

Pulling himself together, he faced the morning light with recognition that this was no time for philosophical wanderings. The reality was that their plan for retreat to the farm, whether futile or not, was their only plan. It was time to get on with it, and in a hurry.

He made a quick call to Bill Rigby at no. 3. 'Bill, soon as you can, get round here, and we'll go and collect the shutters from the compound. If we move quickly, we can have all the houses boarded up by mid-day and be on our way. Frances is on her way round the houses to tell everyone that we are aiming for mid-day departure. Perhaps Carol could also do the rounds to make sure everyone is fully packed. We'll take my Range Rover down to the depot; we've decided to take the guard dogs down to the farm. Will you be okay driving the truck back?'

'No problem, George, its time I got back behind the wheel of a real vehicle. But I'm going to leave you to handle those dogs—they frighten the life out of me.'

'Don't worry, Bill, I'll deal with them. And they'll be caged in the back of the Range Rover by old Mick, the yardman. My worry is going to be getting them out if they develop a liking for chauffeur-driven luxury.'

'That's great, George, but take some meat just in case they're hungry and they think we've turned up as their menu.'

The compound was tucked away on the outskirts of the city to the north of Glebe Pastures in a small industrial estate built by Butler Developments as the firm expanded. For more than twenty years, it had served as the firm's plant yard, storage depot, and joinery shop.

For the last few days, George and Bill had been overseeing the manufacture of sets of carefully measured timber panels for the doors and windows for the Old Hall Estate properties. The workers in the joiner's shop had known better than to ask George what they were for. His increasingly infrequent visits to the compound over the years as he had risen to the top of the firm had distanced him from the workforce as he progressed from being one of the boys to a friendly but firm employer.

For George and Bill, the drive to the compound was beginning to take on an intimidating feel. Once out of the leafy suburbs of the well heeled, the aspiring executives, and the retired gentry, the shock effects of the night's events were apparent on every street corner. No one, it seemed, had gone to work. Small groups were gathering, barricades were going up, and cars, their roofs piled high with valued possessions, were beginning to block the roads. What should have been a half-hour journey took more than an hour.

Arriving at the compound, George and Bill were startled to find that it was already under siege with four youths attempting to batter down the gates with an old car which, judging from the treatment it was receiving, had evidently been stolen. Behind the gates, the dogs were howling on their chains. As the Range Rover pulled up with its brakes screeching, the youths scattered fearing that police or security guards had arrived answering an alert and that the dogs might soon be giving them chase.

There was no sign of Mick, the yardman, dashing George's hope that he might be there to assist them in getting the dogs into the car and in loading the lorry. The compound was deserted. But, Bill, a man of many practical talents, had no difficulty starting and operating the fork-lift loader. Within thirty minutes, the job was done. Noticing that there was still room on the lorry for a few extra timber sheets, George asked for them to be loaded.

'What we are going to do with these?' Bill queried.

'"Attach them to the entrance gates to the estate if we can find some way of doing so. They'll add to security. The gates aren't made to repel battering rams or determined looters. Have a look round and see if you can find anything we could use. But hurry, time's short.'

Within minutes, Bill found some packs of lengthy steel bolts. 'These would work if we had enough panels for both sides of the steelwork. And we'll need to take a sizeable drill back with us.'

'No problem', said George, 'there's a stock of panels over there in the yard. And plenty of drills in the stores.'

It was approaching mid-day when George and Bill got back to the Old Hall. It had proved easier than expected to get the two growling Rottweilers into the cage compartment of the Range Rover. They had all but jumped in, evidently keen to leave the loneliness of the compound for some better life.

The journey, however, had been painfully slow with George trying to keep the Range Rover as close as possible to the overloaded lorry, which Bill was struggling to control, and with the pair of them fighting for space between the ever-increasing traffic.

For two hours after they got back to the Old Hall, it was all hands to the pumps, fitting panels to doors, windows, and the gates, and finalizing loading of the cars. Then at last, they were ready for departure. With tearful farewell glances and forlorn waves to the boarded windows of their once-happy homes, they took their seats for a journey into the unknown.

They would soon be back, they hoped. Life would return to normal. Bad things were happening all over the world, but so had they in the past. Famines, plagues, world wars, set against those, this was nothing; just a bit of foolish financial management. Everyone had been doing it. They were not the first nation to fall into a financial abyss, and they would not be the last.

Rescue plans would already be in hand. The World Bank would step in, the International Monetary Fund would step in, and the army would take control until a new government was formed. With luck, it would all be over in a few days. Or so they all hoped.

George and Frances took the lead in the Range Rover with the two Rottweilers secured in the dog cage. Bill and Carol with their children followed in their big Lexus; Robin and Janet in their Jaguar came next with the Butlers' two spaniels in the back. Peter and Anne brought up the rear in their Volvo.

With all ready to go, George made a brief call to the farm to let John and Mary know that they were about to set off. And then the orderly procession began its fateful journey. When all the cars were through the estate's newly boarded entrance gates, they halted for a while for Bill to park the lorry inside the gates to block intruders and for George to fix to the gates the two industrial size locks and chains retrieved from the compound. Then, closely following the Range Rover, the small convoy made its way onto the Avenue and towards the main road to begin its crawl amongst the swelling ranks of fleeing families towards the junction of the ring road and the southern motorway.

They were still two miles short of the junction when the traffic ground to a halt. Cars and vans could be seen ahead making cumbersome three-point turns, their despairing drivers apparently hoping to make progress in some other direction. A small group of drivers stood in the carriageway ahead of the Range Rover staring down the road, willing the vehicles ahead to get on the move.

'What's the problem?' asked George, approaching the group.

'Dunno, mate, might be an accident, but we've been stuck here for over an hour.'

George was in no mood for standing around. Returning to his little convoy, he announced his intention to find the source of the stoppage, and after helping Frances into the driving seat of the Range Rover in case some forward movement of the cars commenced, he set off at a brisk pace with the two Rottweilers. The presence of the dogs ensured that his momentum was not broken by the groups of anxious families stranded by their cars, but it was still half an hour before he reached the front of the queue.

He stopped, astounded and near speechless, at the extraordinary sight of an unattended army tank on a low-loader blocking the carriageway. As if to add certainty to its purpose, it was sporting a huge and garish 'Road Closed' sign.

'What's going on?' asked George to no one in particular amongst the bemused pack of standing motorists. 'Who put this here, and why? And where are the troops who must have done this. Did anyone see them?'

'Manoeuvres, they told us,' came the reply from one of the pack. 'And they've gone to collect materials.'

George turned and at an even brisker pace than before strode back to his waiting convoy. 'Weird,' said George to himself over and over again as he hurried along. 'Weird and worrying. Why would the army park a tank on one of the main roads out of the city? And why would they do it at a time like this?'

By the time he reached his convoy, he had already decided to say little about what he had seen. He was still too bemused to say anything that would bring enlightenment or comfort to any of his waiting group. He simply walked along the line of cars repeating that the road was closed and that they needed to head for another junction. He would lead the way.

'There's something going on', he said to Frances as he regained the driving seat, 'something that we haven't planned for. The army's blocked the road ahead, and there's no way onto the ring road or the motorway in this direction. Let's hope there is in another.'

George knew the roads well, and he hoped that, even in heavy traffic, they could be on the ring road at a westerly junction and then on to the motorway south within half an hour. It was beginning to get dark, and he had no desire to be on the city roads much longer.

His hopes were soon dashed. Well before the ring road, they were again stuck on one of the city's arterial roads. This time, it was a dual carriageway. George knew that another expedition on foot to find the cause of the blockage would take about an hour.

Too little time for that, he thought, and probably not much to be gained. Leaving the Range Rover, he clambered over the central reservation crash barrier and stopped a cyclist heading back towards the city centre. 'How long is the queue?' he asked, pointing to the long line of cars stretching into the far distance.

'Right the way to the junction', came the reply, 'but you're going nowhere because the road's closed.'

'Not by a tank?' asked George.

'Yes, how did you know?'

'It's beginning to look like a pattern,' said George. 'And I don't like the looks of it.'

Turning back to the crash barrier, he tried to assess what it would take to smash through it. They needed to get back to the Old Hall, to safety, and to think. And they needed to get back quickly. The problem was how to get out of the traffic stopped in front of them and now rapidly building up behind them. Crossing the central reservation was the only way. But was the Range Rover up to it? He went to consult with Bill.

'We might end up wrecking your car', said Bill, 'but let's take a closer look at the barrier.'

A further inspection followed before Bill, perking up, and with a cheering, 'Hang on a bit—I think we may be in luck,' went back to the Lexus and extracted a large adjustable spanner from the boot. 'Never travel without one, habit of a lifetime. Now, let's see if we can unbolt the blighter.'

'Well done,' said George fifteen minutes later. 'Now, let's get through the gap before we're swamped by a mad rush exploiting our efforts.'

Back at the Old Hall, they unbolted the entrance gates, took the boarding panel off the rear door of the Hall and assembled in the Hall's enormous breakfast kitchen. It was a stunned assembly with everyone waiting for someone else to break the nervous silence.

'Should we not ring Mary and John to let them know we've been delayed,' said Anne, after what seemed a lifetime's pause. 'They might be worrying about us. We can't have them sitting up all night waiting for us to arrive.'

'We most certainly should,' responded Frances. 'They are probably worrying already. You know how good they are with their own timekeeping. I'll use the landline in the study. Mobile reception's not too good at the farm.'

'Just tell them we've had to postpone the journey until tomorrow,' said George. 'Say we've encountered technical problems with one of the cars. We don't want to alarm them with news of things that hopefully will amount to nothing.'

And, as he was saying that, the lights went out.

CHAPTER 7

The Fence

No one moved until George broke the silence. "Well, that's fixed it; we're all staying here tonight. Let's dig out some candles and torches. We've even got a couple of emergency battery lanterns somewhere. And can someone give me a hand to bring in some logs? We'll light a few fires and charge up the cooker. We'll soon have it looking like the Old Hall Hotel. Frances will show you to your rooms, and fortunately, tonight we've plenty of vacancies. There's no need to dress for dinner, but it will be cocktails in the lounge at 7.30.'

Despite George's efforts to cheer things up, the atmosphere at the candlelit supper laid on by Frances was a long way removed from the happy sense of collective contentment that usually graced her dinners and suppers. All attempts to lift spirits quickly faded away to give place to quiet whisperings. Periods of silent contemplation ruled the table broken by occasional sobs from the children unintentionally testing to the limits the brave show of fortitude by the adults. The more George urged on consumption of the wine he was patently oversupplying to the table, the more it seemed that they were all turning teetotal.

When the children had been put to bed, the men retired to the billiard room. 'I've been thinking', said George, 'I'm not sure that simply setting off tomorrow morning is the best of ideas. We might get a clear run out of the city, but supposing we don't. Perhaps we were lucky to get back here today. I wouldn't want to risk having to return here tomorrow. If we do, there would be more despair and disappointment, and if we can't get back, well, it doesn't bear thinking about. We need to be sure when we next close the gates behind us that we are going to get a clear run out of the city and on to the farm. We need to do some preliminary reconnaissance.'

All agreed that George was right. No one wanted a repeat of the disturbing ordeal they had been through that day. But all could see that there would be problems. A fact-finding mission on foot would take too long and might be dangerous. A car, or cars, would have to be used, but simply driving around the city in the hope of coming across some way out that was still open was hardly a realistic plan of action. The mission had to be focussed, but focussed on what?

George had been keeping quiet. He was still reluctant to fully disclose what he knew about the two blocked ring road junctions. He had not seen any troops on the city roads, but the army seemed to be blocking the way out of the city. He couldn't work it out, and until he could, it would cause more problems than it would solve if he told the others. He needed to tread carefully.

'I think I have a plan,' he announced. 'I know my way around the city roads pretty well, particularly those around here at Glebe Pastures. Today, we tried to get to the motorway using the city ring road. Tomorrow, it might be best if we tried something different. It will add some miles to our journey, but what I suggest is that we head off into the countryside using one the underpass roads. You probably all know the one I'm thinking of; it's the one not far from here leading out to Welford.

'I normally get onto the Welford road by going up the dual carriageway, but I know a route up to it through the housing estates. If I set out at dawn tomorrow to make sure that the route and the underpass are both clear, we can be on our way to the farm straight after breakfast.'

They were all in favour of George's plan, so much so that they all wanted to go with him. A lively discussion followed on whether it was best for George to go alone or whether it should be a reconnaissance party. But George had no intention of taking anyone else with him; he'd sold the plan to them with an air of confidence that was all for appearances and not for open examination. If it turned out to be a flawed plan, he wanted to be the only one to witness it.

In the end, he managed to persuade them that their presence at breakfast would provide more reassurance than their absence, and they managed to persuade him that if he was determined to go on his own, he should take the guard dogs with him.

He still had to explain his plan to Frances, and at first, she also thought that she should go with him. But with Frances, he was more open about his own doubts, and when he put it to her that if, by some mischance, neither of them were present at breakfast, it might send out the wrong signals. She agreed that she would, as she put it, 'stay to hold the fort'.

When, with dawn barely breaking, George crept down the stairs and made his way to a side door; he found Bill sitting alone in the kitchen drinking coffee. 'No, you can't come,' said George. 'That's an order.'

'I know that,' said Bill. 'I'm just here to see that you get a cup of coffee then I'm going to help you load the dogs, and then I'm going to see you through the gates and make sure they're properly closed after you. I hope that's all right with you, boss. And by the way, I've told Carol that you'll be back for breakfast. I don't want her to think that you've done a runner. Not that she would, of course. But, to put it mildly, she's terrified for the children's sake that anything more could go wrong. And she's relying on you to see that it doesn't. We all are. Best of luck, George.'

George had worked out in his mind the route he would take to the underpass. The short route on the main roads was about eight miles, but although using the housing estate roads would add five miles, he hoped it would be worth the detours. Anything was worth trying to avoid yesterday's blockages. He got off to a good start as he sped down the Avenue, but once he had turned into the housing estates, he soon encountered groups of people assembling makeshift barricades at some of the larger road junctions. He found this more of an inconvenience than a cause for concern.

At each stoppage, a way through the motley collection of dustbins, wheelbarrows, and old fence panels, which the residents had hastily collected, was cleared as soon as it was seen that George was not only on his own but was brave enough to be on his own. He looked like a man with authority and nothing was more reassuring to the rapidly expanding bands of reluctant vigilantes than the sight of a man with authority.

George had half expected and fully dreaded that, before he got to the underpass, he would have to abandon the Range Rover and fight his way through crowds to whatever might be blocking the traffic. But to his relief, the darkened profile of the ring road embankment came into view while he was still at the wheel. Momentarily his spirits soared; his hopes at last were high. But not for long.

Rounding the final bend, he was obliged to pull up behind a small cluster of cars parked at the entrance of the underpass. In front of the cars, a noisy gathering of drivers and passengers stood with heads raised, apparently shouting abuse at the structure's parapet.

George walked slowly towards the crowd then stopped with amazement on sighting the cause of their anger. A fence over two metres high made of steel posts and mesh panels had been installed from wall to wall of the underpass, completely blocking all access. Down the side slopes of the embankment to the edges of the roadway, a fence of impenetrable coiled razor wire had been installed. All possibility of crossing under the ring road by car or over by foot had been deliberately and very professionally eliminated.

Realizing the presence of George and his dogs, the crowd fell into a nervous silence. 'What's going on', asked George, 'and who are you shouting at?'

'The soldiers, they're the people who put this lot up,' came the reply.

'What soldiers?' asked George joining them in their hostile stares towards the parapet. 'I can't see any soldiers.'

'Oh, they are up there all night. And they are armed. They must have done this overnight. It wasn't here yesterday. They had a big truck across the road then. Look up there now through the razor wire. You can see them moving about on the carriageway.'

'Have they told you why they've done this?'

'No, they haven't said a word. Probably under orders not to. There must be something going on the other side they don't want us to know about. But it's not right, blocking the road like this.'

'Well, I agree with you on that,' said George. 'It's outrageous. But perhaps they are more worried about what's going on this side of the ring road rather than on the far side. Does anyone here know if other roads out of the city are blocked?'

For a while, no one spoke. All were quietly digesting George's comments. What was he suggesting? Was he implying that other roads might be blocked? 'What makes you think they might be?' eventually came a voice from the crowd.

'It was just a thought, just a thought', said George, 'but I need to get across the ring road one way or another, and I don't want to waste time just driving around the city to find one.'

'If you're thinking of getting over the road on foot', replied the voice, 'forget it. My house backs on to the embankment, and I've already tried it. You wouldn't have a chance. They've put wire like this all along the roadside. It would cut you to pieces. And they've got jeeps out on patrol on the top in case anyone is mad enough to tackle the wire.'

'Well, that puts paid to that plan,' said George. 'Thank you for telling me. It's back to the drawing board for us all, I think. But best of luck to you all.'

He stayed with them for another minute or two and then, with as cheerful a farewell wave as he could muster, bid them good-bye with a few parting words of encouragement, 'I'm sure this funny business, whatever it is, will be over soon. Don't let it get you down.'

Back in his car, George sat morosely weighing his options. Should he call it a day? Should he check more underpass crossing points? Or should he travel over to see what was happening on the far side of the city? He was beginning to think that whatever he did would turn out to be a fool's errand. The chances of finding a way out of the city seemed to be diminishing at every turn. But the more he thought about it, the more he viewed with dismay the prospect of returning to the Old Hall with nothing more to report than that the underpass plan was off.

There was nothing for it but to persevere. He would head across the city to the eastern side. It was pessimistic to think that just because, for some reason or another, roads on the western side were blocked, he would find them all blocked on the eastern side. But first, he needed to make a quick call on his mobile to Frances, just to let her know that he would not be home for breakfast but that there was nothing to worry about. Everything was under control. She could tell the others that he was still pursuing the plan for leaving after lunch.

He rang her mobile number. He was unable to get a connection! He tried other people's mobile numbers. Again, no connections. His battery level was high, so it must be the network! Could the relay stations have been knocked out by the power cut? But didn't they have auxiliary supplies, generators, and the like? What on earth was going on? No land lines, no power, no television, and now no mobile networks. What did it all point to?

There was only one answer. A well organised plan to curtail their freedom of movement had come into force and with it a plan to ensure there was no way of communicating about it with others. What an evil plan! But whose plan was it?

He stayed, slumped in his car seat, staring ahead, totally stunned. Coping with chaos was one thing. Coping with this, quite another. Someone was aiming for total control of the city, and they were not far from having it in a grip of iron. But how could that be? They had all seen it on the television, riots, looting, and arson. Surely that cannot all have been staged. Only days ago, no one was in control.

He needed time to think. The car radio! Of course, the car radio! He tuned in to the national news channel. Nothing! He tried more. Still nothing! What about the foreign channels? They all cannot have been silenced.

'Reports are coming in that recent disturbances in Norburgh, the capital of Borovia, which led to destruction of national government buildings and much of the city's commercial centre are now under control. The exact number of casualties is unknown, but it may run into double figures. Efforts to organize an international relief force are in progress. Arrangements are in hand to maintain food supplies. Hopes are high that a new government will soon be in place. And now for the sports news . . .'

George winced. Is that all the nation's struggles had come to? Small disturbances in Borovia—not many dead! Yes, they were a small nation in a small country. Yes, they had endured years of precariously balancing on the edge of a very dangerous financial cliff. Yet they were not alone in their predicament. They had all behaved like lemmings. But still their predicament and their misery surely deserved more than passing comment and such deceitful understatement.

Once more, the sense that he was seeing only half the picture of what was going on crossed George's mind. And even half the picture was enough for him to know that he didn't like what he was seeing.

It's time to get moving, he decided, but perhaps not to the far side of the city. Back at the Hall, they might begin to panic if I fail to show up for breakfast. Reconnaissance was over for the day. I've seen enough. And goodness knows how long the journey back to the Hall might take.

But for his air of authority and his menacing dogs, George's return might never have been achieved. At road junctions, more barricades were going up and faster than could ever have been achieved had some orderly authority sought to demand their installation. Beds, sofas, sideboards, and even small sheds and occasional pianos were now being hastily pushed along pavements and piled into impenetrable obstructions. The people were taking security into their own hands. No approvals were being sought for these road closures. The powers of the politicians, the police, and the bureaucrats at the city hall already counted for nothing.

'Good for you! Good for you!' thought George as he patiently explained at each barricade that he was just an ordinary guy minding his own business. But deep down, he worried that it would not be long before their meritorious efforts to maintain a semblance of law and order might be defeated. He'd seen the gangs and the looters on television. It would take more than piles of furniture to keep people like that out.

Arriving back at the Hall, George got the adults together in the drawing room. From all sides of the room, their strained faces focused on him with the intensity of interrogators after every scrap of available information. How, he thought, could he dress up the reality of their predicament? How could he offer them some comfort without resorting to deceit? How could he keep their hopes alive? How could he tell the truth?

'I've only been able to check one of the underpasses', he said, 'but it seems to be under control of the army, and at present, no one can get through. Things may be different tomorrow. I don't know what it's like on the eastern side of the city, or on the northern side, but getting there to find out is not going to be easy. Barricades are going up everywhere.

'We may have to spend a few more days here. You're all welcome to stay with Frances and myself in the Hall, and we hope that you all will. But if you do want to go back to your own homes, Bill and I will assist in removing the shutters. Hopefully the electricity will be back on later today, but if not, I'll go up to the compound to see if there are any generators and lighting sets we can use.'

And then, before he could say any more, the unexpected but unmistakable sound of a helicopter flying low overhead was heard. Rushing into the garden, they were greeted by scores of leaflets, fluttering to the ground like giant flakes of snow.

Those who thought that the leaflets would bring some explanation of the nation's collapse and how it was going to be resolved were in for disappointment. The message on the leaflets could not have been briefer. 'Keep calm; relief is on its way; stay at home.' Whoever was sending out the message and what their intentions were was clearly intended to remain a mystery.

'Just as I thought,' muttered George under his breath. 'There is a plan is to starve us of information, let's hope it's not the same with the food.'

CHAPTER 8

Kettled

Leaving the hubbub of excited conversation in the garden, George returned to the kitchen to ponder what to say next to the residents. He had been on the point of telling them, somewhat reluctantly, about the tanks and the fence blocking the roads out of the city. It no longer seemed the right time. The leaflets had evidently brightened the mood, and he had no wish to pour cold water over their revived hopes by giving them news that could only cause alarm. Knowing what he knew would simply rekindle the fear and despair that the previous day's events had brought upon them.

But they would be expecting him to say something about the leaflets. That bothered him. The wording could be taken as a message of hope, and yet with all the strange things going on, it might be intended as a threat or a warning.

He was still unsure about what he was going to say when Bill entered the kitchen. 'You've got the look of a worried man,' said Bill. 'Can I help?'

'Yes', replied George, 'but it's going to take a bit of explaining. As soon as it would not seem too impolite to leave nor too alarming to do so, I need to get back on the road again. There are things I need to do and things I need to see. But first, I will have to try to cheer everyone up with a few more half truths. Afterwards, how do you feel about coming along with me to the compound to see if we can retrieve a generator or two and some lighting sets? And while we are out, we might just head over to the airport to see if it's still open.'

Bill had been friends with George long enough to know that he would not be pushed into explanations before he was ready to share his thoughts, but he had picked up George's coded message that he wanted to talk. He was not going to turn down the invitation.

'Leave it to me, George', he said, 'forget about the half truths. I'll tell everyone that you've just remembered that you've forgotten to feed the dogs and that as soon as you have done so, we are going up to the compound again. I'll say that we might go on to the airport, but we will be back for dinner. If you have a quiet word in with Frances before we set off, I'll have a quiet word with Carol.'

With the Rottweilers back in the Range Rover and the estate's gates closed behind them, they drove up to the Avenue and, to Bill's surprise, they turned right. Before Bill had time to ask why they were turning right down the Avenue to get to the compound when the quicker way was obviously to go left, George commenced his explanation for the trip.

'Bill, if you're wondering why we are going this way, it's because I want you to see for yourself what I found at the underpass this morning. Something very odd is happening. Something I cannot fathom out for the life of me. You remember when we were stuck for the first time yesterday? Well, I didn't tell you this at the time, but there was a tank on a low-loader blocking the road. It was the same at the second blockage. And then this morning at the underpass, there was a steel fence and soldiers blocking the way. Perhaps I should have told you about all of this before, but I kept on hoping that it was all much ado about nothing and that we would soon be down at the farm.

Now I'm not so sure. Perhaps we will find a clear way out of the city if we keep looking, but I am beginning to have my doubts. Just think of this Bill. Three times out of three, we've been blocked by the army.

And yet we don't know why. Since when in our lifetime did we ever see troops controlling the roads, let alone blocking them. Are they trying to keep us in or are they trying to stop others getting in?'

'Well they could be stopping others getting in, George. Perhaps there's an epidemic or something in the countryside. Cholera, black death, who knows? And why would they want to stop us getting out? What have we done wrong? Unless, of course, they are not our troops. Perhaps we've been invaded by a foreign army? They might well want to keep us bottled up.'

'Bill, you may have hit the nail on the head. That's it. We've been kettled.'

'Kettled?'

'Yes. You know, the way the police do it to control crowds of protesters. They form a cordon around an area and lock everyone in until they're satisfied it's safe to release them one by one. Everyone in the area gets caught like fish in a net. Good or bad, you're held in the net. Oddly though, from what I've seen so far, in this case it looks as though it's our own army doing the kettling. But why would they do that? Our own army!'

'That's a mystery, George. But here's a thought. All the army barracks are in the countryside, safe from the rampaging mobs. Perhaps they want to keep it that way. And perhaps there's a double benefit. They contain the looters and the rioters in the city, and at the same time, they maintain order in the countryside.'

Bill and George continued mulling over the possibilities and probabilities of their kettling theory all the way to the underpass. It was not an easy journey. More and more barricades were going up, and without George's relaxed conversational manner of requesting passage and his unquestioning acceptance of the presence of the barricades, they would never have made it to the underpass.

Bill studied the technique with interest. Left to himself, he would have adopted an aggressive approach to the illegal highway obstructions. Not that he was a fighting man, he would just have been standing up for his rights. But he had to admit it, left to himself, he would not have been standing up at all; he would lying bruised in the gutter.

George parked up the car out of sight of the underpass, and with the dogs by their side, they attempted a nonchalant stroll towards the ring road embankment. Most of the morning crowd had departed, but to George's dismay, a hard core remained and he was soon recognised. 'What brings you back, guv?' asked a familiar voice from the morning's exchanges.

'The leaflets dropped by the helicopter', replied George, 'thought they might have changed things; did you see them?'

'They're just rubbish', came the response, 'trying to frighten us I reckon. But did you see the helicopter? Bright red, not one of ours. What do you make of that?'

'Another mystery of our times,' said George. 'One day, perhaps we'll all meet up and have a good laugh about it. Keep smiling.'

While George had been talking, Bill had been eyeing up the steel fence and the razor wire from as close as was possible without attracting unwanted attention. They strolled back to the car exchanging views on what it might take to break through the fence and the possibility of checking underpasses on other roads after calling in at the compound, which was only a couple of miles away.

Arriving at the compound, it was immediately evident that their diversion had been in vain. There was no point in getting out of the car. The looters had beaten them to it. Little was left to be salvaged, and what little there was left was still being combed over by a determined mob collecting the spoils of unchecked civil unrest. They headed north towards the nearest ring road junction.

Once on the dual carriageway, they made good progress. Traffic was minimal, and the road thankfully free of barricades. Whatever queue of traffic there might have been at the junction on the previous day had evidently cleared. Just a few hopefuls remained, sitting or sleeping in their cars and vans like weary travellers waiting to board a ferry.

'They're optimists,' said Bill. And he was right. At the junction, another unattended tank blocked the road, but this time, the tank sat behind an elaborate arrangement of razor wire and steel fences stretching across both carriageways, the slip roads, and the embankments. The fence erectors had obviously been very busy.

'Nothing doing here then,' said George as he turned round and boldly drove back down the wrong side of the carriageway looking for a convenient crossing point to the city-bound carriageway. Once on the right side of the road, they pulled up on the hard shoulder to study the city street map.

'Here's what I suggest,' said Bill. 'We take a look at this feeder road underpass then we go on to the big eastern interchange and then down to the airport.'

'Suits me,' replied George. 'You're navigating.'

They were now moving into the industrialised side of the city. Fewer street barricades had been erected, but more people were out and about boarding up offices and factories. There was no one about at the underpass. But, as they feared and more than half expected, there was no way through. No tank, but again the steel fence and razor wire obstructions.

'Let's take a closer look at this fence,' said Bill. 'I'd like to see how it's fixed across the roadway. Whoever put it up cannot have had much time to have concreted the posts in. One day it wasn't here, the next day it was. I wish I could find builders who worked at that speed.'

They parked up and cautiously approached the fence. There was no sign of any soldiers in or above the underpass. Bill knelt down on the tarmac and lowered his head to examine the bottom rail. Several times, he repeated this at different parts of the fence then, rising, he went to the middle of the road and grasped in each hand one of the vertical steel fence posts. Still not satisfied with his findings, he then eased his arm through onto one of the horizontal crossbars. Again, he repeated this several times.

'Okay', he said, 'let's go. But before we go, George, have a good look at this fence. Would you say this is the same type as we saw at the Welford road underpass? I wasn't able to get as close as I would have liked with all those people around.'

'Well, to tell the truth, Bill, I didn't get all that close to the fence this morning or on our way here. And this morning, as well as the crowd at the underpass entrance, soldiers were patrolling the ring road above. But the fence looks the same, and why wouldn't it be? They must have had a pre-prepared job lot of plans and materials. It's odds-on that they had a standard design. But does it matter?'

'Yes, I think it does. We need to check the Welford road fence again, but if it is the same as this one, it's not as bad for us as it looks. There's no embedment of the vertical steel rails into the road in this fence. It's more of a big gate than a fence. That could be by design so that the road could be easily opened, or it might be just because they knew they had to do the job in a hurry. But either way, this fence or gate, whatever it is, can be opened in minutes from the other side by sliding back some of the horizontal rails, and from this side, it might be possible to smash a way through if it was hit hard enough.'

'Would the Range Rover do the job?'

'Perhaps, but it wouldn't be going far afterwards. It would be better to use something bigger. The lorry might do.'

Still discussing the implications of what they had discovered, they drove away down to the big eastern ring road interchange. They no longer had any hope or expectation that access to the ring road would be available. The obstruction at the underpass was evidence enough that all access points to or under the ring road were blocked.

As anticipated, at the interchange, there was a tank, more fencing, and no chance of passage. It had been worth checking out, but now it was confirmed. Yes, they had been kettled all right. Kettled, it seemed, by their own army, without explanation or apology.

'We may as well carry on and have a look at the airport while we're here,' said George. 'Not that we are likely to find it open, but we might find some clue as to what's going on.'

They were not surprised to find the access road to the airport blocked. If ever there was going to be a rush to the airport for getaway flights, now was the time. Nevertheless, the sight before them, when they eventually got round to an accessible runway viewing point, shocked them into silence. Huge red airplanes stood by the terminal buildings with teams of red clad figures busily engaged in transferring goods into fleets of red trucks. They gazed in awe at the sheer size of the spectacle, a giant futuristic ballet in red.

Bill was the first to speak. 'This is some relief effort, George. I don't know what I was expecting, but it wasn't this. Who are they? They are not ours. We don't have this amount of kit. We'd be hard pressed to stage a state picnic. This has got to be some sort of international aid scheme.'

'You might think so', said George, 'but I wouldn't bet on it. The timing's not right. It would take weeks or months to get international aid organized on this scale. This lot, whoever they are, must have been on stand-by. They got here within days.

'I'm completely baffled and in more ways than one. How can they have been so well prepared? Everything's happened so quickly. And assuming that all this stuff they're loading down there is food aid, how are they going to distribute it? They'll be overrun by hungry mobs the minute they leave the airport.'

'Perhaps we're barking up the wrong tree George. Supposing it's not food aid, supposing that we've been invaded, and the riots, the looting, and the burnings were all pre-planned by a foreign power. That could account for the power shutdown, the communications blackout, and the kettling. Those crates and pallets down there might all be full of weapons.'

'You've got a point there Bill, but who would want to invade us and why? We're a small, bankrupt, overpopulated nation with no oil reserves or gold mines for anyone to fight over. We've no enemies, no territorial ambitions, and we are no threat to anyone. And whoever invaded any country just for the privilege of taking on the burden of caring for its people? It doesn't make sense.

'And what about our army? Where do they stand in all this? How can it be that they've gone missing at the very time you would expect to see them everywhere? I did get brief glimpses this morning of the troops on the ring road at the underpass, and they looked like our guys to me. They were kitted out in brown, not dressed in red. But I just cannot believe that our army would collaborate with our enemies, if we had any.

'The curious thing is that our army was as well prepared as this lot, but it's inconceivable that they planned the downfall of the government. At least, I hope it is. Anyway it's about time we were on our way. We've a long way to go and a lot to think about.'

They picked out a route that would take them past the docks and then on through the city centre, hoping to get back to the Old Hall while it was still light. They managed to get back before darkness but only just. The unexpected and dreadful events they encountered in the housing areas around the docks trapped them for hours. They never got as far as the city centre.

It was not pleasant driving down the main link road between the airport and the docks witnessing wholesale looting of the warehouses and light industrial units that lined the way yet being acutely aware that they were powerless to do anything about it. But, even if the temptation to try had been there, it had been swept away by acceptance of their personal predicament. They were no more than passive observers. All sense of moral outrage had been laid dormant. They both knew this and said little.

They were within two miles of the docks when they met a stationary line of lorries, a sure signal that the docks and the seaport were closed. George took a right turn into a housing area, and Bill anxiously took out the roadmap. With modest confidence that with good navigation they would soon be in sight of the city centre, although nervous as to what they might find when they got there, they approached without concern the first of the many makeshift barricades they had come to expect.

They were accomplished practitioners in the art of barricade negotiations. They went through the routine of explanations, commiserations, and expressions of goodwill, which so far had served them well. The crowd that had surrounded them, at first hostile, began to yield. They were willing to let them through but only with warnings.

'You'll never make it to the city centre. You're more likely to get killed. You don't want to know about what's going on down there. Go back.'

'We'll be all right,' said George. 'No you won't,' came the reply from the crowd.

The crowd was right. The barricades were getting bigger and more frequent, and then they were in the thick of it. Bottles and bricks were being thrown, corner shops were on fire, terrified families were leaving their homes clutching bags and cases.

Suddenly, George skidded the Range Rover to a halt and, propelled by pure instinct, leapt out to confront a group of youths attacking an elderly couple. Bill followed closely with the dogs. It was soon over. Two youths knocked out cold lying on the pavement. Two youths whimpering on the ground beneath the dogs. Two more sprinting to safety.

'Are you all right?' asked George, helping the couple to gather together their possessions. 'Thanks to you, yes.' said the elderly man. 'We were trying to get to the shelter at the school.'

'We'll help you with your bags,' said George. 'Get in and show us the way.'

After a few hundred yards down the road, around a few street corners, the school was in sight. Fifty yards before it, however, was the last thing that George and Bill expected to see on their journey, a barrier manned by three uniformed policemen.

'Sorry, guv, no one gets past here today. We've got the street blocked at both ends. What's your business?'

It took George only a few minutes to explain their encounter with the thugs and the plight of the elderly couple. The policemen expressed regrets that they had experienced such an incident and willingly allowed him to help the couple with their bags to the queue in the playground.

It was, George thought, the saddest sight he had ever seen, a line of distressed, displaced, and dispossessed people seeking shelter. And this was in his own country. A country in which, only day's ago, the streets were full of expensive cars, and good living was taken for granted.

His sadness turned to anger. How could this have come about? And what were those policemen doing manning a barrier when they should be arresting criminals. It was not right. It was an outrage. But he was beginning to run out of rage.

He returned to the barrier where Bill was in deep conversation with the policemen. He was in the mood to hit a few people, starting with the policemen. Sensing the situation, Bill quickly ushered George into the car.

'Let's be off. We're going to have to go back to the Old Hall the way we came.'

When George had calmed down, Bill told him what he learned. The policemen on the barrier were acting on their own initiative. They knew nothing about any planned relief effort. They were simply part of a group of locally based officers trying to provide protection against the rising tide of violence.

Other groups were forming. They had all stayed in their posts until the police stations were burnt down, and the official chains of command had collapsed. He and George had witnessed a particularly brutal aspect of the breakdown of law and order, forced displacement of people from their homes being carried out by roving gangs of criminals. House grabbing, they called it.

He and George were on the fringe of some of the city's poorest areas. Any attempt to drive further into the inner city estates would be suicidal.

'Thanks, Bill', said George, 'I got it a bit wrong back there. I was beginning to think that the police were cowards, not heroes. I should have known better. Put it down to stress. Now when we get back to the Hall, how much of what we have seen today should we tell the others?'

'Certainly nothing about what we've just been through', said Bill, 'but I think we can put a positive spin on what we saw at the airport. Aid is on its way and all that. It's the kettling thing that's going to be a problem. They won't take that very well. They won't take it well at all.'

'You're right there, Bill. What I suggest is that this evening, we just tell them that we are hoping that, with the arrival of the relief force, the roads will soon be clear and that we will be going out in the morning to check how things are going on. That will give us the chance to get down to the Welford underpass to examine the fence. We'll keep the chatter as short as possible. And the way I feel, we will need all the time we can find for getting a few drinks down.'

CHAPTER 9

Extra Guests

Arriving late back at the Hall, still worrying about how much of their findings to reveal, although relieved to be still in one piece, George and Bill were astonished to find that, in their absence, they had acquired a sizeable collection of extra guests. The kitchen was full to overflowing with every chair and available standing space taken by evidently contented diners.

George's first thought was what a good job Frances was doing with the catering. His second was how she had acquired all the food they were enjoying. As the noise level dropped, he peered through the gloom nervously concerned as to what was going to be expected of him.

Nervousness turned to relief as, one by one, he began to recognise the newcomers as friends and neighbours from down the Avenue. Jim Pritchard was there with his wife, Elaine. Jim, a venerable past captain of the golf club, was now in his seventies but still playing well enough to be one of George's regular partners. The Bradbury family, Martin and Susan, with their two sons, Oliver and Miles, were there. The boys were close school friends of the Rigbys' children. Amanda Brooks, a long-time bridge partner of Frances, was there with her husband, Mark. So was Tony Wesley, another of George's regular golf partners, along with his wife, Sophie, and their only child, Toby, a bright young man doing a year's work placement with the Robinsons before going on to university.

George breathed a deep sigh of relief. For one moment, he had thought that he was about to be presented with a string of new names, which he would immediately forget. In normal circumstances, faced with such a gathering of friends, George might have announced his entry with a little jig and twirl, but on this occasion, he settled for a cheery high hand wave and 'Drinks all round.'

Frances, sensing that his joviality was unusually restrained, got the conversation going again. 'George, you know everyone here so there's no need for introductions. We all met up earlier today, and things being what they are, I've invited them to stay with us. I know you'll be pleased. We've pooled the contents of our larders and had a jolly good meal. Sorry for starting without you, but I was not sure when you'd be back. By the way, did you get the lights?'

'No luck,' replied George. 'I'll tell you the details later. But what about you folk? How did you know we were having a party?"

The details gradually emerged as George circulated through the throng. Frances had set off for a brief walk down the Avenue with Janet and Anne to see how Amanda and Sophie were getting on.

They had found both in a state of shock and near terror. Both were dreading another night in the dark, alone with their families and their fears. Their futures, if they had any, seemed too frightful to contemplate.

Too afraid to go out, they feared that they would soon be starving. Rumours were abounding that gangs of looters were spreading from the city centre towards the suburbs. They had tried to get out of the city but found it impossible. All was lost.

And then Frances had appeared with her friends, relaxed and confident that soon all would be well. They were heading for the countryside and a getaway from everything on a farm. Tonight, however, they would be secure behind the gates of the Old Hall Estate.

George had gone to the company compound to get some lights. To Amanda and Sophie, the very thought of security and a night without fears seemed too good to be true.

'Would it be possible for them to stay at the Hall for the night?'

'Of course it would. George would be delighted. Yes, bring along whatever food you have to spare. No, don't bother about wine. George has more than enough. Get there before dark and bring a few blankets you may be sleeping on the floor.'

Before returning to the Hall, Frances had suggested to Janet and Anne that they call on Mr and Mrs Pritchard. Frances was worried that as the Pritchards were getting on in years, they might not be able to cope with living without lights and no way of finding out what was going on.

They were found in an even greater state of distress than the Wesleys and the Brooks. Frances had insisted that they packed there and then and that they should accompany them back to the Hall. The Pritchards had clung to their arms all the way back to the Estate.

Carol had taken her children to visit the Bradburys. She soon realised that the 'how nice to see you all' welcome they received was simply a show put on for the children. They were trying to maintain a positive outlook, but in reality, they were in a state of shock and despair. When the Bradbury boys learned from the Rigby children that they were going to live on a farm in a valley near the seaside, their plaintive 'can we come too' requests were too much for her to ignore.

'I'll just go back to the Old Hall to ask Frances if there is room for any more,' she had said. For Frances there was only one answer to that question. 'Yes, tell them that they we shall be delighted to have them with us.'

The more George heard, the more he struggled to work out what he was going to say about his day. The guests had brought with them much of the frightening news he had been hoping to keep under wraps. And to make matters worse, they had unintentionally generated a measure of panic amongst the Old Hall residents.

Robin and Janet were now talking about making a run for the airport, and Peter and Anne now wanted to get across the city to visit their elderly parents. There was nothing for it, George concluded, but to be honest but not too descriptive.

The bad news and the good news had to be told. But in what order? Was there a rule of presentation of which he was totally ignorant? As he pondered this, it occurred to him that nothing should be said with the children still present and that he had not, as yet, invited any of the new guests to stay for the night. That must come first.

'I want you all to know that you are most welcome,' said George. 'Things are going to be difficult for a while, so please bear with us if you have to share living space and the sleeping arrangements are not up to your usual standards. Normal service will be resumed as soon as possible.

'Frances tells me that you've all brought candles and torches. Thank you for that, we're going to need them until the power comes back on. I don't know when that will be or how long we will all be staying here in the Hall, but I think you all know that unless the general situation improves within the next day or so, we are planning to relocate to a farm in the country until things settle down.

'Accommodation will be tight, but again, you are all welcome to come with us. The more the merrier, I always say. Take your time making you mind up, there's no need to decide before breakfast.

'Now, if you'll excuse me, I am going to see what can be done about lighting log fires in all the rooms with fireplaces. Thankfully, we've plenty of logs and plenty of fireplaces. I'll leave it to Frances to settle you all in, starting with the children. Oh, and one last thing, could I have some help in moving the cars around?'

As they all started to move around and head for the bedrooms, Bill sidled up to George. 'Well done, George. You should have been in the hospitality business. But what's all this about the cars?'

'Security, Bill, and a chance to have a quiet word with some of the adults. Can you round up the drivers and get them outside with their car keys?'

When the drivers were gathered together, George explained his plan. 'I don't want to over dramatize things, but we cannot take the risk of overnight intruders getting into the estate. They might struggle to get into the houses, but they could steal or damage the cars. Then we would be in a fix. So what I propose is that Bill should put the lorry close up to the gates, and then we pack the cars tightly around the lorry. As an added precaution, we'll chain the Rottweilers behind the gates. They're trained for guard duties, and nobody in his right mind is going to take them on. I need to get the Range Rover out early in the morning. I'll explain why when we are all back inside, so I'll take the place directly behind the lorry.'

Once everyone was back in the kitchen and the children were out of the way, George, tapping the table with a spoon to emphasise the need for attention, commenced his uncomfortable address.

'I don't need to tell you that we are in a tight spot. We've all seen things that we never expected to see in our lifetime. Worse, still we are completely in the dark as to what is going on. And I don't just mean that we've no power and no television.

'Bill and I have been out and about for the last two days trying to find out what's happening. It's hard to make sense of it. The good news, if you could call it that, is that some form of relief force appears to have taken over the airport. That may not be good news for you, Janet and

Robin, but I'm sorry to say that I think your chances of getting into the airport, let alone getting a flight out, are nil.

'The seaport, by the way, also appears to be closed. We can't work out whose planes and people are at the airport, but strangely everything is coloured red, the planes, the people, and the trucks. It's some sort of red brigade. Let's hope they are the promised relief brigade and not a hostile force. Well, that's about the limit of the good news.

'The bad news is that the police and the emergency services appear to have gone missing from the streets. We met a few brave souls trying to do their best, but law and order seem to have broken down in the inner city area, and it looks as though it's spreading.

'Worst of all, however, particularly for us, is that all routes out of the city have been blocked. Whether that's to keep people in or to keep people out, we don't know. Bill and I think it's to keep us in. It looks to us as though we've all been kettled. However, all is not lost. We think there is a way out. Tomorrow morning, I'll be setting off early with Bill for a closer look at an underpass we think we can get through. So keep your spirits up and enjoy a drink or two. With all the bottles we've collected recently, we could open an off-licence.

'Finally, Peter, I know that you and Anne are worried about your parents, but I don't think you should attempt to cross the city on your own. Bill and I will look them up tomorrow when we are out if you give us their addresses. Now, I'll try to answer any questions, but I don't promise any useful answers.'

The discussions that followed covered a lot of ground, but as George had expected, there were far more questions than there were answers. Is the money we've got in the bank still safe? How can we get it out? What will people do if they have no money? How are we going to buy anything if we can't use crowns? Will we be able to use our credit cards and cheques? How will people know when to go back to work? How will we people get paid? Will our pensions be all right? Are we still insured? Who's looking after the hospitals and nursing homes? What will happen to our homes when we're away? When will we have a new government?

And so it went on until late in the night. Questions! Questions! All questions of vital importance. But George had no answers. Nor did anyone else. Like hapless passengers on a ship heading straight for a highly visible iceberg, the unthinkable was now reality. Thank goodness for Captain George, he still seemed to have a rescue plan.

CHAPTER 10

Threats and Fears

The night passed without apparent incident. A chilling silence had descended over the darkened city perversely disturbing the sleep of the nervous occupants of the Hall. But the guard dogs had remained reassuringly quiet apart from a single short burst of barking, and when George and Bill examined the gates and the parked up vehicles in the early morning gloom, they at first found nothing of concern. Their anti-intruder efforts, it seemed, had either worked or had been entirely unnecessary. It mattered not. It had been a job well done.

They settled the dogs into the Range Rover, and Bill set about unbolting the gates. All was not well! The wooden panels they had fixed to the outer face of the gates now carried the threatening message, 'Get Out Now or we Burn You Out' crudely sprayed in white paint. The intimidators were nowhere to be seen.

'Well, so we have had visitors,' Bill exclaimed, standing back from the gates as though the message might change the longer he looked at it. 'What do you think we should do?'

George appeared to be dumbstruck. His mind reeled as he considered the implications and possible actions. To run or to stay? Flight or fight? Never before had he been pressed to make such decisions. What did business acumen and sporting prowess count for now?

Gradually, his mind calmed down. It was not what he would do for himself that mattered. Who cared if he appeared as a coward or a hero? The only thing that mattered now was the safety of his charges. But what, in the circumstances, was best for them?

'I'm tempted to tell everyone to pack immediately and that we will be leaving within the hour, Bill. But what happens if we can't get through the underpass? We could be stuck in no man's land and a sitting target for villains. That's far too risky. We have got to be sure we can crash our way through the fence before we leave here.

'And we must not forget that we have said that we would go in search of the Robinsons' parents. I would feel very bad about letting them down.

'The best thing I think is to stick to our plans for the morning, but first we will have to tell the others what's going on. I'll go and see who's about, and I'm going to look for some paint to blank this rubbish out. I'll be back in a few minutes.'

George, carrying his paint, returned with Peter and Robin. 'There it is', said George, 'there's the problem.' Both stood silent, visibly shaken. 'How soon can we leave?' said Peter.

'Not just yet,' replied George. 'We need to take another look at the underpass. But we'll leave the lorry and the cars behind the gates, and we'll leave one of the dogs chained up here. Have a word with the other chaps and see what they think about forming a guard duty roster. You could sit in pairs in one of the cars. But don't worry, I can't see anyone being brazen enough to attempt to move in while we are still here.'

When eventually they were ready to go and with the gates secured behind them, Bill and George sat for a while, planning their route to the underpass and scanning the trees lining the verge for signs of the would-be intruders. Nobody was to be seen, and nothing but the dawn chorus of the birds in the spinney disturbed the quiet.

'I'll be sorry to leave this place,' said George. 'We've got it all here, city life and bird life, town and country, all on our doorstep. Does the thought of leaving bother you, Bill?'

For once, Bill had no quick reply. Chin in hand, perhaps holding back a tear or two, all he could say was 'We haven't been given much of a choice. We just have to make the best of what's left for us. Now, which way are we going this morning?'

'I was thinking that we should take the same route as I took the other morning through the housing estates', replied George, 'but if we get a clear run on the main road, that will be quicker. Let's give it a try.'

They headed up the Avenue towards the main road. One hundred yards short of the junction, George brought the car to a shuddering stop. Ahead of them red clad figures were busily erecting a barrier across the end of the Avenue. 'Well, well, well', said Bill, 'now's the time to have a little talk with our new neighbours, assuming of course that they speak English.'

The language barrier proved to be no problem. But getting the men in red to say anything was more difficult. Only one of the group of four looked up as Bill and George approached to ask what was going on, and he was clearly not in the mood for casual conversation. The most they could extract from him was that the main roads were being closed to ordinary traffic to allow relief supplies from the airport to be distributed around the city.

George's attempts to find out what country he was from and who was behind the relief effort fell on deaf ears. Bill's attempts to find out why they were dressed in red did no better.

Realising that, short of barging their way past the barrier, there was no way past, and that getting involved in an affray at one barrier might well lead to their arrest at the next, they retreated to the Range Rover and headed down the Avenue to the housing estate roads.

Taking the same route as they had the previous day, they reached the Welford road and the underpass without incident, impeded only by numerous stops at the resident's makeshift barricades. At some barricades, George was recognised as the big man in the white Range Rover who had been through before, and he was greeted with a growing measure of camaraderie. At others, he had a bit more explaining to do. But always, George maintained without effort an affable dialogue and a cheering presence.

'If we could all pull together like these people, wouldn't that be wonderful?' he said to Bill as they pulled away from one of the barricades.

'Yes', replied Bill, 'but can you imagine trying to get the Avenue folk out manning barricades, let alone building them? "Good grief, no you can't have my grand piano nor my dining suite, whatever it is you want them for." But anyway, most of them have already done a runner, and that's the difference, isn't it? These people have to stay because they've nothing else.'

'You're full of little surprises, Bill,' said George. 'I never saw you as such a deep thinker. But you may well be right. Where does that leave us though? Are we not trying to do a runner?'

'No, we all talked about moving abroad, but we chose to stay. Not for us cocktails on a flash hotel balcony in Monte Carlo or skiing in the winter sunshine in the Alps. We'll be lucky to find a village pub with lights on and with a barrel of warm beer in the cellar.'

'Thanks for that, Bill. I've got the picture. I was just wondering what our plans for retreat to the farm might look to those stuck here. But enough of this depressing talk; let's see what this fence is made of.'

Much to their relief, the fence across the roadway was identical to the one they had seen the previous day. As Bill had suggested, a good hit with a powerful vehicle would show it to be no more than a big gate.

The lorry would get through, and so would the Range Rover. But would they be driveable afterwards?

They were still debating this when the second shower of airborne leaflets descended upon them. This time, the instructions were more specific than in the first airdrop. All police and emergency service workers were to report to the airport without delay. To allow distribution of food supplies, all unauthorised vehicular traffic was prohibited from using main roads. Pre-packed food parcels would be available without charge from supermarkets on proof of identity. Only pedestrian access would be allowed to supermarket sites. Community workers and care home managers should report in person to the police manning the supermarkets and other food distribution centres. Power supplies would be restored on a part-time basis within a few days.

'Suddenly, I feel a bit better', said Bill, 'but only a bit. What makes this red brigade lot think that the police will show up at the airport? I'd think twice about leaving my family alone without protection. And what makes them think that people can get to the airport anyway? Not everyone goes round with a pair of Rottweilers.'

George continued to study the leaflets. 'Do you know what this says to me, Bill? It says, we'll provide some food to keep you from starving, but the rest is up to you.'

'Not much change then.'

'Probably not. But I hope I'm wrong. We need law and order just as much as we need food, perhaps more. Think about it, Bill. The police lost the battle for law and order when they were on the streets. What chance do they have if half of them are handing out food parcels in supermarkets? All in all, I don't think we should hang around in the city to find out how this all pans out. The sooner we get to the farm, the better. But first, let's go and find Peter and Anne's parents.'

After an hour's difficult driving along side-roads and occasional bursts along main roads until ordered off by the red clad erectors of barriers, they reached the northerly suburban housing estate of Keston with its multitude of tree-lined crescents and cul-de-sacs. This was the area marked on their map as the home of Anne's parents.

They found them happily engaged with their neighbours building a substantial barricade out of tightly packed refuse bins and garden benches. No one was going to get into their cul-de-sac without a great deal of effort.

'How are you all getting on?' asked George after introducing himself and Bill.

'Very well, thank you. We were quite well stocked up before all this trouble thankfully, and we'll be off to the supermarket tomorrow to collect our free food parcels.'

Would they like to leave?

'Good gracious, no. It's quite fun really, particularly now that there's nothing to watch on television. We are all a bit worried about our pensions and savings though. But it will be alright when things get sorted out, won't it? And how are Anne and Peter getting on? Are they all right? Off to a farm for a nice change, are they? Well that will be nice. Give them our love.'

The address for Peter's parents showed it to be only a couple of miles from the city centre on a radial road leading to the suburb of Eastcote. The road itself was typical of the ribbon development by which the city had started its expansion half a century or so earlier. The houses on the stretch of road they were looking for were attractive medium-sized detached dwellings, set back from the road, with gravelled drives.

'Here's the house', said Bill, 'that's the number.'

It was immediately obvious that there was trouble ahead and that there had been in the past. The state of the cars and vans on the drive gave everything away. It was a long time since any of them had been inside a repair workshop or a car wash.

'We've come to see Mr and Mr Robinson' they announced to the unshaven, string-vested, and overweight figure who answered the bell call with a half-opened door. 'Are they at home?'

'Never heard of them,' came the reply. 'Clear off.'

'They lived here until yesterday. This is their home. How long have you been here?'

'None of your business.'

'You think so. Fetch the dog, Bill, and get the muzzle off; we're going in.'

'They left yesterday. They've gone to the shelter.'

'Where's that?'

'The schoolhouse down the road.'

'They had better be. And remember this. When we come back, which we will, it will be with a pack of dogs, a pack of Rottweilers. And if there's any damage to this property, none of you will be leaving with happy memories of your stay here or with your legs intact.'

The schoolhouse was packed. Every chair had its occupant, and whole families were sleeping on the floor, stressed to exhaustion. A small group of middle-aged ladies, having commandeered the kitchen, were hard at work making drinks and sandwiches. Without them, George and Bill would never have identified Mr and Mrs Robinson.

They were tucked into a corner, hidden by their baggage and clearly suffering from shock. 'They came in yesterday,' said one of the tea ladies. 'I know them well. They're a nice couple, evicted from their homes like many of the people here. They've hardly said a word. It must have been very frightening for them. How do you know them?'

'Peter, their son, asked us to try to find them. He's a neighbour of ours. It looks as though we'd better take them back with us. Thanks for your help. And keep up the good work here. You're doing a great job.'

The journey back to the Hall was made in near silence. The Robinsons seemed to have fallen asleep on the backseat. Bill and George, lost in their own thoughts, were anxious not to do anything to disturb them.

It was another slow drive. The barricades were getting bigger and more numerous. Worse still, huge crowds were beginning to form in the vicinity of supermarkets, completely blocking the roadways, and making it impossible to pass. Tedious diversions were the only solution.

Passing a hospital, Bill and George were surprised to see that, once again, the men in red were in evidence, controlling entry and unloading lorries. The momentary uplift that gave did not last for long. The signs of forced evictions, or house grabbing, as Bill now preferred to call it, were definitely on the increase in some of the streets where the residents had relied on the police rather than barricades to keep out intruders. A menacing trend of moving house without the bother of exchanging contracts was developing, and who was to know where it would all end.

After negotiating their way through one particularly difficult barricade, Bill whispered to George, 'When we get back, there's something we need to talk about. It's about the barricades on the route to the underpass. We can get your car through all right, but what about the others? How are we going to explain why we're leading a convoy of cars through without giving the game away?

'I've been thinking the same', replied George, 'but I haven't come up with any answers yet. We'll talk about it later.'

When at last they reached the Avenue, Bill surprised George by suggesting that, instead of driving straight up to the Old Hall, they should turn right and then take the first turn left. 'There's something I want to look at,' said Bill. 'Stop when I give you the shout.'

The object of his interest turned out to be an ambulance station set back from the road with a garage on one side and a small office block on the other. The big concertina doors of the ambulance station were closed, and there was no sign of life on the forecourt. Nor were there any signs of life in the buildings on either side.

'Park up on the forecourt', said Bill, 'but keep the engine running; we may have to make a quick getaway. I'll be back in a few minutes.'

Bill crossed the forecourt and clambered over the tall side gate to the left of the building, disappearing from view. Moments later, and to George's surprise, he reappeared clambering over the side gate on the right-hand side. Back in the car and rendered breathless by his exertions, he urged George, in a few gasping words, to head speedily for the Old Hall. He was still breathing too heavily to speak when they got there.

Peter was on guard at the gates when they arrived at the Hall. Taking one look at his parents dozing in the back of the Range Rover, he sprinted off to get Anne and to get the keys to the cars and the lorry blocking the entrance. Whilst Anne shepherded his parents to a quiet room in the Hall, he joined George and Bill clearing a way through the cars for the Range Rover. By the time they had reinstated the vehicular blockade and Peter had again sprinted back to the Hall to see his father, Bill was at last able to explain to George what he had been up to.

'You remember a few miles back when we were talking about how we were all going to get to the underpass, well, a thought suddenly came to me. The problem is in the numbers. My maths may be wrong, but on my count, our little party of eleven has now grown to twenty-four. We're no longer talking about a small group; we're now talking about a proper convoy.

'I couldn't see how we could keep it together. It's enough getting one vehicle through the barricades. Make that a convoy of six or eight vehicles, and it hasn't a chance. Somehow or other, we need to get everyone into three or four vehicles. What we really could do with is a bus.

'And then it occurred to me that we haven't seen a single ambulance on all our travels. Nice big heavyweight vehicles with few windows. The sort of vehicles that are given clear passage even at barricades. And then I remembered the ambulance station. That's why I asked you to make the detour. I just wanted to see if there's anything available for short-term hire.'

'So what were you doing climbing over those gates?'

'I was looking to see if they've got anything in stock, and they have, six of them.'

'Bill, you'll get us shot. But you may be on to something. All day long, I have been worrying about the route to the underpass, ever since we saw the red brigade putting barriers on the main road. I hadn't planned on trying to get our line of cars through the housing road barricades, even when we only had four cars to bother about.

But you're right about the bigger convoy. It hasn't got a chance. How could we explain what we were up to? Any hint that we were leaving the city, and within minutes, they'd all be in their cars and vans racing to get to the front of the queue. And we'd be stuck once again behind a line of vehicles going nowhere. I suppose we could try to smash our way down the main road, but I doubt that we'd get far without being apprehended. The red brigade will have some form of walkie-talkie communication.

To be quite honest, Bill, I was beginning to think that we might have to sit it out at the Hall until things cool down. We've got the numbers to hold off invaders, but will that be enough? I doubt that we've got the food to hold out much more than another few days. This ambulance idea of yours is worth looking into. But do you really think that we could borrow or steal a few?'

'The way you put it, George, we haven't got much option but to try. The first step would be to get back down to the ambulance station on foot to have a good look round. We need to find a way into the building, and we need to find the ambulance keys. We'll have to do this before it gets dark, so we can see what we're looking for. Do you think we should tell the others?'

'Well, they are due a few explanations, Bill. We'll certainly have to say something about today's events and give them some idea on when we hope to leave, if at all. But we can't have a full house discussion just yet. I suggest that we get a small group of representatives or something together, put them in the picture, and see what develops from that.'

CHAPTER 11

Decisions

George started the process of forming a group of representatives by calling everyone together and declaring that some important decisions needed to be made. He and Bill had seen the leaflets dropped that day, but from what they had seen on their travels, questions remained on how speedily food supplies and law and order could be restored.

The men in red seemed to have taken control of the main roads, which might interfere with their plans for leaving. There would be time later for full discussion, but the immediate priority was to take some preliminary soundings of how people felt by sitting down with a small group of representatives. Nominations were requested. 'Just put your hands up if you are interested.'

The group that eventually sat down together comprised George and Bill, Janet and Peter from the residents, and Martin and Amanda from the guests. George got the discussion going by explaining that the original expectation that they would be able to leave for the farm when it suited them had been dashed by the difficulties of getting out of the city. They now had to decide whether to go ahead with attempts to leave or whether to stay and make the best of their enforced confinement.

There was no need to make a decision there and then. There would be time later for more thought and talk. But if they did decide to leave, they needed to have an exit plan they were reasonably sure would be successful. From what Bill and he had seen, such a plan could not be based on simply driving away in a convoy of cars.

What was needed was a small convoy of bigger vehicles. They had ideas of how such a set of vehicles might be acquired, but it involved illegal activity. He and Bill did not wish to undertake some necessary investigations, which sensibly needed to be done within the next hour or so and which themselves would be illegal, if the general view was already that staying put was better than leaving. He and Bill had spent much of the last few days away from the Hall, and they would like to hear what those around the table sensed to be the general feeling.

The discussion which followed suggested that most of the adults were still of two minds. Janet made the point that, until they knew whether their dwindling food supplies could be replenished, it was difficult for anyone to come to a reasoned conclusion. However, she felt that if food could be assured, the majority might prefer to stay and look after their properties rather than take the risks of travel.

Peter, influenced perhaps by the ordeal of his parents and the worrying time he had spent on guard duty, suggested that if everyone was aware of the full horrors that might be coming their way, the majority were just as likely to vote for leaving irrespective of the food situation.

Martin declared that he felt something of an intruder into the debate. His shared Janet's view that more was needed to be known about food supplies before any general consensus could be assumed. He felt the same about the uncertainties of restoration of law and order. Until the intentions of what George called the red brigade were known and the effectiveness of whatever measures they might be taking to gain control of the streets could be seen, he couldn't even say what his own view would be on staying or leaving.

Amanda was of the view that what really mattered was not the balance of pros and cons of this or that but was confidence in the group's leadership. In the end, everyone would be looking to George.

George thanked them for their contributions, adding that they had very helpfully assisted in resolving the question of whether he and Bill should look further into possible travel arrangements. In the light of what they had heard, they were now confident that they should look further, and that is what they would do. They would leave immediately to carry out further investigations and would be back within an hour or so.

After dinner, and with the children out of the way, there would be a general discussion involving everyone. But while they were away Janet and Amanda could, with the help of the other ladies, carry out the very important task of assessing how long the present stocks of food would last.

George and Bill were well prepared as they set off down the Avenue on their first criminal outing. Bill carried a large bag of tools, and George carried an assorted bag of potentially useful items including torches for dark rooms and two pairs of ears muffs in case they activated any noisy alarms. Both were suitably dressed for the occasion in jeans and anoraks.

Road traffic was minimal, but unusually large numbers of pedestrians were around for an area where the majority of households had at least two cars and going out on foot was only ever done as a recreational pastime. Not all the pedestrians looked entirely comfortable in their surroundings. Many seemed intent on keeping their heads down as though employed as pavement inspectors. Their only interest in George and Bill was apparent admiration of the Rottweiler at their heels.

Whilst they greatly welcomed this unplanned anonymity, they were uncomfortably conscious of the need to show no sign of concern that their once select neighbourhood had, in a matter of a few days, taken a very evident turn for the worst. It had not taken long for the underclass of the city to discover that the upper class had largely abandoned their homes in the panic of the times. The squatters, intruders, house grabbers, or whatever name they were given, were not just on the way here, they were already here.

'Our turn next', muttered George under his breath, 'it makes you want to stay and fight, but to what end?'

The ambulance station was set well back from the carriageway behind its large forecourt. The six massive sets of concertina-type doors took up the entire front of the building. To either side of the building, high pedestrian gates secured the premises.

After examining the gates and selecting the left hand one as his target, Bill produced from his bag a large steel jemmy and a lump hammer. I'm not going to ask you to climb over,' said Bill. 'Once was enough for me, and it would be more than enough for you; just hit the shackle hard, and as soon as I've levered some clearance, we'll soon have it open.'

He was right. Closing the gate behind them, they made their way along the plain brick sidewall of the building to a paved courtyard at the rear housing, a collection of sheds and a scattering of plastic chairs and tables. A run of windows broken by three doors occupied the wall overlooking the courtyard. Although all the windows had steel grill attachments, there was no obvious sign of any burglar alarm box.

Peering through the windows, they could see that two of the doors seemed to give access to storerooms. It was not obvious what was behind the third door, which stood between the other two. They moved to the unexplored sidewall. Like the other sidewall, it had just one small grilled window but no doors.

'It has to be the middle door at the back,' said Bill. 'It must give access to a corridor. That's the one for us.'

'What are we going to do if an alarm goes off?' asked George.

'Well I say that we should carry on regardless. Who's going to answer any alarm? And if we leave the dog chained here by the door, who's going to come in after us?'

'Good thinking, Bill,' said George 'Now let's see more of your breaking and entering skills.'

The door was no match for Bill, and as anticipated, it led to a corridor, which further examination revealed led to other corridors serving offices and communal rooms and entry to the ambulance bays. They found the keys to the ambulances neatly displayed in a wall-mounted cabinet in what appeared to be the station manager's office.

'That's the easy part done', said Bill, 'but I'm not sure how we can get these big fellows out onto the forecourt. I would guess that the doors are electrically operated. Yet how would they get them out if there was a power cut? They can't have overlooked that.'

'Manpower,' replied George. 'Let's give it a try.' It worked, and they stood back admiring their efforts.

'Now, we need to be careful,' said Bill. 'Don't push them back too far; we don't want every man and his dog coming in. We've found out all we know for the time being. They're here for the taking. But perhaps not for long if the red brigade can get the police and the firemen back to work. If we are going to take them, well, some of them, the sooner we do the deed, the better. But now is not the time. It's still too light out there, and there are too many people about. Dawn would be the ideal time. Let's close up and get back.'

They walked back to the Hall in deep concentration. George was worrying how he could get a set of ambulances and a lorry through the barricades. Bill was worrying about how many ambulances they would need and how many of the group's drivers would be capable of driving an ambulance. And they both had a dread feeling that they were acting on an impulse of audacious magnitude.

Were they seriously considering the theft of a set of ambulances? What sort of a crime was that? Would the defence that they were really only intending to borrow them mitigate their punishment? And what if they were apprehended on route and torn to pieces by an angry mob? What madness had taken leave of their senses? That question was soon answered.

As they turned from the Avenue into the drive to the Estate, they saw immediately that it was already under siege. The gates were still closed, and the guard dog behind them was barking furiously. But In front of the gates, an unsavoury throng of individuals with a motley collection of vehicles had taken camp.

Bill froze. George reddened. Rushing forward unthinkingly and without care as to the response he might produce, he roared at the top of his voice, 'Out! Out! Now! Or you're dog food. And don't even think of coming back." And saying that, he leant forward as though to release the Rottweiler from its leash.

The throng, rushing to put maximum distance between themselves and the dog, scattered and scrambled back to their cars; then, retreating to the safety of the Avenue, they disappeared with a fist-shaking show of bravado and strings of obscenities. George and Bill stood inwardly shaking until the last of the vehicles was out of sight.

'Well done, George,' gasped Bill. 'I'd almost forgotten what a fearsome fellow you used to be in your rugby shirt. I hope we've seen the last of them.'

'Not a chance', replied George, 'they'll be back.'

Later that evening, with his friends and guests gathered around, George knew that the time had come to put all the cards on the table. The decision that had to be made was his. But they deserved a hearing. Nervously, he commenced his recital to the background and reality of their situation.

'It's a few years now since some of us here in the estate planned that if ever the nation's woes brought us to the brink of catastrophe, we would get away from the troubles. We bought the farm at Lostock as a rural retreat, and that is where we would be now if all had gone well. Unfortunately, very little has gone well, and I take responsibility for the fact that we are still here. I mistakenly thought we had time to see how things would develop. Regrettably, as you all know, the troubles are now on our doorstep. I apologise to you all for landing you in this predicament.

'Earlier today, I had a chat with Janet, Amanda, Peter, and Martin to see how you felt about the big question we must now decide. To stay or to leave? What I have to say now is just my view on what we should do. But please, ask whatever questions you like, and if the majority of you see too much risk in what I am going to propose, let's carry on talking.

'This is how I see it. Firstly, our food supplies will last us only a few more days. It may be that the relief effort, which seems to be underway, will help us out, but from what I have seen on my travels with Bill, I don't think we can rely on it.

'The same applies to the restoration of law and order. Efforts are being made, but it will take time to put things right, weeks, months, perhaps years. We only have days. Most concerning for us is that the very things that once made this area so safe and desirable now make our properties targets for the sort of people you saw today outside the gates. And there's one thing you can be sure of. If the cavalry does come riding over the hill, they won't be stopping here. It's the city centre they'll be heading for.

'So what do we do? I think that we should leave, and I believe, from the soundings we've taken, that most of you think likewise. We won't be leaving tonight, and it won't be tomorrow. There are a few more things that must be done. But unless some miraculous change of fortune occurs encouraging us to stay, we will be leaving early the following morning.

'I won't go through the details now, but don't be surprised if, when you look out tomorrow morning, you see a fleet of ambulances parked up and waiting to take us on our way. Bill and I have arranged to borrow them for a day or so. They'll be safer than the cars. Now, let's have an open discussion.'

The discussion went on for over an hour. Contemplation and expression of the anxieties and uncertainties of the life that beckoned reduced some of the gathering to tears. There were so many questions but so few answers. Questions that went over old ground on why it had happened and who was to blame. Questions about when it would end and what would follow. But no one expected answers to these outpourings of communal grief; the relief came in the talking.

George was happy to sit quietly listening to the talk of this kind; his views, like everyone else's, were no more than opinion and guesswork. However, some aspects of the discussions were a little more focussed on the practicalities of their planned retreat to the countryside. What might they find when they got out of the city, and what fate would befall them if they were apprehended before they reached the farm? When might they be able to return to the Old Hall, and what will have happened to their homes and cars in the meantime? How would they survive at the farm, and how would the locals react to their presence? When would people be returning to work, and when would there be schooling for the children?

As George listened to the discussion on these, again saying little, he was beginning to see problems that he had either overlooked or not wished to confront. But much to his relief, no one queried how they were going to get to the underpass and, once there, get through it.

'We've covered a useful lot of ground, and you've raised some very good questions', said George as he brought the discussion session to an end, 'but I don't need to tell you that I don't have all the answers. In fact, I have very few. We'll find out in good time what's in store for us, but I do believe that it will be better for all of us to be in the countryside rather than in the city for the next few weeks, months, or however long it takes to put things back together again.'

And with that, George, thanking everyone for their forbearance and contributions to the discussion, called together the car drivers and asked them to join him with their car keys on the drive.

'Sorry to drag you out chaps, but we need to move the cars. Very early tomorrow morning, Bill and I will be going to collect the ambulances. Bill will be doing all the driving to get them here, and he needs to have a clear run through the gates for each of the four trips he will be making. And when we all leave the following morning, we will again need a clear run. I'll keep the Range Rover out, but I suggest you lock all your own cars up in your garages.

'Now there's just one more thing. We can't take the risk of intruders getting in overnight and spoiling our plans for the morning, so I'm looking for volunteers for guard duty. On a shift basis, of course.

'We'll only have the lorry and the dogs at the gates, but I've got an idea for creating the impression of a bit more. You know that little tractor I keep in a garden shed, well it's got headlights powered by its engine. If we tuck the tractor in behind the lorry with its engine running and lights on but out of sight from any climbers on the gates, it may be enough to deter them from thinking they've got easy entry.

Whoever's on guard at the gates can sit it out in the Range Rover and use the horn as an alarm if needs must.'

There was no shortage of volunteers for guard duty with Martin and Robin taking the first shift, Peter and Tony taking the second shift, and Mark and Toby taking the final shift. George was getting a few hours of much-needed sleep when he was disturbed by a quiet knock on his bedroom door followed by a whisper, 'George, they're back!' Within minutes, he was on the drive with an agitated Tony grasping his arm repeating in disbelief, 'They've lit a fire on the road.'

'Have they tried to get in?' asked George as they headed along the dark corridors of the Hall to the doorway and out towards the gates.

'No, but if you climb on the lorry, you can see them.'

George climbed onto the lorry. Shadowy figures could just be made out in the trees lining the entrance road to the estate. A dozen, perhaps less, thought George. The fire, which seemed to be made out of timber planks, was no more than a few yards from the gates. It extended across the full width of the road.

'What are they doing?' whispered Tony who had now attached his arm to Mark. 'Not a lot', replied George, 'but this is the last thing we need.'

Bill and Peter had now joined them at the scene. 'Shall we set the dogs on them?' asked Bill as George got down from the lorry.

'That's what I would like to do', said George, 'but perhaps that's their plan.' The dogs rush out and they rush us from the bushes. Anyway, we can't start a commotion just now. Within the hour, we're hoping to be quietly and secretly bringing in the ambulances. Not much chance of that now, but we have to stick to the plan. It's all we have left.

'And if it's only those people out there who know we've got the ambulances, who cares? They're not likely to be dashing off to find someone in authority to report a theft. And they've got their own agenda, which will not include sharing their intended spoils with the rest of the ragtag and bobtails who've moved out here. No, I think we should just ignore them.'

'Do you mean bring the ambulances in while they're still here?' asked a surprised Peter. 'Isn't that a bit risky. And what about the fire, you can't just drive over it.'

'Well, we'll just have to shift it, and I think I know how we can do that. Bill, you're the handyman around here. Remember the dozer attachment I have for the tractor, how long would it take to fit it?'

Bill frowned. 'About half an hour if someone gives me a hand, but who's going to drive the tractor? It's tiny.'

'I am', said George, 'and it's not that tiny. I was a very big child. Perhaps that is why I was an only child. Anyway, over the years, I've learned to do all sorts of tricks with that tractor, and one involves driving it standing up. That's how I got it over here to the gates.

'But it's not the fire that really bothers me. The bigger problem as I see it is maintaining security at the gates whilst we bring in the ambulances. The plan is that I'll drive Bill down to the ambulance station taking one of the dogs which we will leave down there to keep people away. I'll then drive back in front of Bill as he brings up the ambulances, one by one.

'The whole business shouldn't take more than fifteen minutes. But here's the problem. During that time, the gates will have to stay open. And I don't like the thought of that one bit.'

'Why not use four drivers and cut the exposure time down?' asked Peter.

'For two reasons, Peter. One being that, without some training, which you will be getting tomorrow from Bill, only Bill can safely drive the things. The other is that it's best that only Bill and myself are involved in obtaining them. So far as everyone else is concerned, they have been kindly lent to us, or borrowed if you think that sounds more convincing. No, what we need is a show of strength at the gates, which will deter the enemy from getting too close.'

Neither Peter nor Tony saw much prospect of assembling a credible show of force, but Robin, who had joined them at the gates, was far more positive.

'Leave it to me,' he said. 'We've got the numbers. In fact, if we rope in everyone, excluding the children and the elderly, I reckon we can outnumber them. I'll rustle them up. When do you want them on parade?'

'Make it one hour from now', replied George, 'watches set.'

CHAPTER 12

The Paddocks

With dawn just breaking, George examined his troops. It was a good turnout. Robin and Janet, Bill and Carol, Peter and Anne, Martin and Susan, Amanda and Mark, Tony, Sophie, and Toby, and even, somewhat to George's concern, the elderly Pritchard and Robinson couples. Frances had been persuaded that she was the best person to stay in the Hall with the five children.

Bill started up the truck and backed it away from the gates. George started up the tractor, now looking quite impressive with its dozer blade fitted, drove it up to the gate then placed the Range Rover close behind it. One of the dogs was coaxed into its cage.

The troops, George decided, should be formed into three semicircular ranks with Robin, Peter, Martin, Mark, Tony, and Toby in the front rank; Janet, Carol, Susan, Amanda, and Sophie in the second rank; and the four elderly folk in the third rank. Martin volunteered to hold the lead of the dog selected by George as the more controllable of the two ferocious animals.

From a distance and in the early morning half light, the serried ranks could be taken as a formidable human barrier. A force to be reckoned with.

As quietly as he could, Bill unlocked the chains and opened the gates, not quiet enough though to avoid alerting the would-be intruders that something of interest was about to happen. They moved from the darkness of the trees towards the gates sensing that their moment had come. They rapidly retreated as the tractor, with its dozer blade scraping the surface, clattered into view with George standing high at the controls. He hit the fire at the best speed he could muster, dislodging some of the burning timbers which he could now see were scaffolding planks, presumably stolen. A shower of sparks momentarily lit the darkness but lasting long enough to illuminate the ranks of supporters behind George at the gates.

Within minutes, the timbers were pushed aside, and the tractor, with what had at first looked like an attacking charge, turned and was back inside the gates. Seconds later, the white Range Rover sped from the drive and disappeared down the Avenue. The guards at the gates stood still as statues in the eerie glow of the scattered remnants of the fire. Only the chirruping's of a modest dawn chorus broke the menacing silence.

No one moved from the trees. Whatever was going on was not over yet.

And then, seemingly as quickly as it had disappeared, the Range Rover was back. Not alone, but closely pursued by a dementedly driven ambulance. No sirens, no blazing headlights, just an incomprehensible chase towards some hidden disaster. The ranks opened and closed. The vehicles were gone with the speed of a waking dream. This was no time to leave the trees.

It was the Range Rover again, flashing once more towards the Avenue. Some calamity must have occurred, nothing to do with us but not something to welcome. Here they were again, the Range Rover and another ambulance. This must be some calamity. Was it time to flee? No, stay in the trees; he's coming out again. Stay quiet, stay still; it's not us they're after.

Another ambulance! And now he's off again! How many can there be? That's four! And now they're closing the gates! It's a though we weren't here. That's enough for tonight; one more, and we'll call it a day.

Silently, they departed.

When the residents, proud of their show of strength, had seen enough of the ambulances and ready for breakfast were back in the kitchen, George set out the plan for the day. He would be leaving early to do some final route checking. He had thoughts on how their passage through the barricades might be eased, and he would need some help loading the Range Rover with crates from the wine cellar. Bill would be giving driving lessons to volunteer ambulance drivers.

The group of representatives needed to meet to allocate places and fix the seating plans. Each ambulance would be carrying six people but full use should be made of the stretchers with priority for the children and the elderly. Lots of blankets were needed to be provided. They were not planning to stop for inspection at the barricades but it would be best if it looked as though the ambulances were on normal duties.

Space would be needed in one of the ambulances for the Rottweilers' cages. The dogs would be staying behind the gates that day, so the cages could be removed from the Range Rover before George left. The cages needed to be firmly secured in the back of the lead ambulance. Because they would all be leaving at dawn tomorrow; all packing must be done before nightfall. Before retiring for the night, they would stage a rehearsal of their departure.

With the cages removed from the Range Rover, George found there was room for ten cases of mixed bottles. There were, he thought, only eight barricades on the housing estate route to the underpass, but a couple of extra cases would do no harm. Anyway, some of the barricades were bigger than others.

Loaded up and with the lorry and tractor out of the way, he nudged through the cautiously opened gates. All was quiet and not so much as an abusive or threatening message on the gates to bother about. The embers of the night's fires remained by the roadside, but otherwise, the early morning events might have been imagined. Perhaps they were no longer under threat. Perhaps the would-be intruders had been frightened away. Perhaps they could stay and fight their way through crowds at the supermarkets for food supplies. Better still though that they all stopped for lunch at a country pub tomorrow on their way to the farm and put all this worry behind them.

Although George had little doubt that the only feasible route to the underpass was through the housing estates, he couldn't resist the temptation to drive up the Avenue to the main road to see what was happening. The red brigade was still in charge. The barriers were still in place. It was the run through the back road barricades to the underpass or nothing.

He turned the car and headed for the housing estates. As soon as he reached the first barricade he jumped out of the Range Rover and greeted the guards with his rehearsed cheery patter. 'How are you fellows keeping today? Anything to report?'

The guards looked at him with curiosity. 'Are you with the police or something? And where are your dogs today?'

'Well, I'm just keeping an eye on things around the city. There's some awful things happening you know, and some are not far from here. Gangs of vagrants are breaking into people's houses and taking over their properties. There's looting and burnings going on. Have you had any problems like that in your roads?'

'Not yet, we haven't, but we'll be ready for them if they show up here. Some of the lads have seen them though. They went out yesterday on a bit of an expedition, trying to see what's happening in the city centre. They didn't get there. Ran into disturbances a couple of miles out. Had a bit of trouble getting back, what with roads closed by redcoats and crowds outside supermarkets. Have you been there yet?'

'I gave it a try, but it's hopeless. The city centre's a no-go area at present. It won't be possible to get there until the police are out in force again. Hopefully it won't be long though. You saw the leaflets yesterday? If they can be relied on, we'll soon have food and power supplies.'

'Well we won't be hurrying to the supermarkets. It's going to be chaos. And just as likely that if you do get your hands on a food parcel, someone's going to mug you for it. Anyway, we've a job to do here keeping things safe.'

'How are you managing for food then?'

'All right, so far. The local shops still have stocks and we've set up a local system of rationing. No one's being allowed to clear the shelves in our shops.'

'Good for you; keep it up. Now before I go, you asked about the dogs. I didn't have room for them. I'm carrying something else today. Here's a case of bottles for you, a gift from some well-wishers. I may have another case for you soon.'

'Thanks mister. Thanks very much. But what's your name?'

'George, just call me George. Bye.'

'Hang on a minute. Hang on. We've all been guessing about your number plate, GB1. Are you George Butler, the man who built the houses around here?'

'Why do you ask? Don't tell me there are some cracks in the walls.'

'No, they're very well built, guv. But it's nice to see that the man who built them is still interested in us.'

It took George more than an hour to negotiate his way through the seven remaining barricades using the same routine and getting much the same reception at each one. But he'd made some new friends. Quite a lot. And he was beginning to look forward to visiting them again when all this was over.

Perhaps they were overreacting to the crisis? Would these quiet suburban roads ever be a target for looters and brutal gangs intent on illegal occupations? Somehow it didn't seem likely.

These roads had neither the tensions nor despairs of the densely packed inner-city streets, which left the poorer people so vulnerable; nor did they have the obvious vulnerability of the handsome avenues of the rich with their secluded mansions. Perhaps these people would be safe without their barricades. But who was to know?

Maybe what he was witnessing was reaction to shock, not to physical fear. What future would the people here have without jobs, means, and a supportive government? Yes, that was probably it—team spirit, pulling together, and manning the barricades. What better way to put the fears for the future out of mind, if only for a few days or weeks. Whatever it is, you just have to admire them.

He left the last of the barricades and headed towards the Welford underpass for one final check. He needed to fill in some time. Heading straight back through the barricades might seem a bit odd, even to his new friends. And he had promised Frances that he would go to the paddocks to make sure that her horses were still being well looked after.

Then came the shock. The junction with the underpass road sported a red painted barrier bearing a 'Road Closed' sign. It was not manned, and it was easily passable, but its presence brought him to an abrupt halt with a spate of inward curses. Why had he overlooked the possibility that the red brigade might take control of the underpass roads? There was only one way to find out if they had done so.

He parked the Range Rover and ventured on foot down the road towards the underpass. There they were, two of them, smart and forbidding in their red uniforms, standing by a red-painted sentry hut. As though not satisfied with army's steel fence closure efforts, they had placed one of their own red wooden barriers across the entrance to the underpass right up against the steel fencing.

What now, he thought as he returned to the car and sat staring with dismay into the far distance. Could the breakthrough still be done? No, it wasn't possible. Crashing the fence was one thing, knocking down and probably killing two people was another. And what an utterly despicable act that would be, deliberately carrying out hit and run murder in stolen ambulances. There would be no lenience in the sentencing for that offence.

He took out his road map and worked out a route to the paddocks at Kentford. He would think on his way. A network of minor roads and tracks left over from the times the whole area was farmed still survived inside the ring road edge of the city giving access to a drab belt of fields given over to what was known locally as horse culture.

George had never understood or shared Frances' desire to have her own riding horses. Much as he loved horses, he preferred to see them in racing stables, perhaps because he had long held the view that no horse big enough to safely carry him had ever been bred. Still it was better to use the fields as paddocks than to leave them fallow. And Butler Developments had no immediate need to build on them, the time would come.

Frances' horses were kept in a group of stables run professionally by a retired trainer who, in previous years, had been in charge of the substantial string of racehorses owned by George's father. Knowing that he was totally reliable, George had no doubt that Frances' horses would be well looked after. Still, he knew that she would feel better if he had seen them for himself. He found Eric, the trainer, in the yard, apparently talking to one of the horses.

'Hello, George, what brings you here? I haven't seen Frances for a day or two.'

'Eric, you may not know this but the government has collapsed, and the nation's in a state of meltdown.'

'I always said they were useless. Good riddance to bad rubbish.'

'Yes, you may be right there, Eric, but there's rioting and looting in the streets, people are fighting for food, and our money is now worthless.'

'Mine's not. It's all in dollars. Has been for years. If you didn't know that collapse of the crown was a racing certainty, you must be an idiot. Your old father would turn in his grave.'

'Well, I take it that you're all right then, Eric. You won't be wanting these bottles I've brought for you.'

'Leave them there. I'll look after them. But you still haven't told me what brings you here.'

'Frances asked me to call to let you know we may be away for a while and to thank you for looking after her horses. She sends her regards. I'll let her know you asked after her. By the way, just before I go, I see that you get a good view of the ring road from here. What's going on up there?'

'Nothing. Nothing but army trucks for days now. There must be a war going on somewhere.'

'Any idea what's happening on the other side, and why there's all that razor wire along the top of the embankment? There's no way over, is there?'

'No way over, but there is a way across. It's no use to you though, George, you've put on too much weight.'

'Come on, Eric, come clean. What's the score?'

'Well, you know young Billy, whippet of a lad, wants to be a jockey; poor fool. Lives in the cottage here with his mum and dad. Well he's got a lass in Kentford village a mile or two over there. Gets across to see her every day.'

'How does he get over?'

'He doesn't get over. He goes under. Through the drainage culvert.'

'Can I take a look?'

With a measure of reluctance, which somewhat surprised George, Eric led him across a muddy field to the toe of the ring road embankment. They edged down a steep bank thick with weeds to a big concrete pipe about four feet in diameter, its end covered by a rusty but easily removable metal grill. A slow drainage ditch ran into the pipe.

George winced at the thought of trying to crawl through the culvert. It had to be about fifty yards long. Young Billy was a brave lad if he went through that every day. George crouched down to look up the culvert.

'Is that a trolley I can see there?' he asked. Eric mumbled that it was something Billy used to lay on to keep out of the water. Looking closer, George could see that a stout rope attached to the inward end of the trolley was dangling into the water. He was about to ask Eric about the rope when he thought better of it. A fair guess suggested that the trolley was designed to carry more than just little Billy. Another fair guess suggested that Eric might be a beneficiary of whatever purpose it served.

When they got back to the farmhouse and the stables, George, after saying goodbye, turned and looked towards the big old barn. 'Is that where you keep your hay and tractors Eric? Do you mind if I have a look to see what condition it's in these days?'

'Why not, it's your barn.'

George silently gazed at the fine old timbered roof, apparently assessing the need for any necessary repairs, but inwardly thinking, "A man could hide quite a few ambulances in here. And if I'm right about the culvert, the people around here will not be in need of food parcels."

He waved goodbye to Eric and headed back towards the Old Hall. His passage through the barricades could not have been easier. A quick flash of his headlights to indicate his approach, a friendly wave through his lowered car window, and within an hour, he was back at the Old Hall. The siege party, he was relieved to see, seemed to have departed, alarmed perhaps at the mysterious goings on behind the gates.

The residents and guests had not been idle while George was away. The drivers had been trained, the passenger seating had been settled, and most of the luggage everyone planned to take was securely in place. Fixing the cages for the Rottweilers had not been forgotten. All they needed to do now was to get a good night's sleep.

Well, that was how George put it. But he needed to get Bill on one side and to let him know that all was not well. Tomorrow, the two of them were going to have to make some difficult decisions. He tracked Bill down and loudly suggested to him, for the benefit of everyone within earshot, that they needed to go outside to see about the lorry.

'Bill, we have a problem, a big problem, and it's not one we've planned for. The redcoats are down at the entrance to the underpass. Two of them on sentry duty today, complete with a sentry hut. We must assume they'll be there tomorrow. If they are there, I don't see how we can go through with our breakout plan.

'But there may be an alternative. When I saw them there today, my first thoughts were that we had been struck with total disaster. Our plan to leave through the underpass was our only leaving plan. And we've already concluded that staying put is not an option. For a time, I almost felt suicidal. Just as I thought we'd sorted out the problem of the barricades and the only question left was whether the Range Rover could smash the fence, which, I'm sure, it can, the redcoats turn up.

'Then as I was down at the paddocks at Kentford, checking up on what's happening with Frances' horses, a Plan B came into my mind.

We'll set off for the underpass just as intended. I'm confident that if I drive ahead of the ambulances in the Range Rover, we'll get through all the barricades without difficulty.

'We can stop just short of the underpass road to see if the redcoats are on duty. If they are not, we carry on with Plan A. If they are there, we move to Plan B, and you all follow me to the paddocks. Once there, we bunker down in the big barn with the ambulances out of sight to think about our next moves. We won't starve, there's a way of getting supplies under the ring road from Kentford village. Now, what do you think of that, Bill?'

'George, if that's the only Plan B, I'm with you. But why do you think we can't get through the underpass if the redcoats are there?'

'Because we'd almost certainly kill them with our charging vehicles.'

'Not if we got the redcoats out of the way before we charged.'

'How would we do that?'

'Set the dogs on them. They'd soon rush for the safety of the sentry hut to shelter behind the door. Then we'd hit the barriers at full speed and be gone.'

Later that evening and unable to sleep, George found himself on the driveway of the Old Hall walking round the ambulances, staring at the stars and hoping that the Lord would forgive him his sins and allow them all a miraculous flight to safety. For their sake, not for his. He deserved punishment for getting them into this mess. He walked down the drive and clambered onto the back of the lorry for one last look over the gates before retiring for a second time to try to get some sleep.

His worst fears were realised. The would-be intruders were back amongst the trees and, once again, apparently collecting wood for a fire. It was not an auspicious answer to his prayers.

CHAPTER 13

Escape

Despite being mentally and physically exhausted, George found it impossible to sleep. Too many thoughts were racing through his mind. How could he face tomorrow morning just driving away from his cherished home not knowing when, if ever, he would return? What state would it be in if he did return?

How was it possible that the wealth of the nation, accumulated by generations of hard-working decent people over many generations, now seemed to have vanished or be up for grabs by those with the biggest sticks? Why had democracy let them down? Was that the fault of the people or the politicians? How could law and order be restored and maintained in a country with no money and no possibility of ever repaying its debts?

Who was going to feed the nation and look after the vulnerable? What work was available for the millions in the city with its businesses and government in ruins? Was it likely that other nations that had lived within their means would come to the rescue of a nation which, for years, had lived as though money grew on trees? Who was it that seemed to by trying to help them now, and why?

Would things be much better if they ever got down to the farm? What chance was there that they would ever do so? What if they were captured by the army or by vigilantes on the way? And how would they ever get the ambulances out of the Old Hall Estate and past the people behind the gates?

George must have dozed off because suddenly an entirely new plan for dealing with the people at the gates came into his head. He needed to treat them as people! He had taken them to be enemies but they had never resorted to actual violence. He had taken them to be villains when they might be no more than opportunists. Perhaps they were just ordinary people as fearful for the future and their families as he and the others at the Old Hall were.

Perhaps he could talk to them. And what was the point in fighting them? They were going to get into the estate anyway as soon as it was left empty. He and his group wanted to get out, and they wanted to get in. They just had to talk.

As soon as George detected from noises in the kitchen that preparations for departure were underway, he called a meeting of the residents to put to them his thoughts on trying to do a deal with the people at the gates.

The basis of the deal would be that occupation of the Estate would be allowed until such time as the residents returned. Providing that the properties and the grounds were kept in good condition and free of damage and re-entry was given without challenge, no legal action against the occupiers would be taken by the residents. To ensure that the occupiers were not left without homes to go to at the end of their stay, free housing would be provided by Butler Developments.

The residents were unanimously in favour. Getting out without a fight and getting back in without one would solve a lot of problems and ease a lot of minds. Departure would be delayed to allow time for talks.

When the morning light improved, George climbed onto the gates carrying a hastily made placard bearing the simple message, 'Help Us and We Will Help You'. He stood for a few minutes, but no one ventured from the trees. Either they couldn't read the message, or they feared a trap. Well, if they were not going to come to him, he would go to them.

He crossed the wide grass verge towards the trees, carrying the placard like a seasoned demonstrator. He could see that they were gathering into a huddle as though seeking group protection from something he might have concealed on his person. They were evidently more frightened of him than he was of them.

As he approached, they nervously backed off and fearing they were about to run, he barked, with all the authority of a man of his size, 'Stay where you are. All of you. I want to talk to you.' They stood, eight of them, all early middle-aged males in jeans and anoraks, trembling like schoolboys caught smoking behind the bicycle shed by a fearsome headmaster. 'Who's in charge?' barked George. No one spoke.

'Never mind,' said George, lowering his tone to indicate his intentions. 'We've got some business to do together, serious business. You can all join in.'

Once George had explained who he was and what he had in mind, the atmosphere eased, and it was not long before they were telling George their story. They were dockworkers living in one of the poorer parts of the city. Even before the government collapsed, they could see their lives falling apart. What little money they got, when they did get paid, went nowhere with prices rising daily. They, and their families, would have been heading towards starvation had it not been for what they called dockers' perks.

Local crime was on the increase, and it was no longer safe to walk the streets alone. After the collapse and as things got worse, stories began to circulate that people in the rich parts of the city were fleeing the country with their money and that no one was stopping their homes being taken over after they'd left. Everyone was on the lookout for a find.

When things got really bad in the city after the lights went out, they had decided that it was time for them too to try and find somewhere safe for their families. They had come across the Old Hall Estate by chance and, because of the shutters on the houses, thought it was already empty. They were frightened of entering when they heard the dogs but thought it worth staying around for a few days to see what was happening.

They had tried to move things along by painting threats on the gates and by lighting fires in the road. They meant no harm. The last thing they wanted was violence.

A little bit of bartering went on. Mainly about what sort of houses they would be getting, where they would be, and whether they could use the cars left behind at the Old Hall. The promise of new houses on a suburban estate and use of the lorry was more than enough to clinch a deal. They were more than delighted with George's kind offer, made after they had agreed terms that while their families were at the Old Hall, their children could play with the little tractor. 'But make sure they look after it,' said George. 'It's 45 years old, and I haven't finished with it yet.' And then, like a bunch of old friends, they all went down to the Hall with George to tidy up the details and to sign up the agreements.

'That all went well,' said Bill as he went out with George for a last look around before departure. 'I liked the explanation you gave them for the ambulances—on loan to us to get some sick children to hospital! Just as well, the children weren't skipping around! Now, we are going to have to wrap them up in blankets! But why did you tell them that we were going to Barton and not to the farm?'

'It's something I've been thinking about,' replied George. 'I was thinking's about a lot of things last night. We've been so engrossed in how to get out of the city that we haven't talked enough about all the details and what we are going to do when we do get out. Let's run through the details again to make sure we're on the same wavelength.

I'll drive the Range Rover to the Welford road with you up front as passenger and distributer of bottles at the barricades. Robin will drive the lead ambulance, followed by Peter, Martin, and Mark, driving the others in that order. At the Welford road, I'll approach the underpass with the dogs, and you will crash the Range Rover through the fence with the ambulances close behind. Once the other side of the ring road, Mark's ambulance will stop to pick us up, and as soon as possible, we'll all stop, and you and I will take over the lead ambulance.

Now, somewhere along the way, we're going to have to ditch the ambulances; we can't just drive them all the way to the farm. What would we do with them if we did get them there? But more likely than not, somewhere along the way, we're going to get stopped by the police or the army and have to hand them over. The longer we stay in the ambulances, the greater the chances of us getting arrested like thieves caught red-handed. So it would be far better for us if we could quietly park up the ambulances as soon as we can and transfer to some other mode of transport.'

That's one reason I mentioned Barton. It's a big town with lots of traffic going in and coming out. We won't find much heading towards St Jude. Another reason, as you know well, is that Frances and I have interests at Barton, an apartment on the seafront and a boat in the marina. I hadn't originally thought of going via Barton, but it won't be a disaster if we have to do so. Anyway, perhaps we should keep quiet about where we're going until we know what's in store for us.

Before we set off, Bill, I think we should tell everyone, including the children, to leave all talk about our destination to you and me. If pressed, they should say we're going to a hotel in Barton. Not that I'm hopeful of one being open, but you never know.'

Rubbing his cheeks with his hands as though to indicate the level of his deep concern or deep concentration, Bill took his time in responding. 'I agree with you, George, that we need to get rid of the ambulances as soon possible, but I can't, for the life of me, see where alternative transport is going to come from. There are twenty-four of us. We can't just call a taxi. And one thing's for certain, it's no use us just abandoning the ambulances by the roadside and trying to hoof it to Barton or wherever. We would look like a bunch refugees struggling along with our sad bundles of belongings.

We need to find a spot where the ambulances won't look out of place and where we can melt into the surroundings. A big car park would be best, or we could try for my transport depot, but that's north of the city and miles out of our way. But come to think of it, I wouldn't want to see them there, parked up and waiting to be collected as evidence of our crimes.'

'Do you know, Bill, I think I know the very place, the motorway service area on the M South at Greenfields. It's on our route; we can get in off the service road, and what is odd about a few ambulances on a motorway service area. With your skills, we might even be able to steal a few parked-up cars or lorries to complete our journey, but we'll deal with that problem when we get there.'

Bill thought it an excellent idea.

The drive to the Welford road went without incident. It was a good start. The Range Rover, with George at the wheel and Bill in the passenger seat, headed the convoy a few hundred yards ahead of the tightly bunched ambulances.

Before reaching each barricade, George flashed his lights repeatedly as a warning that he was approaching at speed. He then crunched to a halt, shouting through his lowered window, 'Thanks, guys, no time to stop, I'm on escort duty today. Stand clear of the ambulances, they're close behind.' Bill had only seconds at each barricade to leap from the passenger seat and put down a crate of bottles. And then they were gone, leaving behind a bemused but not unhappy team of guards.

The convoy pulled up as planned just before the Welford road. George and Bill crept stealthily along the hedge and around the corner until they could see the entrance to the underpass. Two redcoats were chatting at the barrier. No soldiers were in evidence on the ring road. They crept back to the convoy.

George took the dogs from the lead ambulance, and Bill took the wheel of the Range Rover. The ambulance drivers were given the 'get ready' signal, and George, with a dog either side, head erect, and back as straight as a ramrod, strode boldly down the middle of the road towards the sentries. The sentries ceased their chatting and shuffled nervously.

Fifty yards from the barrier, George, making no secret of his intentions, bent down to unleash the dogs and then, still holding them by their collars straightened up, faced the guards and bellowed, 'Go boys, go.' The sentries were already on the move. With little more than a trouser leg to spare, they were behind the door of their hut.

Still breathing heavily, they watched with amazement as a white Range Rover roared into view and, still accelerating, crashed with a mighty bang through the barrier and the steel fence. Seconds later, four ambulances, lights flashing and sirens blazing, followed through.

What was all that about? They were in no hurry to leave the hut to find out but, having got their breath back and realising that the dogs were no longer pounding on the door, they opened a narrow gap before cautiously putting their heads far enough round the hut to see down the underpass. There was nothing to be seen except broken timbers and steel rails and a battered Range Rover listing on the far verge. The ambulances, the striding giant, and the terrifying dogs were all long gone. This was going to take some reporting.

Out of sight of the underpass and a few hundred yards down the road, the ambulances stopped to make their pre-planned driver changes. George took the wheel of the lead ambulance with Bill doing the navigating. It was twenty miles to the gated access road, well known to both George and Bill, where it was possible to get directly into the service area without going onto the motorway. The gate was very rarely closed. Their chosen route avoided the big villages but passage through two smaller villages could not be avoided.

Well before reaching the first of the villages, they could see from activity in the fields and the amount of traffic on the road that life outside the city was close to normal. But then, as they came toward the first village, they could see that it was not entirely normal. A barrier manned by civilians blocked the road.

With no more than a moment's hesitation, George turned on the siren and the flashing lights and put his foot down. Instinctively, the barriers were opened allowing the ambulances to speed through. 'One down, one to go,' said Bill, wiping his brow after releasing his tight grip on the seat.

'I don't know whether you noticed it or not', said George, 'but we've just passed an inn that either had electric lights or some very bright candles. Try your mobile phone, Bill, and see if you can make a few calls.' All of Bill's efforts failed. Normal service had not been restored.

Passage through the second village matched that of the first. The fields were flying by, and all was looking well. And then, with less than three miles to go to the service area, a persistent overhead buzzing alerted them to the fact that they had company.

'Can't tell whether it's police or army', said Bill, straining his head through the window to get a better look at the helicopter, 'but they're on to us.'

'We might as well keep going,' said George. 'We're almost there.'

Contrary to their expectations, the gate at the access road was not open. It was not only firmly bolted, it was also bearing a sizeable 'No Entry' sign. George pulled up, and flagged the ambulances behind to stop.

Bill jumped down to examine the gate, and with the strength of a man used to heavy lifting, he pulled up the two lengthy central ground bolts and signalled George to nudge his ambulance up to and into the gate panels. The lock and chain snapped with a bang, and the gate fell open, allowing the ambulance convoy to glide quietly down towards the car park. The helicopter passed noisily overhead.

The sight before them as they rounded the final curve in the access road came as a complete surprise. The service area was now serving as an army camp. 'Act normal,' said Bill as they parked up the ambulances. 'Ask them where the toilets are.'

From the helicopter, a smart young Captain marched briskly towards them.

CHAPTER 14

Colonel Millar

In the ivy clad administration building of the military headquarters at Camp Blackstone, Colonel Millar stood at his office window awaiting a telephone call. He watched with mixed feelings the latest batch of recruits jogging round the perimeter of the extensive playing fields under barking encouragement from a muscular training instructor.

The army could be proud of the opportunity it was giving to so many people from all walks of life to answer the nation's call. But could it be proud of the part it was playing in what might turn out to be the nation's dissolution? They were stretched to the limit with what they were doing, and they were doing it well. The rush of volunteers to join them was proof of that. So was the supportive reaction from all the people under their control despite the restrictions and hardships being imposed upon them. Never in their lifetimes could they have imagined such things happening to them. They were taking it well, there was no disorder, and no one had died.

But they were only part of what had once been a small but proud nation. It was the plight of the others that bothered him. Those they had fenced off in the city. It had seemed a good plan, the only plan in the circumstances that had befallen the nation. But already, the reports coming in from the city suggested that it was going to fail.

Sooner or later, they were going to have to get involved. And that would drag the army into the very things it had sought to avoid, conflict for which it was neither equipped nor manned and responsibilities that even the government had found impossible to meet and manage. A lot might have to be asked of the young people out there. He hoped they were up to it.

The telephone rang. It was Captain Jacobs. 'I've got the ambulances, sir, and the occupants, all twenty-four of them, plus two dogs.'

'Good man. Where are you now?'

'At the Greenfields camp, M South service area.'

'How did you get them in there?'

'They drove in sir. Well, smashed their way in would be more accurate. They broke open the access road gate.'

'How very odd. What sort of a crowd are they?'

'A mixed bunch, sir, five children and nineteen adults. All pretty well-heeled I would say. In fact, from the amount of cash they've got packed away in their bags and cases, you'd think they'd just robbed a bank. One of them, a big fellow who seems to be the leader, has a case with thousands of dollars in it, perhaps hundreds of thousands. We haven't had time to count it yet. I've taken them all over to the Travel Hotel conference suite to keep them out of the way.'

'Well done. Call me back when you've questioned them. Now, what have you done about the damage at the underpass?'

'Everything is under control, sir. A platoon's out repairing the fence, a breakdown truck's bringing in the smashed Range Rover, and I'll be drafting a report on the incident in case we need something on record.'

The colonel moved back to the window. They could do without this distraction. Up to now, the fence had done its job. A few hardy idiots had taken on the razor wire and made it through. But all had paid the price and ended up in hospital. These idiots had taken on the fence and the risk of getting themselves, and others, killed. And yet they were anything but a bunch of drunken youths. They were apparently from well-off families, and they had their children with them. As the realisation of what this suggested dawned, the colonel moved slowly back to his desk and sank into his seat.

The plan for the city had failed. Only pure desperation could have driven these people to steal ambulances to effect an escape. How bad could things be, and what sort of terrors had they faced? He rang Captain Jacobs with an instruction that the captives should be given breakfast and treated with care. He then rang General Aspel telling him of the breakout incident and his concerns about the city. It was not a comfortable conversation. The general had a lot to lose if things went badly wrong. His entire army would be in the deep end of a very dirty pool.

It was nearing mid-day before Captain Jacobs rang back to report on his questioning of the captives. They had told him that they were a group of friends and neighbours trying to reach Barton to escape from hunger and violence in the city. Their houses were under siege from roving bands of vagrants even more desperate than themselves. House grabbers or house thieves they called them. People who were occupying houses left empty by people who had fled abroad and forcibly entering others still occupied. Food was in desperately short supply, and people were fighting over the relief rations. Maintenance of law and order appeared to have collapsed.

The escapees had 'borrowed' the ambulances to get out of the city because they would have had no chance of getting out in a convoy of cars. They were adamant that the ambulances were only borrowed and not stolen. That is why they had headed for the army base on the service area. They were looking to hand them over. Their plan was to stay in a hotel in Barton until things got better in the city. The money they were carrying was their own money, prudently saved and converted to dollars over many years and months.

Amongst the group was Bill Rigby, the owner of Rigby Transport, and George Butler, the owner of Butler Developments. He seemed to be the leader of the group and the owner of the two Rottweiler dogs that had attacked the sentries at the Welford road underpass. He was the one with the huge stash of cash, which amounted to over three hundred thousand dollars.

Overall, they seemed to be an honest and truthful bunch of people, but one or two things did not add up. One of the men, a Mr Harvey, a retired bank manager, had become a bit stressed and kept making the point that they had every right, as citizens of Borovia, to go wherever they pleased in the country and that he had every right to go his cottage in Bowland if he wanted to do so. It also seemed odd that no one could tell him which hotel in Barton they were heading for.

Colonel Millar listened attentively to the captain's report. 'Did I here you say that one of the men was called George Butler?'

'Yes, you did, sir. He's the one with the money and the dogs. And by the way sir, we think he was the owner of the Range Rover that crashed through the underpass fence. It's been recovered, and it's now here with us at the service area camp. It carries a personalised number plate, GB1. Do you know him, sir?'

'Not personally, captain, but I know of him. We're going to have to deal carefully with this, very carefully; we've caught a very big fish. He's not just the owner of Butler Developments, he's a big landowner, one of the biggest. A lot of his land is out here in the countryside, although most of it is let-out to local farmers. He doesn't do farming himself. He's also President of the National Rugby Association and a big shot in the golfing world. He's not into politics, but he's got a lot of friends in high places.

'Lay off the questioning for the time being, I may have to deal with Mr Butler myself. Just tell them all that they are staying under arrest while we carry out further investigations. But put it nicely. Say it's for their own safety. Hint that travelling in stolen ambulances may not have made them many friends.

'I've a feeling they are going to be with us for a few days so make them comfortable. Try to find rooms for them at the hotel and to keep them confined. We don't want them wandering around the camp, and we certainly don't want any more spectacular escapes.'

'That won't be a problem, sir. I'll get on to it right away.'

The colonel sat musing for some minutes. Technically, he was holding George Butler and his friends on suspicion of the theft of four ambulances. That would be about the last thing the general wanted to hear coming on top of his earlier warning of bad news from the city. And if the accounts given to Captain Jacobs of the breakdown of law and order in the city were reliable, his warning was beginning to look something of an understatement. But hear the news, the general must, and there was no time to waste. He rang the general.

'General, its Colonel Millar again. That breakout incident I told you about this morning has taken an unexpected turn. The owner of the Range Rover that crashed through the Welford underpass fence and the organiser of the theft of the ambulances is on our list of names. It's George Butler.'

'Good grief, Millar, how did that happen? I thought he'd flown with the rest. If anyone had the means to get out of the country, he did. I wonder what made him stay. Obstinacy, probably. He always was something of an odd ball.

'But if he is the last man standing, we could hardly have encountered him in more unwanted circumstances, detained by the army in possession of stolen ambulances. We need to turn this round very quickly. Those ambulances have got to be returned today. And preferably with our Mr Butler at the wheel of one of them. If he led them out, then he can lead them back again.

'We'll decide what we are going to do about him later, but treat return of the ambulances as top priority. Do whatever is necessary.'

Within the hour, George found himself seated at table in one of the hotel's conference rooms facing a very stern-looking Colonel.

'We'll skip the formalities for the moment, Mr Butler; just tell me how you got hold of the ambulances and how you managed to get them out of the city.'

George saw no point in lying or even seeking to bend the truth. He had done what he had to do, and that was that. The sooner the truth was out, the better.

The colonel sat engrossed by the details of George's account of the difficulties he, and the other Old Hall residents, had encountered in trying to get out of the city and the lengths they had gone to in planning their escape. He uttered not a word until George had finished, and then, after what seemed to George to be an eternity of silence, he cupped his chin in his hands and gave George a long hard stare.

'We have a problem, Mr Butler, both of us. Can you get those ambulances back to where they belong? Today would not be too soon.'

'Not without a bit of help,' replied George. 'I presume you'll give us a clear run through the underpass, both ways.'

'Of course. Now, do you want to use your own men as drivers or mine? Mine would be in plain clothes, not in uniforms.'

George thought for a moment. 'What I need to make this trip go smoothly is an undamaged white Range Rover fitted with my personalised number plates, eight cases of wine, and Bill Rigby sitting beside me in the passenger seat. And as for the drivers, I would prefer your men. Mine have seen enough action for today.'

The colonel smiled and called in Captain Jacobs. 'Captain, Mr Butler here wants a smart white Range Rover, and he needs it within two hours, fitted with his personalised plates. Borrow one, requisition one, or steal one. Get intelligence on the job and start with the dealership at Barton. He also wants eight cases of wine. Raid the mess stores if necessary, but don't take the good stuff.'

The guards at the barricades were getting used to seeing George's car approaching at speed. They were not overly surprised that, once again, he was followed by a fleet of ambulances. But where was he getting all this wine from?

Re-entry to the ambulance station proved no problem, and but for a few dents and scratches to the front of one of the ambulances, no one could have guessed of their absence for an exciting day out in the countryside. The barricade guards were mildly disappointed that George failed to stop as he sped past once again towards the Welford road, but they could see that the Range Rover was fully packed with passengers leaving little room for disposables.

Safely back at the service area camp, George and Bill made speedily to the hotel bar for a few much-needed beers, but it was not long before Captain Jacobs interrupted them.

'I hear that your trip went well, gentlemen. Colonel Millar sends his thanks for your co-operation. He may want to see you in the morning, Mr Butler. We hope you all have a good meal tonight and a good night's sleep. The first for a few days, I should think.'

'That's very kind of you, captain, said George. 'Tell Colonel Millar I shall be pleased to see him. By the way, when will we be able to leave?'

'Not until you've sorted out some transport, I imagine,' replied the captain. 'And that reminds me, can I have the car keys back please?'

CHAPTER 15

The Colonel's Plan

By the time Colonel Millar arrived at the hotel the following morning, George, for the first time in over a week, felt on top of the world—eight hours sleep, a hot shower, a fried breakfast, and the burden of responsibility for his charges transferred from his shoulders to a surprisingly benevolent army. He was clearly back in the Lord's good books. A bright new day had dawned, even though it was pouring with rain.

Colonel Millar was also in a brighter mood. Despite an unusually disturbed night's sleep, he was looking forward to the day. Having gone to bed with nothing but worries on his mind, he now had a plan for dealing with some of them.

If he played his cards well, he could move the problem of what to do with Mr Butler to the general's desk, and he could be seen to be actively trying to resolve the appalling situation in the city. He wasn't looking for medals, but it was time to put some distance between himself and the nightmare of the firing squad that was beginning to haunt him. But first, he had to get the general's consent to activate of his outlandish proposals.

The general listened, patiently at first, but then with increasing enthusiasm. Something had to be done, he knew that. But his thoughts had been running along different lines than the colonel's. Neither of their plans was going to turn retreat into outright victory, but the colonel's plan gave more scope for salvaging something even if it achieved very little.

And presented with enough positive spin, it should be enough to keep the donors on board until a lasting rescue plan could be devised. Things were going badly for them, and something was needed to halt alarming talk about possible withdrawal of their support. The colonel retired while the general made a few phone calls.

'It's on', said the general, 'but not a word more than necessary to our man, Mr Butler.'

The colonel borrowed the captain's office for his meeting with George and commenced with the usual pleasantries. George responded in kind. The colonel thanked George for co-operating with return of the ambulances, and George thanked the colonel for the hospitality they were receiving.

'Well, now we've got that business with the ambulances out of the way, Mr Butler, tell me how you propose to get to Barton; it is Barton you are heading for, isn't it?'

The colonel gave George another of his hard stares. Wincing inwardly, George gave an unconvincing, yes. Then, warming to his task, he began a mostly honest explanation of how it was that he, and twenty-three others, found themselves stranded without transport on a motorway service area.

They had intended to travel by car and they had set off in full confidence of a trouble-free journey to their destination. Unable to get out of the city because of road closures, they had returned to their homes only to find, after exploring various alternative routes, that not only were other routes blocked, but also that their homes were under siege. Desperate to get out of the city and realising that this would not be possible in a convoy of cars, they had borrowed the ambulances. Foolish as it might seem, given their present predicament, they had put little thought about what they would do once they had handed the ambulances over. Perhaps the army could help them get to Barton.

The colonel repeated his hard stare. 'Am I right in thinking, Mr Butler, that you have a farm and some holiday cottages near St Jude and that Mr and Mrs Harvey, Mr and Mrs Rigby, and Mr and Mrs Robinson also have holiday cottages in the same complex?'

'We do, but how do you know that, and why does it interest you?'

'Army intelligence, Mr Butler, and diligent study of local authority housing records. Now the reason we are interested is because that is where we think you are all heading for.'

'Yes, that was the original plan, but we abandoned that when we abandoned hope of getting out of the city in our cars. I still don't understand why it interests you.'

'Because we would like to help you and your friends, Mr Butler, and whilst getting you all to Barton would be no problem, getting you all to St Jude could cause us difficulties we simply cannot risk encountering.

'As you well know, there has always been a vociferous minority in Bowland claiming some historic right to independence. In recent years, unfortunately some would say, these separatists as they are called have gained increasing support to the extent that they now have the makings of a viable political party.

'One matter high on their agenda is strict immigration control, supposedly to preserve their unique identity, but we believe there is also economic motivation. We're in little doubt that it would suit them well to detach themselves from the nation's economic woes with the aim of keeping their agricultural wealth for themselves.

'If they do succeed in their bid for independence, that will be a disaster for the nation in many ways, and it will be particularly bad for the army as sizeable numbers of our troops are based there. Anyway, to keep them quiet whilst we struggle to deal with the bigger picture, we are allowing the separatists to provide some of the manpower for the checkpoints at the estuary viaduct at Stourmouth and at other river crossings. Those of you who already own properties in Bowland should be allowed through without difficulty. The rest, I suspect, will be turned back at Stourmouth.'

This was the last thing that George had expected to hear. It had never occurred to him that he and his friends might not be welcomed by the good folk of Lostock and St Jude and that some of his friends might even be barred from entering Bowland. Was the nation really disintegrating so quickly? Could centuries of patient nation building be lost by a mere twenty years of foolish overspending?

No, thought George, there must be more to it than that. Somehow, the bonds that brought us together in the first place and have held us together ever since have been broken. The collective strength of 'all for one and one for all' traditions that saw the nation through plagues, wars and famines, where was it now?

'Are you all right, Mr Butler?' the colonel asked in a tone of genuine concern, bringing George out of his reverie. 'Can I get you anything?'

'You're very kind', said George, 'but it just struck me that, in little more than a week, our world has been turned upside down—imprisoned in our own city, deprived of information and means of communication, left fighting for food and our property, and now debarred from travelling in our own country. Who planned all this? And tell me why, colonel, it was our own army that blocked the routes out of the city. And who are these people in red controlling the city roads and distributing food supplies?'

'One day, Mr Butler, if our paths cross again, I will do my best to answer all you questions, but now is not the time. All I can tell you now, all I'm authorised to tell you now, is that the army is doing all it can do with its limited resources to prevent the entire nation descending into lawlessness. And, as I have said, we will do our best to help you and your friends. Now, back to your travel plans, have you any thoughts on how we can help you?'

'Well, with what you've told me about crossing the estuary, it's clear that, at least in the short term, we need to get down to Barton and to fix up some accommodation. Once there, we'll have to decide on whether to split up the group, although I don't like the idea. What's the chance of us buying some cars locally?'

'You would be better placed doing that in Barton than here in Greenfields; this is not an area where people go around carrying enough cash to buy five or six cars. And by the way, Mr Butler, how did you come by all the cash you are carrying? Captain Jacobs mistook you for a bank robber.'

'It was all acquired perfectly legitimately, colonel. Nothing more than three years of prudent savings held as a matter of caution under the proverbial bed. I trust you haven't left your family cashless, colonel.'

'On my salary, Mr Butler, I couldn't match your three-year savings in my lifetime. But back to business, I've a suggestion to put to you. We'll transport you all down to Barton, and we'll scout around and find a hotel for you, with you, of course, paying your own bills. We'll even look after the Rottweilers for you until you are more settled.

But, in return, there's something I would like you to do for us. Tomorrow, a convoy of trucks will be entering the city with food supplies and with an additional mission. It will be heading for that part of the city you went through yesterday when returning the ambulances. We would like you to lead the convoy.'

'Tell me more', said George, 'and why me?'

The colonel leant back in his chair and gazed at the ceiling. 'You know as well as I do, Mr Butler, about the problems in the city; you probably know them much better. The problem that troubles us most at present is the breakdown of law and order. It's preventing the orderly distribution of food supplies.

'Unless we can rectify the situation, there is a real danger that the donors, or the red brigade as I believe you call them, will pull out. The consequences for the city of that would be catastrophic. We have to get the police and emergency services back on the streets. To do that, we will have to do more than rely on pleas in airdropped leaflets. We need to provide face-to-face encouragement and persuasion that returning to duty is required and is rewarding. That is where you come in.'

George decided that it was time for him to do a bit of ceiling gazing. 'Colonel, if I can help in any way in relieving the problems in the city, then count me in. But what role can I possibly play? I doubt that you're expecting me to go round knocking on doors asking if a policeman or fireman lives in the house and, if one does, if he will please get his uniform on.'

'No, of course not, Mr Butler. Your role would be to act as a facilitator. You seem to have to have an unusual talent for getting through barricades without hostility and engaging in friendly conversation with those manning them. We were all most impressed at the ease with which you returned the ambulances.

'But this time you won't be stopping with cases of wine; you'll be stopping with truckloads of food supplies. The unloading will be done at such shopping or community centres as suggested by your friends at the barricades. Whilst the unloading is going on, you, and the soldiers with you, will be exhorting the crowds which will undoubtedly form around you to assist in getting local police and the like back to work. Leave it to them to do the doorknocking.'

George thought about this for a while. 'I'm with you all the way, except that I fear there will be antagonism towards the soldiers. There are strong feelings in the city about the army, and they're not good feelings.'

'We understand that, and for that reason, the soldiers will be in plain clothes, which brings me to something else I need to discuss with you. Your friend, Mr Rigby owns a fleet of colourfully painted lorries, well recognised on all our roads. They're presently parked up at his depot north of the city. We would prefer to use these rather than army trucks. Their presence in the city would assist in signalling a return to normality. Do you mind asking him if we can borrow them?

'And just one more thing. Captain Jacobs will be travelling with you. He wants to see the situation in the city, firsthand. He would like to sit down with you as soon as possible to plan out the route details. Would you be happy with these arrangements?'

'Yes, but am I at liberty to tell the rest of my party what I'll be up to and why we will not be leaving tomorrow for Buckland?'

'You can tell them that they will be leaving the day after tomorrow for a hotel in Barton and that yourself, and Mr Rigby, if you wish to take him with you, will be helping the army tomorrow with some transportation tasks. Yes, and you can tell them that, before they leave, we will provide you all with ration books. You're going to need them. Things are not back to normal yet here in the countryside even if the lights are on and most people are back at work.'

'I was wondering about the lights; what about telephones?'

'No mobiles yet I'm afraid, but some landlines are in operation. And that, by the way, is something you can promise the people in the city. You can tell them that restoration of power supplies and communication networks depends upon restoration of law and order and that, if they all do their bit to help, others will do theirs.'

'It all sounds all right, colonel, but there's something I think you've overlooked; I'll need the white Range Rover again.'

The Colonel smiled. 'General Aspel will love this. It belongs to his wife. She may not even know that we borrowed it yesterday.'

CHAPTER 16

Bill's Plan

Even before he reached the end of the corridor leading away from the captain's office, George had an uncomfortable feeling that he had been well and truly outplayed by the colonel. Had he been mugged, or had he been hugged?

He had intended to demand some answers from the colonel. Who is in charge of the nation? Who gave the army authority to fence in the city? Who are these people in red? He'd come away with nothing. Worse still, he'd been slyly manoeuvred into co-operating with the army in another of its mysterious activities. Or had he?

Perhaps the colonel was a good chap, weighed down with colossal responsibilities. Someone who recognised the predicament that he and his group had got themselves into. Someone who sympathised with their plight and was anxious to help them out of it. He had certainly let them off lightly on their illegal possession of the ambulances. Perhaps he was the one needing help the most. He was not sure. It was time to have a chat with Bill.

He found Bill trying to make a telephone call at the hotel reception desk. 'Still no luck, George, no mobiles and only restricted landlines. How did it go with the colonel?'

'We need to talk Bill. Let's take a walk outside. This place may be bugged.'

George recounted his discussions with the colonel. 'I hope you don't mind, Bill, but I've more or less lent your lorries to the army. I'm sure they'll be in good hands.'

Bill adopted his customary face, rubbing before saying anything. 'George, I sometimes wonder how you got that degree of yours. Let me get this straight. We've avoided the rap for stealing the ambulances, but now you're planning to drive round the city into the arms of the red brigade who are no doubt still on the lookout for the hooligans who nearly killed two of their number yesterday, and you've agreed to do so in the Range Rover belonging to the general's wife without her knowledge. And I'm invited to join you. I wouldn't miss it for worlds.

'But, joking aside, George, the colonel's plan is hopeless. It's doomed from the start. The sole reason that the ambulances got through the barricades on both trips is that they never stopped at the barricades. You saw to that. Can you imagine what would happen if a lorry load of food stopped? It would be rushed in the same way that the supermarkets were rushed. No one would be going anywhere. No one would be getting anything.'

'I hadn't thought about that, Bill, not that I had much time to think about anything. It was all over too quickly. But what do we do now? I don't fancy going back and telling the colonel that the deal's off. Not that I can because that's probably his helicopter I can hear taking off now. And I'm supposed to be sitting down with Captain Jacobs in half an hours' time to finalise the route details. We have to think of something and quickly. I was looking forward to telling everyone we would be leaving here the day after tomorrow.'

'Remind me again, George, remind me why the colonel is so keen on this trip to the city.'

'Well, it seems that this red brigade lot expected that they would be delivering relief supplies to a city where the police and emergency services would be in control of the streets. Now that they find that is not the case, they are threatening to pull out.

'The colonel was very careful about how much he told me, but he seems to think that a successful trial run into the city showing that local distribution of food not only works but can be used to persuade people to return to their duties will be enough to keep the red brigade on side. I don't know whether it will or it won't, but what else can be done?'

'The obvious answer, George, is that the army could go in and get a grip. What did he have to say about that?'

'Not a lot, Bill. All I could get out of him was that they are doing the best they can in the circumstances. He wouldn't be drawn on the details.'

Bill went into thinking mode again. 'It's a funny business, isn't it? I wonder what the relationship is between the army and the red brigade. One day, perhaps we'll find out. But you know, George, if it was left to me, I'd be telling the colonel that a much better plan than going in with my lorries would be going in with the red brigade's lorries. That would put them in touch with the people directly, cutting out the middleman. And another thing, how long are we going to be kept here leading convoys round the city? This isn't a one-day job, it could go on for weeks.'

'He promised that we would be leaving the day after tomorrow', said George, 'but you're right. And I bet if all goes well tomorrow, he'll be leaning on us to stay around until the job's done. And as you say, we could be here for weeks. We need to have a rethink.'

They sat in a quiet corner of the lounge with a cup of coffee. A plan was emerging. It was all about food distribution. Bill was big in food distribution. That's what he did for a living. The red brigade had hit a problem trying to put too much of the available food into too few places. They needed to get closer to the people, but they were afraid of doing so.

All the signs were that they were far from being a combative fighting force. If they were to travel into the housing estates, they obviously felt that they needed protection. And where were the people who should be giving them protection, the police and emergency services? In the housing estates, frightened and impoverished. How could the two be brought together? Bill had the answer.

'Supposing that this afternoon, you and I go back into the city, in the Range Rover if we can lay our hands on it. We tell the people at the barricades that tomorrow red brigade trucks with food supplies will be coming their way, but they will only stop for off-loading if local police are at the barriers to control the operation. Otherwise, they will have to wait until the trucks can get back on another day.

'Tomorrow, we can then lead a convoy of trucks, as suggested by the colonel, through the barricades we're familiar with. I'll bet a pound to a penny that the police will be there. We tell the police, and any other support services that have turned up, that if they report to the airport the next day, they will be given duties escorting more food trucks around the city.

'For good measure, we try to persuade the colonel to arrange payment of their wages at the airport. To the funders of the red brigade, that will be small beer. Yes, and if the colonel is really set on the use of my trucks, he can have them.'

'Bill, you need to come in with me when I go to see the captain. Your plan is a mile better than the colonel's. I don't suppose the captain's going to be too enthusiastic about putting it to the colonel though. It might well cause a bit of offence if they think we're trying to run the show.

'The captain will probably cough and splutter a bit, so we're going to have to tread carefully. We need to give him the chance to sell the plan as his own. Still, it's worth giving a try. We'll give it a shot, and if it works, the day after tomorrow, we are off on our holidays.'

They found the captain poring over a set of street plans spread across the desk in his newly acquired office. 'You asked to see me, captain. I hope you don't mind, but I've brought Bill Rigby with me, the owner of the lorries the colonel thinks we should use tomorrow. Bill's got some other ideas, which I think we should consider.'

The captain paled as he listened to the revised proposals. They were so much better than the orders he had been given, but it would be unthinkable to say so openly. And now, he had the unwelcome task of explaining to the colonel that tomorrow's mission needed a good deal of change to make it of long-term value.

Bill and George sat quietly, looking for clues in the changing frowns and grimaces on the captain's troubled face. George decided to put him out of his misery. 'Captain, do please tell the colonel, if you need to speak to him, that Bill and myself are quite happy to go along with whatever plans the army might have for tomorrow's mission. And if you don't mind, we would prefer not to be identified as the originators of any changes if you can manage that. Just in case things go wrong.

'And there is something else I would like you to put to the colonel if you get the chance to speak to him. It's about the white Range Rover. I would like to buy it. Cash, of course; I won't quibble about the price. But it needs to be a quick deal if Bill and myself are to use it this afternoon. Your welcome to join us but preferably in plain clothes.'

'Stay around the building,' said the captain. 'I've a few calls to make.'

After lunch, the three of them set off together in George's newly acquired white Range Rover. The calls had done the trick. The colonel was happy to pass the parcel to the general. The general, a gambling man at heart, was never one to pass over the opportunity for quick winnings. His wife could get a new Range Rover for her old one, and he could get the red brigade, as everyone now seemed to call the donors, straight into the front line. The trucks could be loaded directly at the airport, avoiding the planned airlift, and the populace of the city would be put to the test of supporting the police. He would let the top brass at the donors know about his change of plan in due course. They would almost certainly interfere it if they knew about it in advance.

They headed first for the city airport. The captain wished to check that work was in progress on loading the trucks for an early start the following morning and to brief the drivers on the route they would be taking and the day's operational rules. He was still in uniform, but he carried a bag of civilian clothes. That was a good move as not all the red clad sentries had been prewarned that they had clearance. That would have to be smartened up before tomorrow. The airport sentries were better prepared, and within an hour, the captain's work had been done.

Bill and George spent the time viewing the enormity of the relief effort from a lounge viewing window. What a pity it wasn't working, they thought. Bill, whose eyes had been working to capacity from the time they entered the airport, had picked up something of particular interest.

'Have you noticed, George, that much of the signing carries the letters DRE? Does that mean anything to you?'

'Not a thing', said George, 'but we'll spring it on the captain sometime today.'

Captain Jacobs retuned to the lounge suitably dressed as Mr Jacobs. 'I hope you've got a spare uniform', said Bill, 'or are we coming back here?'

'Yes, we are Mr Rigby, I will have some reporting to do.'

He seemed somewhat ill at ease and had little to say except to confirm that all was going well, that there would be ten trucks in the convoy and that each would a crew of five including the driver.

'We better be going,' he said. 'It won't be much of a diversion, but I'd like to take a look at some of the housing areas in the north east sector as well as those we've planned to see in the north west.'

Neither Bill nor George thought it appropriate to query the reason for the change. The captain was obviously under orders. There was no point in making life even more difficult for him.

They turned out of the airport onto the dual carriageway leading north. It was only four days since Bill and George had last travelled the road in the opposite direction, but to both, it seemed like a lifetime. Nothing much had changed. The industrial estates on either side of the road remained deserted. The looting and vandalism they had seen on the first trip seemed to have stopped, but whether that was because the red brigade were in control of the main road or because the first fevered wave of lawlessness had abated, neither could tell. With such desolation, despair could not be far behind.

George broke the gloomy silence. 'It can't go on like this much longer, the nation is dying; something must be done.'

'That's why we're here,' said the captain. 'Let's hope we can accomplish something.'

When they reached the fringe of the first residential area along the road, the captain, who had studiously been tracking their progress against the street map on his lap, asked George to turn sharp right into one of the feeder roads to the housing estates. A few hundred yards down the road, they could see why.

The large supermarket, which had obviously been selected as an aid relief distribution centre, had been rendered totally inaccessible by hundreds of parked cars. This was not a new sight to Bill and George, but to the captain, it was clear proof, if proof was needed, that the relief effort had collapsed. The colonel was in for some very bad news.

'You chaps have been getting around the city quite a lot; is it like this everywhere?'

'Everywhere we've been', replied George 'but it's human nature, isn't it? No one's going to stand back from the stampede if they've got families to feed. Would you, captain?'

The captain made no answer. They sat for a while as he fiddled with his maps. 'There's no point then of going off to other supermarkets if they are all like this. But let's do something useful while we are here. Let's find a couple of barricades in this part of the city for tomorrow's truck drops; we'll still have eight truckloads left for the planned drops in the west and north-west.'

Turning into the Eastcote estate roads, they soon found a substantial barricade at a major crossroad junction. This was not one Bill and George had visited before, and they had to start from scratch with their introductions.

The guards listened with surprise at the strange offer being made to them. Get out round the streets! Get the police, the firemen, and the ambulance crews into uniform and out at the barricades in the morning! In return, we get a truckload of food parcels! That, and we get the promise of power being restored! Who are these characters? A trio of comedians? Could this be some sort of trick to pile more misery on us?

The trio took it all in. No, they explained, this was serious, very serious. This was an opportunity not to be missed. Perhaps the last chance to help restore normality. Miss this, and today's hardships might look like paradise in a week's time.

'Come on, chaps', said George, 'just go and tell your wives about the offer. They'll get the police out. But just one word of caution though. You all know what's happening outside the supermarkets. Well, we don't want it to happen here. So keep the operation local for this first delivery. Once you've established your repeat deliveries, then it's the time to spread the message about restoring law and order as far and wide as you can.'

There was a murmur of approval from the crowd, and after George's now-well-rehearsed parting words of encouragement and goodbyes, the trio was on its way again. 'Put a bit of distance between here and the next time we stop again,' suggested the captain. 'Let's head back to the dual carriageway.'

The next stop was in a slightly more affluent housing area, not far from the estate where they had found Anne's parents apparently enjoying their ordeal of imposed austerity. They selected the largest of the barricades they encountered to deliver their message to the people. They were, as Bill laconically observed, big on building barricades, although some were little bigger than a heap of chairs.

'It shows spirit,' said George. 'These people will get the police out.'

It soon became apparent, as the guards took in the significance of their offer, that they would indeed get the police out. Woe betide any shirker who preferred to stay at home. A full complement of uniformed officers would be in attendance at the barricade from first thing in the morning. Was there anything else they could do to help the cause?

The mood in the car was beginning to lighten up. The captain was almost cheerful. Bill and George were positively looking forward to the repartee, which they knew would greet them when they got to the barricades beyond the Welford underpass road where they would be instantly recognised and accepted as the best of friends. Now was the time to ask the captain about DRE.

'These people in red who will be driving the trucks, they're from the DRE. How are we going to explain that at the barricades?'

The captain gave George a quizzical stare. 'Who told you about the DRE?'

'Oh, everybody knows about it, it's common knowledge.'

The captain looked alarmed. 'It's not something we should talk about. All that we have to say at the barricades is that the red brigade, as I think you call them, is a sort of international relief force. Don't get drawn into any details of who they are. The people behind this red brigade are totally averse to any publicity at the present time. All will be revealed in the fullness of time.'

Bill and George exchanged amused smiles. The captain was probably as much in the dark as they were but reluctant to admit it. He was trained to give orders and obey orders. It was not for him to query who the paymaster of the day was. He might not even want to know.

The passage through the barricades between the underpass road and the Avenue was a revelation to the captain. At each stopping point, it seemed that people were coming out of their houses to greet them. The news that food trucks would be arriving the next day was greeted with cheers. These were not the chilling encounters that he had expected and dreaded. What was he to make of it? What would the colonel make of it?

He was mentally writing out his report when they reached the Avenue and turned right towards the main road south. His thoughts were soon broken by the curious sight of grand houses with battered cars on their drives. As he was about to ask George about it, George unexpectedly turned onto a leafy private drive, at the end of which a mansion could be seen, standing back behind stately gates and a high brick wall. George stopped the car, and with a brief 'We'll be back in a minute,' disappeared with Bill through the gates.

'What was all that about? asked the captain as they climbed back into the car.

'Just visiting a few friends,' said George 'It would have been rude to go past without giving them a call.'

'Everything all right, was it?'

'Yes, they were a bit surprised to see us, but everything is in good shape.'

'Fifteen all,' muttered the captain in an intentionally audible whisper.

Chapter 17

Relief Deliveries

When George and his company of fellow travellers assembled later that evening in the hotel's private dining room, which Captain Jacobs had thoughtfully commandeered for their use, the conversation rapidly moved to the question of when they would be on their way to Barton. Although they had only been at the hotel for little more than one day, restlessness was already beginning to set in. The immense relief they had all felt on arrival at finding themselves in the safe hands of a friendly force of soldiers and free from the fears they had endured in the city had reduced some of their number to tears. But once settled into the hotel and familiar with its comforts, the limitations of confinement on a motorway service area soon became apparent. And it was obvious just from the demeanour of the civilian staff at the hotel that life outside the city was going on much as normal and was a million miles away from the torments within it. They had been through the bad times, and now they were ready for the adventure of a new life, starting with a holiday by the sea-side.

They were still enjoying their pre-dinner drinks when Captain Jacobs poked his head round the door and beckoned to George that he would like a quick word. He had good news. His report on the day's drive through the city suburbs had gone down well with his superiors, and tomorrow's trial food distribution run was to go ahead as planned. They would be leaving the camp at 08.00 hours in the Range Rover.

A bus carrying twenty soldiers in plain clothes would be following them. There would be ten red, relief force trucks in the convoy that would be loaded up and ready to leave the airport at 10.00 hours. Each truck would have a driver plus a crew of two red-clad relief workers for offloading and two special force soldiers in plain clothes, ready to deal with any difficult situations.

George would lead the convoy in the Range Rover with Bill navigating. He would be directing operations from the backseat. The expectation was that they would be back at the airport by 16.00 hours and back at the service area camp by 18.00 hours.

The following day, George and his party should be packed and ready to leave the camp at 10.00 hours for Barton. They would be travelling in an army bus, and they would be dropped off at the Pines Hotel, which would be expecting them. For security reasons, the Range Rover would be taken down to Barton by an army driver and would be delivered to the hotel later that day. Ration books, which should be carried at all times since they also served as identity documents, would be handed out before they left the camp. As requested, the two Rottweilers would be placed in the army's kennels at Camp Blackstone until it was convenient for them to be retrieved.

The captain declined George's invitation to join them all for a drink, and so after checking that everyone was present, George got on with the business informing the assembly of the good news about their departure to Barton and the potentially bad news about the separatists who were creating difficulties at the estuary crossing into Bowland.

Lively discussion groups formed around the room. The topics were various. The Pines Hotel was one of the best hotels in Barton, and whilst there was keen interest to see how it was maintaining its four star standards in the face of national austerity, there were also concerns that the costs of any prolonged stay could prove a heavy drain on available cash resources. Would it be open to them to relocate to some other hotel of their choosing?

The proximity of the hotel to George and Frances' holiday apartment was also of interest. Was it coincidence, well-meaning thoughtfulness, or was there some ulterior motive behind the selection of a hotel no more than a stone's throw from the prestigious block, Carlton Towers, which housed the apartment? Were they to be kept under observation for the same security reasons, whatever they might be, hinted at by Captain Jacobs in his reference to getting the Range Rover down to Barton?

But these discussions were little more than idle chatter. The subject that generated far more heat was the news about the separatists. For generations, a small minority of the people of Bowland had pursued their apparently harmless and hopeless aims of establishing a sovereign state with its own currency and its own incomprehensible and unpronounceable language. And for generations, the people of Borovia had responded with benign tolerance and patronising indifference bordering on amusement.

How could it be that the separatists were now dictating who could and who could not enter Bowland and do so hand in hand with the Borovian army? And how could the separatists be so unprincipled in striking for independence at a time when the nation they had so long been part of was reeling on the ropes and in dire need of support at all levels? These were very hot topics, which were still being debated long after dinner.

The following morning when Bill and George collected the Range Rover and drew up at the hotel's doorway to pick up the captain, they were mildly surprised to find that the transport for the soldiers was a civilian bus, not the army bus they had been expecting. They were soon in for a few more surprises.

Captain Jacobs had clearly been busy since early morning. As soon as they left the camp, he announced that there needed to be a change of plan. Intelligence reports were coming in that pedestrian and vehicular traffic in the regions of the planned food distribution stops had been increasing since dawn. News of the plan, although spread only by word of mouth, was evidently travelling like wildfire.

To avoid the possibility of the convoy getting caught up in congestion or worse, still being ambushed while stationary, all the trucks would remain at the airport before being called up to the drop locations, one by one if that proved necessary. It all depended on how big and how orderly the crowds were at the barricades. If it came to the worst, it might not be possible to make all the planned drops in one day; they would just have to deal with whatever circumstances they encountered and do as much as they could.

The prospect that they might not complete the full round of drops weighed heavily on George's mind for the rest of the journey. It made sense that they should follow the previous day's route and commence with the drop nearest to the airport, but starting with what was likely to be the most difficult drop meant they might never reach the easier drops.

And as he saw it, that would be a disaster. He had built up a bond of trust with the residents of the Glebe Pastures housing estates, and he was sure that they would be out on the streets, waiting excitedly and peacefully for the food delivery he had promised them. He couldn't contemplate letting them down.

And if the captain had it in mind to spread the deliveries over two days, that was just as bad. He had promised his friends and neighbours stranded at the service area that they would be leaving tomorrow. They were probably packing their bags already.

Somehow or other, he had to take charge, but he had to do so without upsetting the captain or seeming to be challenging his authority. The captain had been designated as director of the operation. He was the team captain for the day. And if his sporting achievements had taught George anything, it was that support for the team captain was essential for success.

They were nearing the airport by the time George hit upon an idea to resolve his dilemma. 'Captain, when we get to the airport, what's the chance of laying our hands on a megaphone or some other type of loudhailer? If it's crowds of people we have to deal with, I'm more than prepared to stand up and encourage them to help us, not hinder us. And if they are behaving themselves, I'd like the opportunity to thank them and offer them the prospect of better times ahead.'

Whether or not the captain guessed correctly or otherwise what George was planning for any crowds standing in the way of smooth progress of the food trucks, he kept his thoughts to himself. If George wanted a megaphone, he could have one, and someone had better find one somewhere on the airport. And if George wanted to take over crowd control, so much the better. The captain had no desire to become involved in any fracas. Returning to the camp with a black eye or even worse would not do anything for his reputation.

On arrival at the airport, the captain left Bill and George in the Range Rover while he went off to brief the truck crews that they would be leaving on a call-up basis instead of in convoy and to instruct the search for a megaphone. He was back within half an hour accompanied by two red-clad attendants, one carrying a collection of megaphones and a walkie-talkie set, the other carrying two sizeable step ladders and a hooter.

'You're not leaving anything to chance then', quipped Bill, viewing the assortment of paraphernalia with interest 'but who's going to play the hooter?'

'You are', replied the captain, 'and I'm sure the pair of you will make a great double act.'

A good mile before they reached the first of the Eastcote barricades they had visited the previous day, it was evident that the captain's fears of crowd problems were well founded. The people were out in force, straggling along the footpaths and the carriageways towards the rumoured event that might relieve their miserable plight.

Stopping and starting, the Range Rover was making little progress, and it was only with Bill's realisation that the hooter might prove useful earlier than intended that they were able to blast their way through to the barricade. So dense was the crowd at the barricade that identification of the guards was impossible, and even though a good number of people in uniforms could be seen, it was far from obvious how they could be brought together to engage in discussion, less still to act as a cohesive control force.

George realised the reality of the situation in an instant, and wasting no time, he pushed Bill out of the passenger door, extricated the stepladders, and cleared a space on the pavement. High on the ladders, Bill sounded the hooter, and George began his megaphone address to the suddenly silenced crowd.

'Yesterday, along with my friends, I made a promise at this barricade that if the local police and emergency services personnel assembled here this morning and were seen to be in control, a truck carrying relief food supplies would offload in this neighbourhood. We are here today to keep that promise, but we need your help. Your enthusiasm in turning to support your community is a tribute to you all, but it is also a problem.

'We need to have the streets clear to get the truck here, and the police and emergency services personnel, who I can see are here in good numbers, need to have the space to assist the offloading and then to control distribution. So what I want you all to do, except the uniformed personnel, is to return to your homes so that we can get things organised. I would like all the uniformed personnel to come forward to the barricade for a briefing session; please let them get through.

'Now, before you depart, let me just tell you something most important about these relief food supplies. They are being donated to us by some international body that seems to want to remain anonymous. As I understand it they will maintain supplies as long as we maintain law and order. That's the deal; now, let's show them that we are keeping our side of the bargain. And finally, a round of applause for all the brave police and emergency service workers now at the barricade and who you will be seeing much more of in the next few days.'

As the crowd dispersed and Bill and George stepped down from their ladders, Captain Jacobs left his seat at the back of the Range Rover, warmly shook George's hand and whispered, 'Well done. I'll call up the truck.' A somewhat embarrassed George smiled weakly and whispered in return, 'That's half the job done; now, let's organise our uniformed friends here.'

Scanning the area around the barricade, George could see that a mix of about a hundred police and emergency service workers were anxiously awaiting instructions. He began by thanking them for volunteering and describing the huge weight of responsibility that had fallen on their shoulders with the collapse of the government and its control of law and order. He emphasised over and over again that the fate of the city was now in their hands, but if they all pulled together, they would get through the ordeal they presently face. Evidence of that would be with them within minutes as the first truckload of supplies to be handed over to them was already on its way from the airport. It would be for them to decide where the truck was to be unloaded and how the supplies should be distributed.

Tomorrow, they should report to the airport to register that they had formed a community control group. Further truckloads of supplies would then be delivered to them on a regular basis. He concluded with an assurance that, if sufficient community control groups could be formed, the restoration of power supplies would not be far behind, and with an apology that he could not stay to take questions as he had many more barricades to visit.

The red painted truck came into view. The crowd gasped and began to clap as though George had pulled a rabbit from a hat. It slowed to a halt. No one stepped forward.

Bill immediately spotted the problem. They were genuinely surprised. They were not prepared and probably never believed a supply truck would turn up. They needed a leader, and they needed one quickly. He scampered back up his stepladder, his hooter in one hand and a megaphone in the other. Three quick blasts on the hooter were enough to silence the excited chatter.

'We need a volunteer to lead your community control group,' he bellowed through the megaphone. 'Hands up anyone willing to take on this task.'

A uniformed police inspector, smart and eager looking, who had positioned himself at the front of the crowd was as quick on the uptake of the situation as Bill, and without waiting to see if any other candidates would emerge, he ascended the stepladder vacated by George and announced that the ideal place for their headquarters would be the community centre and that they should all make their way there immediately.

'My name's Inspector Lewis,' he said as he stepped down from his ladder. 'Who are you gentlemen, and who should I report to at the airport tomorrow?'

'I'm Michael Jacobs,' said the captain moving forward quickly to shake the Inspector's hand. 'I have a liaison role with the relief force. This is George Butler of Butler Developments, and this is Bill Rigby of Rigby Transport. George knows the city like the back of his hands, and Bill knows the city even better than George. They're both kindly helping to put the relief force in touch with local communities. Now, tomorrow at the airport, report to Mr Angelos Arraviets; he is the logistics manager, and he will be expecting you.'

'That was a close shave', said Bill as they set off for the next barricade, 'in more ways than one.'

They northbound dual carriageway was again deserted, and within ten minutes, they were on the fringe of Keston and the turn-off for the housing estate they had visited the previous day.

'It's much quieter around here,' said the captain. 'I think we can safely call up the truck for the Keston barricade and have it parked up ready for entry. We got a very positive reception at the barricade here yesterday.'

'It would not surprise me', said George, 'if they have bunting strung across the road and a band waiting to greet us. I may have to think of a new routine.'

There was no bunting and no band, but there was a line-up of uniformed personnel at the barricade holding back the excited crowd of householders. A new routine was clearly needed. The veiled threats could be omitted. Encouragement and support would suffice. Megaphone diplomacy would be inappropriate. George spoke from the pavement to the attentive crowd leaving the stepladders in the car.

After the formalities of thanks and introductions, it was more of a discussion than a speech. George was able to tell them that the truck was on its way. The captain told them of the procedures for reporting to the airport and obtaining future deliveries from the airport. They talked about formalising a community control group and an elected leader. It turned out that they were already well on the way to both and that they had already selected the local sports hall as the food relief distribution centre.

With the two drops in the north-east suburbs successfully completed, the captain was beginning to have doubts about his revised call-up plan. The eight scheduled drops for the north-west and the west suburbs were all scheduled for barricades in housing estates that seemed, from the previous day's tour, to be comparatively well ordered. They would save time and put on a better show if they reverted to the convoy plan. Bill and George agreed. They parked up in a lay-by and waited for the convoy to reach them.

For Bill and George, it was an enjoyable experience driving up to barricades where they were on first-name terms with the guards with a convoy of food relief trucks in the rear. They did not expect trouble, and they did not have any. The police and emergency services were out in force, and the distribution centres had been selected and made ready.

There was increasing curiosity about George and his trips through the barricades, but general acceptance that too much questioning of whatever it was he was up to might not be in their best interests. He was able to bat away without difficulty the occasional timid queries about his dogs, the ambulances, and the source of his copious supplies of wine. The only question he struggled to answer was when they would be seeing him again. George had no idea. He'd been so intent on getting out of the city that he had hardly given a thought to when he might return. He was lost for words.

Bill was again quick on the uptake. 'As soon as we can make it. We've a lot of ground to cover, but we'll be back.'

'Tell me about your plans,' the captain asked as they drove back to the service area. 'Do you envisage a long stay at Barton or Bowland if you ever get there?'

'I think we'll take it a day at a time,' replied George. 'It's out of our hands. But I do wish we knew whose hands it is in. Let me put it to you this way, captain. When we guessed years ago, correctly as things have turned out, that the day might come when it would be safer to be out of the city than in it, we never imagined for one moment that the best reason to be out of the city would be that you chaps in the army would be on one side of a fence and the people in the city on the other. So the best answer I can give you is this, as long as you chaps stay out of the city, so will we.'

An uncomfortable period of reflective silence followed until Bill, never happy in such situations, tried a more direct approach to breaching the captain's reticence to explain what was going on. 'These people in red, captain, who's in charge of them, and who is funding them?'

'It's very complicated', said the captain, 'and without disclosing highly confidential information, it's difficult to explain. But there's an old saying that beggars can't be choosers, and if the only donor in sight insists on remaining anonymous and the beggar has a family to feed, confidentiality is the price of survival. That's how it is, and we in the army don't like it any more than you do. But let's not spoil a good day's work with this. The high-ups are going to be greatly relieved when they read my report.

'We have a lot to thank you two for. It's just as well you came our way, although if you do engage in future escapades, try using more conventional means of transport. It's been quite an imaginative task reporting on the means you took to join us as new recruits.'

Chapter 18

Barton

It was a bright morning as the party of Old Hall residents and friends assembled noisily and cheerfully at the hotel's entrance to await the arrival of the promised bus to Barton. The two-hour journey went without incident and was a time for relaxed contemplation and reflection. Most of the adults were lost in their own thoughts and had no need for conversation. All of the children were too engrossed in sightseeing to engage in chatter. It was a time to sit back and go with the flow.

The bus was comfortable, and everyone had plenty of room to spread around and view with interest the normality of life in the countryside. There was nothing boring about this normality. Four days of confinement in the city followed by three days confinement on a service area had transformed their regard for normality. Each sighting of tractors in fields and villagers on bicycles drew excited attention as though they were tourists on a package holiday travelling through the Alps. Even the swelling volume of traffic they encountered as they reached the outskirts of the town was hailed as evidence of better times ahead. The closer they got to the town centre, the more their excitement grew. They were expecting a ghost town. This place was alive and bustling.

As the bus turned onto the cliff-top promenade, they got their first view of the sea and the piers. It was a view known to everyone from holidays and day trips. A view replicated on millions of postcards and in millions of photograph albums. But this day, it was a very different view. Instead of quite sandy beaches and a placid sea extending miles to the horizon with only the occasional yachts and small fishing boats to act as focus points, it was difficult at first sight to recognise what they were viewing. The sea was full of boats of every kind; the beaches and piers were covered by a mass of brightly coloured stalls and huts. Was it a regatta, a carnival, or some previously unheard of beach market?

They were still staring with bewilderment when the bus pulled into the hotel car park. They were expecting it to be empty. They were expecting to be the only guests.

They were beginning to expect the unexpected. The car park was full to overflowing, and after circling the packed rows of cars, the driver settled for discharge of his passengers at the front entrance. They struggled with their cases through the noisy foyer to the busy reception desk and joined the queue, marvelling as they waited at the enticing aromas wafting from the dining room. Their expectations of survival on a Spartan menu had obviously been misplaced; the sooner they booked their tables for dinner, the better.

George and Frances went straight to their apartment at Carlton Towers, surprising Alan, the resident manager, by their first arrival on foot in his twenty years' service. 'Where's the car?' he asked as they crossed the lobby to the lifts. 'You haven't walked here all the way from Norbugh, have you?'

'It's a long story,' replied George. 'We came by bus with a group of friends; they're all booked in next door at The Pines. We are all on our way to Buckland, if we can ever get there. Just as soon as we've unpacked, I'll come down and have a chat with you in your office. But it's good to be back and even better to see that everything's still in top-notch condition. We hadn't expected these lifts to be working. We were all set for a long slog up the stairs. And you're looking fit and well, that's another bonus.'

'Let me help you up with dogs,' said Alan, taking the leads of the two spaniels from Frances. 'We don't want people talking. If anyone asks about a bit of barking, I'll say that those raucous, big black-back gulls are nesting on the roof again. And what about some sandwiches for the pair of you? I'll send Tom round to the hotel; they do a good selection.'

When George and Alan settled down for their chat, the first thing that George wanted to know was what on earth was going on in Barton. 'It was like this,' said Alan. 'About ten days ago, when things started turning really nasty in the city, there was panic here in the block. As you know well, many of the residents are elderly, and talk of financial collapse frightened the life out of them. Thank goodness that, when the lights went out a few days later, there was enough fuel in the diesel tank to keep the generator going. Without that, I simply do not know how we would have got through.

'The food shortages hit us very quickly, and Tom and I did nothing else for two days but collect as much cash as we could and buy whatever we could. Some of the residents were very generous in putting money into the pot for the good of everyone. Then the soldiers came round with ration books, and things started getting back to normal. The power came back on, people went back to work, and the town started to come back to life.'

Alan paused and shook his head as if still reeling in disbelief and fearful that what he was about to say would be regarded as ridiculous. 'Then suddenly an extraordinary thing happened. It was a bit like a gold rush. Everyone who had a boat was out fishing to supply homes and restaurants with the catch of the day or was ferrying prized possessions to sell on the quaysides across the water for dollars. You'd make a fortune with that boat of yours down in the marina. I can see it now, "Butler's High Speed Fishing and Ferrying".

'But seriously, you can't believe how much fish they're catching. I've never seen anything like it in twenty years. It's good stuff though. You'll see that tonight when you tuck into your grilled sea bass at The Pines.

'Anyway, the word must have got out about the trade to be done in Barton because people started pouring in from everywhere, and they're still coming. I've even had people coming here and asking if there are any apartments to rent.'

'I was going to ask you about that,' said George. 'Some of my friends at The Pines might be in for a longer stay in Barton than they're expecting. But do go on. How are things on a day to day basis for ordinary people here?'

'Well we've no telephones yet and no television, and I haven't seen any newspapers in the past week. It must have been like this in the dark ages; perhaps everyone then was kept in the dark. But that bothers me, and I think it bothers us all.

'Sometimes, I feel like hiding in my office to get away from the stream of questions from the residents. I don't think they expect answers, but I hate repeating that I just don't know anything more than they do. I didn't realise it before all this happened, but we are the must-know-everything generations, and in some ways, having no news is worse than having no food.

'The other big problem we have is that, when you do find shops or petrol stations open. they won't take crowns in payment. It's supposed to be illegal, but there's no one out there stopping it. Fortunately for us, this ration-book system of handing out free food parcels being operated by the army seems to be working, and no one's going to starve. And if you've got dollars, then, as you've seen for yourself, you can get all the extras you want on the street markets.

'But taking everything into account, we're doing all right here in Barton as long as it doesn't go on forever. And if the rumours going the rounds are right, we're a lot better off than the people in Norburgh. They even say that the city has been fenced off from the rest of the country.'

'Sad to say, it has, Alan. There's no way in, and there's no way out. And things are bad, particularly in the inner city areas. I was down by the docks a few days ago, and it was a frightening experience. I would not want to go back there again; it's lawless." George stopped. He had intended to say more, but he could see that he had already said more than enough. Alan had turned as pale as a sheet. 'Are you all right, Alan?'

'My daughter and her two young children live near the docks, Mr Butler, and I haven't heard from them for nearly two weeks now. Do you think they'll be all right?'

George winced. What a blunder. 'Let's hope they are,' he said. 'Has she got a partner to look after her?'

'No, do you not remember last time you were here, that she was staying with us after her marriage breakdown?'

'Sorry, Alan, I forgot about that. You must be very worried. Leave this to me. It's just possible that I might be able to get some information on them, but it needs a bit of thinking about. I'll do my best. Write down the names of all the family and the last address you have of them on this piece of paper, and add the name and address of the children's school, if you know it."

'That's very kind of you, Mr Butler. Kath will be so relieved if we can get some news. She's been wanting them to come and stay here with us for months now. If you do find some way of contacting them, can you let them know that we have the bedrooms ready for them? But they might need some help in getting out of Norburgh; did you find it difficult, Mr Butler?'

'To say that it was difficult, Alan, would be the ultimate understatement. It took five days of constant searching for a way through the fence and then a lot of luck of the sort that doesn't come twice in a lifetime together with application of some very risky brute force before we managed it. The way we got out could not be repeated by us or even by trained escapologists.

'I'm not saying though that all other possibilities are ruled out. If I can track down your daughter and her children and they need help, I won't spare any effort or expense in getting them to safety. Just give me a day or so to think about it.

'But tomorrow, Alan, I have another task. I need to find out how difficult it is to get into Bowland, not for me personally but for my twenty or so friends round at The Pines. I've heard that entry restrictions are in force at the estuary crossing. Have you heard anything?'

Alan had indeed heard something. He'd encountered it. Only yesterday, he'd been turned back by officious barrier guards at the Stourmouth side of the viaduct. His mistake had been to truthfully tell them that he wanted to get into Bowland to scout around the farms for fresh eggs and vegetables for the elderly residents he was looking after in a block of flats at Barton. He was told in no uncertain terms that Bowland's food was for Bowland's people and not to bother trying his luck again. He had been too shocked to question their authority at the time, but he'd reported the incident to the soldiers at the Grange barrier on his return.

The soldiers had told him that the guards were just troublemaking separatists flexing their muscles, but there was nothing they could do about it.'

'But I'll tell you what', said Alan, "if I had your boat, I'd be sailing daily to St Jude and everyone in the block would be getting eggs and bacon for breakfast. Why don't you just ferry them over in the boat?'

'Don't say I hadn't thought of it. But keep this to yourself, Alan. My boat is just for show. I've got my Coastal Skippers Certificate and all the rest, but left to me, the boat would never leave the marina. And generally, that's as far as it gets.

'What better for a bit of weekend business hospitality than a drive to Barton, champagne and lunch on the Sunseeker, and a gentle cruise around the bay? Who wants to go to sea? There's no one out there to impress.

'When we do go over to St Jude for some of our more adventurous clients, I hire a proper skipper. Perhaps that's what I may have to do for my friends at The Pines. But that apart, you've set me thinking. When we do all get to Bowland, assuming we do, the boat might come in very useful if berthed at St Jude. Thanks for that. Now, before I go, Alan, you mentioned flats to let here in the block. Are there any?'

'Two or three, perhaps even more if there was some way of contacting the absent owners. But one way or another, we can take in a few of your friends here at the Towers. Quite a lot of the residents would welcome lodgers in times like these. And some of the apartments must have two or more empty or underused bedrooms. You can safely tell your friends that we will look after them.'

After George had thanked Alan for his positive approach, he took the lift back up to his apartment with a lot on his mind. He sat with Frances for two hours, munching his sandwiches and discussing what they should do next. Frances was more in tune with the personal aspects of the situation than George. While George was worried about the logistics of getting twenty-four people into Bowland and the difficulties of housing thirty people at the farm and its cottages,

Frances was more concerned about what the various families wanted to do now that they had seen that life in Barton was apparently far from frightening. Some might prefer to take what was on offer at Barton rather than risk the unknowns of life in Bowland. And there was the difficult position of the families from the Avenue and Peter Robinson's elderly parents who might be refused entry to Bowland.

Knowing that George would be uncomfortable talking to people face to face on what might involve delicate personal decisions, Frances suggested that she should spend the afternoon talking to the families on an individual basis and letting them know that if they did wish to stay in Barton, there was a good possibility that apartments at Carlton Towers could be bought, rented, or available as lodgings. She would try to get sufficient feel of the numbers happy to stay in Barton and those still anxious to get to the farm in time for George to announce at dinner his plans for tomorrow.

When George told Frances about the plight of Alan's daughter, Sally, and her two children, Frances was more than a little concerned. She had watched Sally grow up, get married, and have children. She liked them all, just as she liked Alan and his wife, Kath. She could imagine the ordeals that Sally and the children might be enduring in the city and the ordeals Alan and Kath were going through in not knowing what had happened to them.

From what she had heard from George about the alarming situation he and Bill had encountered in the inner city and from the distressing accounts of the dock workers they had let into the Old Hall Estate, Sally and the children could be in dire circumstances or even extreme danger. George would have to do something. Whether that might involve trying to pull strings with his new-found army contacts or going into the city himself, something just had to be done.

George agreed. And he was not unhappy that Frances was taking a strong line on the need for action. The greater the pressure, the more he was encouraged to attempt the seemingly impossible.

Sheepishly, he confessed to Frances that he did know a way in and out of the city that did not involve stealing ambulances and crashing through barriers. It was at the Kentford paddocks. Unfortunately, it involved the unbearable confinement of crawling or being hauled through a long, wet, and probably rat-infested drainage culvert. He'd told Bill about it but no one else in case the very thought of it caused panic. Eric knew about it and probably used it; so also did a local lad, Billy.

'Would that be Billy the stable boy', asked Frances, 'the little lad who wants to be a jockey?'

'That's him,' said George, 'uses it to visit his girlfriend in Kentford village. But I don't see how little Billy can help us.'

'Perhaps he could,' replied Frances. 'I couldn't go through a culvert like that on my own. But with Billy holding my hand, whistling and chatting as he always does, I might just manage it. And another thing, George, we know people who know the docks, and I'm sure that, with their help, we can find Sally.'

George was intrigued at the turn the conversation was taking. His intention had been to run a few thoughts past Bill after dinner on the possibilities for a search and rescue mission. But already, the mission seemed to have acquired a new leader. He was not sure whether he should appear enthusiastic about Frances' participation in the actual operation or horrified at the idea. He was not even sure of his own feelings on the matter.

Something that he had known nothing about only two hours ago was taking over his powers of reasoning, not to mention those of

Frances. He decided to move the conversation along without giving too much away.

'Frances, before we do anything about Sally, we need to give some thought to where we and all the others are going to be over the next few days. Assuming the Range Rover turns up as promised, I would like to do a trial run to the farm early tomorrow morning, just the two of us. We'll be able to test the difficulties of the barriers, and we can keep our eyes open to see what sort of vehicles are out and about on the route. I doubt that we'll see any buses, and even if we do, I can't see them being much use to us, but horseboxes would be of interest. Would you want to stay at the farm or to come back with me?'

Frances was not to be diverted from her mission. 'That's a great idea, George, and I'm really looking forward to the trip, but I'll be coming back with you. But always remember, George, that the following day, we'll be going to Kentford in search of Sally. And then, while we are at the paddocks, I can say hello to my horses again.'

George could see that he was losing the battle. He settled down for an afternoon snooze while Frances went to The Pines to gather what information she could on preferences for staying put or moving on.

The entry phone rang, bringing him to a shocked awakening. It was Alan with news that his Range Rover was on the surface level car park and that he had the keys. George sprinted to the lifts. It was a long shot, but Captain Jacobs might be the delivery man and might still be around to take on the burden of rescuing Sally in return for all the help he had received.

It was a forlorn hope. The driver had gone. The problem of Sally remained.

In late afternoon, Frances was back with news that everyone except the two elderly couples, Mr and Mrs Robinson and Mr and Mrs Pritchard, were keen to move on to the farm. But that was not the end of it. She had agreed that the Bradbury family could have the use of the remaining spare cottage and that Amanda and Mark and the Wesleys could stay with them in the farmhouse. All that was needed now was transport to the farm and passage through the barriers. George wondered what he had done in his past life to deserve all this. All he wanted now was another hour's sleep before dinner.

As Alan had forecasted, they were not disappointed by dinner at The Pines. The food was excellent, and Frances had arranged the use of a private dining room. The pressure was off, the drink was flowing, and in Bill's words, 'They could do this for a living.' It was celebration all round, except for George who was struggling with the mental arithmetic of the transportation needs and the problem of wading through a fifty-yard culvert without an attack of claustrophobia.

CHAPTER 19

Bowland

The early morning journey along the coast road to the Stour estuary took less than one hour. With the sun behind them and the road unaccustomedly quiet, Frances and George were able to enjoy the clifftop and valley views without the demanding concentration normally required of both drivers and passengers on the nation's favourite scenic route. Instead of the stop-start, nose-to-nose grind, amongst a never-ending line of packed saloon cars, they were able to sit back and let the miles fly by.

On reaching the little town of Grange, which sat on the near side of the estuary, they were happy enough with their progress to stop for breakfast at one of the town's many old-fashioned tea shops. Once again, life in Borovia was as it should be. Who would want to live anywhere else? Everything, it seemed, was back to normal, but then by the barrier at the viaduct, which in the past had served only to regulate traffic at peak times, stood the soldiers.

Politely, Frances and George were asked to produce their identification papers, state their destination, and explain the reason for their trip. Within minutes, they were waved through, but George, noting that there was nothing surly about the soldiers and that nothing was queuing behind them, eased himself from the driver's seat and started a friendly discussion.

The soldiers were happy to talk. This driver was taking an interest in them; most of the others were too full of their own concerns. When they had exhausted the weather, food rationing, and the diminishing prospects of Borovia's football team in forthcoming internationals, George blandly asked, 'And how are things in Bowland? We've not been down to the old place since the troubles started.'

'They're doing all right,' said the most talkative of the soldiers. 'They're well away from Norburgh, and that's where most of the trouble is. They've got farms and fishing, and they're beginning to think they don't need the rest of us. There's talk of independence, but it won't come to that. Well, we hope it won't. That would be the end for Borovia, and if it did come to war, well, I don't want to think about it.'

'No, we can't allow that to happen', said George, 'but do you think these independence people will cause us any trouble? We've heard they're manning some of the barriers and making a nuisance of themselves.'

'They are', said the soldier, 'but they'll only get away with it for as long as we let them, and it's better to know your enemy than drive them into hiding.'

With a friendly wave and cheerio, George jumped back into the car and drove slowly onto the viaduct, keeping close to the kerb so as not to interfere with the passage of the ambulance coming up from behind. Once it was past, he tucked in closely behind it as they sped towards Stourmouth

The toll barrier went up as soon as the ambulance was sighted, and without any loss of speed, it disappeared into the town. George slowed to a halt, making sure that the barrier had closed before he reached it. The last thing he wanted today was a clear passage. He wanted the full works, in-depth interrogation, spotlights, and all the rest. He wanted to see how much of a nuisance these people could be when in the mood.

He offered up his toll with the appearance of someone anxious to get moving.

'Your identification papers please; we need to see them for both of you.'

'Why's that? We were cleared through at Grange. We didn't clamber up onto the viaduct you know. Not in this Range Rover.'

'The barrier stays down until we see your papers. It's up to you.'

The guard studiously studied the identification documents handed over by George with a contemptuous flourish. 'Do you own this property, Valley Farm, Lostock?'

'We do. Why do you ask?'

'Residency rules. Do you live there?'

'What residency rules are these? And what is it to you where we choose to spend our time?'

And so it went on for some minutes, the guard getting more and more exasperated and the two uniformed soldiers standing nearby getting more and more amused. A chorus of honking horns from the cars behind eventually won the day and, their papers returned, George and Frances were released to continue their journey. Frances was not amused by George's performance, but he was not abashed.

'It had to be done,' he said. 'We've saved some of the others the embarrassment of turning up in cars and being refused entry, and we've saved wasting our own time trying to shuttle them all through. All we have to do now is think up of some other way of getting them through. And anyway, I enjoyed it. They're way out of order with all that nonsense about residency rules.'

Fifty yards down the road, they turned their heads to watch a Grange bound ambulance speed towards the viaduct and pass unchecked through a rapidly raised barrier. Neither said a word.

The reception they received half an hour later when they reached the barrier at Lostock went to the other extreme. John jumped from his roadside chair and, in his excitement at seeing the Range Rover, accidently fired a blank into the air from his old service revolver.

'At last you're here! And both looking so well. Take over Martin, will you? I'm off to the farm. We've got some celebrating to do.'

The emotionally charged Frances and George stepped from the car and gave him a hug. 'It's good to be back, John. Sorry it took so long. And how's Mary?'

Mary was running down the lane thinking someone had been shot. Years later, it was still remembered with great amusement.

Coffee was served, and Graham and his family were brought in to say hello to 'Aunty' Frances and 'Uncle' George. Together, they strolled for an hour around the farmhouse and the cottages, admiring the views and the quiet of the countryside.

Buzzards were heard and then spotted. A group of roe deer was seen by the woods across the fields. Farmer Brown steered his tractor and trailer through the sheep and cows in the riverside meadows to join them at the fence and to welcome Frances and George back to Bowland.

Then it was round to see Mary's proudly displayed vegetable garden, new in the making, but already with neatly lined-up rows and cloches. It was entirely due to the efforts of others, she insisted. The ladies in the village had supplied all the plants, the grandchildren had done all the work, and she was just the supervisor.

They moved on to the chicken runs and the duck pond. The egg production was not yet on industrial scale, joked John, but they had high hopes and realistic targets. The scale of the rabbit hutches at the side of the barns also gave the impression that they were built for production rather than for housing pets. But John's reticence to reveal the details of his intentions suggested that his education of the children on the nutritive benefits of the cuddly occupants was far from complete. And just when Frances and George thought they had seen it all, they were taken round to the back of the barns to view the very latest showpiece exhibits of the Valley Farm self-sufficiency project, four monster pigs contentedly grunting in their sties.

Frances and George were lost in admiration of what had been achieved so quickly and by so few. Their own dreams of an Arcadian retreat had stopped short of the realities of working the land and managing livestock. But now that they had seen the reality of Mary and John's efforts, their minds were racing to what could be achieved when they were all at the farm together. They could be a serious production unit and fitter and stronger for it. They could market the surpluses or donate them to the poor. Yes, there was work to do, and it was time to get on with it. But first, they had to get everyone to the farm.

Apologetically, they explained to Mary and John as they sat in the farmhouse with more coffee, they were only on a short visit and that, after lunch, they needed to return to Barton to complete some business. Almost immediately, they wished that they had done a little more preparation for the reunion. They were happy to explain why they were on their own and why they would be going back to Barton later in the day rather than staying at the farm. They were less happy to discuss the detail of all they had gone through getting out of the city.

John and Mary were obviously settled into their new lifestyle, but the same could not yet be said of Graham and Rebecca. They were evidently still in shock. It was too early for honest reminiscence, and not everything was looking as rosy as their first exchanges of greetings and well-wishing suggested.

Mary and John sensed the reservations as soon as they asked about security of the properties at the Old Hall. Frances went pale, George went pale. 'Nothing to worry about,' said George. 'We've got some people in looking after them.'

It got worse when John asked how they had managed to get to Barton. Time stood still waiting for a reply. 'We went down on a bus,' said Frances unconvincingly after an uncomfortably silent interlude. 'It was quite a nice ride.'

Gradually, the rules became clear. Particularised questions were out. Generalisation was in. Topics could be introduced but not pursued unless taken up by all with enthusiasm.

And so, up to and through lunch, they talked about life at the farm and the extra guests who would be joining them. They talked about the state of the nation and how long it would be before things were back to normal. And bordering on the fringe of what was permissible, they talked about the spread of separatism. By the time the good-byes for the day were over, they were all exhausted by the tension.

'I'll drive, said Frances. 'You look washed out, George.'

They passed through the barriers at the estuary without any problem. Neither the civilian guards at Stourmouth nor the soldiers at Grange showed much interest in their identities once they revealed that they were heading for Barton. George dozed, on and off, but coming to the first of the Barton barriers, he suddenly straightened in his seat and asked Frances to stop long enough for him to have a word with one of the soldiers.

'What was that about?' asked Frances as he got back into the car.

'I was just asking him about the location of the Barton ambulance station' replied George. 'We turn left at the next set of lights and then right at a small round-about.'

'No, George, not again. I saw the looks you were giving those ambulances this morning at the estuary barriers. Don't even think about it, or you'll be looking for another wife.'

'I'm not thinking of stealing or borrowing one. It's just that, from talking to Alan yesterday, it seems that Barton's now a bit like a frontier town; anything goes if you've got the cash. And then I got to thinking wouldn't it be nice if we were able to buy a surplus ambulance here in Barton, where I'm sure there is a surplus, so that we could donate it to the good folk of St Jude, who I don't doubt are in need of an ambulance. Bill could drive it. We've got other things to do tomorrow. It would only take him a couple of trips to transport everyone to the farm.'

'George, the way you put it, how can I say no? But you've got me thinking now. An ambulance might come in handy in rescuing Sally and her children. Let's see if we can buy an ambulance, but don't go giving it away just yet.'

They found the ambulance station as directed and parked on the forecourt alongside the two ambulances out and ready for action. 'I hope they've more inside', remarked George, 'or we are going to be out of luck. You come in with me Frances; it will add dignity to the proceedings.'

They entered by the office doorway and asked to see the station manager, announcing themselves as Mr and Mrs Butler of Butler Developments. A surprised-looking station manager, Mr Gerrard, ushered them into his office.

'What can I do for you?' he asked. 'I hope you are not planning to buy the site to put up more flats; we've more than enough round here already.'

George smiled, 'Don't put ideas into my head, Mr Gerrard; this would make a very nice site. But we are here to see if there's any chance of buying something far more modest. We are looking to buy an ambulance.'

Mr Gerrard sat back in his chair and wondered what to say next. Were they pranksters? No, they looked too prosperous for that.

Were they gangsters? No, they looked too relaxed for that. Were they imposters? No, he'd spotted the number plate. They must be for real! But what were they up to?

They were still both smiling. Humour, he decided, might be the best way of dealing with them; they might be suffering from the stresses of the times. 'We don't actually sell ambulances here I'm afraid; we just drive them around picking up people who aren't fit to walk.'

This is a man I could do business with, thought George. Get straight to the point. 'In normal times, Mr Gerrard, we wouldn't have dreamt of approaching you like this, but these are a long way from normal times. We're just back from our place near St Jude, and it seems that there's a shortage of ambulances in parts of Bowland. To help out down there, we would like to donate an ambulance to the local people if we can lay our hands on one.

'We're patrons of the Valley Farm Community Group, a recently formed organisation aiming to support people in need. It occurred to us as we were driving back that, with the fuel shortages and the difficulties of paying wages, you might be willing to sell one of your older ambulances if you have one to spare. We have the means to pay whichever way suits you best, cheque, card, or cash. If it's dollars you need, we'll pay in dollars. We were thinking of thirty thousand, but we could go higher. It would all have to be above board, of course, and properly authorised.

'Would it be possible for you to discuss our offer with your superiors and let us know later in the day if a deal can be done? Come round and see us this evening at our apartment at Carlton Towers. If we are not in, we'll be having dinner at the Pines Hotel next door. You're welcome to join us.'

Before Mr Gerrard had time to respond, George was shaking his hand and saying good-bye.

Back in the car, Frances was caught between chastising George for his lies and applauding him for his imagination. 'George, you've already got a tractor to play with back at the Old Hall; you don't need an ambulance as well. And by the way, you forgot to ask him to throw in a couple of drivers' uniforms. But seriously, do you think they'll play ball?'

'Odds on', replied George, 'and even if they haven't got a spare of their own, I'll bet they soon find one.'

He was right. At six-thirty, a three-man delegation was at the apartment. By seven, a deal had been done. For thirty thousand dollars in cash, an ambulance could be collected from the station the next day but only after eight in the evening. It would have enough fuel to reach St Jude.

George managed to persuade them that it would be best to include a couple of uniforms to avoid awkward questions at road checks. They wished Frances and George well with their charity work but declined with regrets their kind invitation to dinner that evening. On another evening, when the world was a better place, they would be delighted to join them for a night out.

George made a quick dash for the hotel leaving Frances to join him in half an hour. He needed to track down Bill and give him a few things to think about over dinner. As expected, he found him in the bar preparing himself with a few quick drinks for the rigours of the extended polite conversation, which he knew from experience was the downside of large gatherings.

He welcomed George with open arms. It had been a long day with the children. George, for his turn, could hardly wait to tell Bill his plan for getting everyone to the farm. They would be travelling by ambulance, he knew how to get one, but it would need more than one trip. Sadly, he would not be with him in the ambulance as he would be going by car.

Bill assumed a thoughtful pose and slowly sipped his beer. 'Sorry, George, but I haven't got a uniform, and anyway, my days of pinching ambulances are over. They're awful things to drive. So how are we getting to the farm?'

'I've told you', replied George, 'by ambulance. I mean it. But it's not as bad as it seems; the ambulance we will be using is ours; I've bought one so that's not a problem. Well, that's the good news. The bad news, if you like to call it that, is that we don't get it until late tomorrow evening and that's bad because it gives us enough time tomorrow to tunnel our way into the city and rescue a trapped family. What do you think about that for a day out?'

'George, they'll be taking you away in an ambulance soon. But go on, tell me the worst; where do I fit in?'

'Bill, you fit into the tunnel. I'm too big. And Frances has got the bit between her teeth on this one; she thinks she's going through, and I can't have that.'

'None of this makes sense to me,' said Bill. 'What's it all about?'

'It's like this, Bill. Alan, the resident manager at our apartment block has lost contact with his daughter and her two young children. Their last known address was in the docks area of the city. Alan and his wife are desperate to get them out, and I promised to help.

'I probably should not have done so, but I told Frances about it, and I also told her about the tunnel under the ring road at Kentford paddocks, the one I mentioned to you when we were worried about getting out through the Welford road underpass. Frances is determined to embark on a rescue mission even if it means crawling through the tunnel. Given my size, I'm terrified at the thought of it; that's one of the reasons

I bought the ambulance, although I don't fancy using it even as a last resort.

'But I can't have this thing hanging over me for days. I made a silly promise, and now I'm stuck with it. So tomorrow morning, I'm going up to Kentford with Frances to take another look at the tunnel. I just thought you might like to come with us.'

'Remind me again. How big is this tunnel?'

'About four feet in diameter with about a foot of water in the bottom the last time I saw it.'

'It's not impossible then but tight. Count me in for tomorrow. Tonight, I'll work on the possibilities. But tell me this though, supposing we can get through the tunnel, what are we going to do when we get to the other side? Don't tell me that you're planning to foot it to the docks, knock on doors, and then carry the children back, one under each arm?'

'Bill, you worry about the tunnel, and I'll worry about the rest. But I have a plan.'

CHAPTER 20

The Canoe

Colonel Millar lay staring at the ceiling. He was trying to remember why he joined the army. It could have been the attraction of the brightly coloured uniforms of fusiliers and guardsmen in his inherited collection of cigarette cards, or it could have been to enjoy a life of excitement away from the boredom of an office desk.

Whatever it was, it was not to spend night after night lying awake worrying about things that should not be his business. He'd joined the army to fight wars or something like that. Stopping other people from fighting wars, perhaps.

The politicians should be the ones worrying about feeding the people; they were the ones who had caused the problems with their false promises and lies; they were the ones who had spent all the money. But they were gone, and he was here, trying to think how optimistic he could be at his meeting with the general and how they could persuade the men with money in Geneva that the nation was on the road to recovery.

The curse which burdened the politicians was now on him. What else was left but false promises and lies? It was his turn now.

One thing at a time, one thing at a time; he kept repeating to himself trying to push from his mind the one thing that he knew had to be done to get his plan so proudly presented only four days ago back on track. It had been a good plan and two thirds of the city was benefitting from it with regular relief supplies and improved security.

Confidence had been restored in the suburbs, but it had still to reach the inner city. What a delicate thing confidence was, installed with ease by some and destroyed with ease by others. There was nothing for it but to eat humble pie. One way or the other, he had to get Mr Butler, or 'Big George', as the general had taken to calling him, back into service. Face to face, that's how he'd do it, at Barton, Bowland, or wherever he was. And he'd do it today.

He rang Captain Jacobs with instructions to track down Mr Butler and let him know that Colonel Millar was on his way to see him on urgent business. His meeting with the general would probably go on until lunchtime, but he would be free in the afternoon and evening if necessary.

As it happened his meeting with the general went quite well, particularly once the general was informed that 'Big George' had agreed to lead convoys into the inner city. He rang Captain Jacobs to find out the arrangements for the meeting with Mr Butler, a formality of address he could not even contemplate abandoning.

'It's not good news, sir,' the captain replied, in a tone which already conveyed the negativity of the message. 'As of now, I'm still trying to find him. He's not in Barton, and he's not in Bowland, but his car's in a picnic carpark at Kentford village, west of Norburgh. We don't know what he's up to, but he's behaving rather strangely.

'We've been getting reports in from our men at town barriers, and we're following the Range Rover with the tracker we fitted. What we do know is that yesterday he travelled with a woman, his wife by the description we have, to a farm near St Jude.

'On the outward journey, he seemed to be trying to wind up the civilian barrier guards at Stourmouth over entry restrictions. On the return journey, he quizzed our own barrier guards at Barton on the location of the ambulance station. We've made discreet enquiries at the station, and nothing's been stolen yet, but we'll keep it under observation.

'Now today, the Range Rover left the Barton promenade at 09.00 hours and was driven to the Barton marina. It stayed there for an hour before leaving Barton heading north. Our reports from the barriers all show that a woman was driving and that two men were in the back. It was carrying a small canoe on the roof rack.

'At Kentford, it parked up where it is now. The woman's sitting in the car reading a book, the canoe's no longer on the roof, and the two men have disappeared. I'm sorry I can't be more helpful, sir."

'Captain, you say the men have disappeared. I take it that that you're searching for them.'

'We are, sir, but we're doing it discreetly as we assume one of them is Mr Butler. We've had men up and down the River Kent all the way down to the River Avon, but there's no sign of them.'

'Somehow, captain, I can't see Mr Butler in a canoe. I picture him in a far bigger craft, something like the Sunseeker he has berthed at Barton marina. And anyway, he's too big to fit into a small canoe. That canoe is just a ruse. Perhaps he's trying to kid us that he's going to attempt some ridiculous stunt of boating downriver to Stourmouth with his friends. More likely though, he's just trying to throw us off his track.

'My guess is that he's heading for the city, and he probably knows that we've fitted up the Range Rover with a tracker. Whatever he's up to though, he doesn't want us to know about it. I wonder if he left some of his pile of cash behind, and he's out to recover it.

'We'll find out when we catch up with him, but for now, what we need to focus on, captain, is why Kentford? It's very close to the ring road, but is there something else? Have any reports come in from the ring road patrols of any unusual sightings, and what about the land between Kentford and the ring road? That's where you're most likely to find him, not on the river bank.'

'We had thought about that sir, but there are two problems. One is that, when they built the ring road past Kentford, they erected a long length of sound barrier fencing; the other is that, at the same time, they planted up the land between the road and the village with trees as amenity compensation. We can't see the village from the road because of the fence, and we can't do much discreet searching between the road and the village because it's now open-use woodland, complete with picnic parking areas. And the picnickers are out in force today.'

'Very well, captain, we may have to accept that we've lost track of him for the time being, but we can be near certain that he's going to come back to the Range Rover sometime today.

Our priorities remain the same. One, it is imperative that I have a meeting with him today; two, we keep him out of mischief as far as is possible; and three, we do nothing to alert him to our interest in him. He should not be arrested under any circumstances. And, if it's not too late, put his house at Glebe Pastures under observation. You may know of it, it's called the Old Hall.'

'I do believe I do, sir,' replied the captain thoughtfully.

Ray Ford sat at the counter of his water-sports store, sipping coffee and wondering who might come in next through the door. There was no telling anymore. Nothing was certain since the collapse. His youthful regulars had disappeared like swallows in autumn, and all to be seen on the horizon was ruin.

Then suddenly, out of the blue, a new flock of unlikely looking customers had descended at his door. And this lot had a surprising amount of money jangling in their pockets for citizens of a bankrupt country. His silenced tills had started ringing again or would have if they had been set up to register dollars, a situation he would just have to live with. There must have been more money under beds than in the banks.

And what a funny lot they were, he mused. You wouldn't have wanted to be at sea with any of these would-be mariners at the helm. Most probably thought they served drinks at the harbour bar. And as for the three odd balls that came in this morning, the mind simply boggles. First it was wetsuits they were after, six sets. Best not to think about it. Then as they were leaving, the little fellow spots the kayaks and the canoes, removes the seat from the smallest one-man canoe, and gets the big fellow to lie down on his back in it. 'This could be just the job,' he said, and then they were off with it fixed to the roof rack, the lady driving and the two of them in the back giggling like schoolboys. And a less likely set of villains could hardly be imagined. That plain-clothes detective, or whatever he was, didn't fool me. He was after them all right. But why should I have known why they wanted the canoe? None of my business, and that's what I told him, 'You don't ask questions if you want to survive in these hard times.'

Eric's first thought when he saw the two, black-clad menacing figures approaching was to hide in the stables. Not only were they both much bigger than him, but one was bawling at him in a threatening manner. On second thought, not the stables. These two would certainly frighten the horses; they might even want to steal them. He bolted for the barn and hid behind the bales. The big one knew his name, and it also knew someone called George. What now! It was tearing at its face. It's a hood! It's George! The rotten prankster, nearly gave me a heart attack.

'So you thought we were the creatures from the black lagoon coming to snatch the horses, did you, Eric? No, we were just passing through on our way into the city. This is my pal Bill. He's harmless, so long as you don't cross him. By the way, we 'd like to borrow your pickup truck for an hour or so. Would that be okay with you?

'And there's another thing. We'll leave these wetsuits here in the barn, and we've left a canoe in the culvert. Make sure little Billy doesn't make off with them, and tell him that if he's here when we get back, we may have a small job for him, good pay guaranteed.'

'And what's my reward, George?'

'Your reward, Eric, will be in heaven. We're on a rescue mission involving some children. But if anyone comes asking, you haven't seen us and you know nothing, and for that you can keep the canoe. Twice the carrying capacity of your old trolley and far more comfortable.'

The new residents of the Old Hall Estate were getting used to George's visits, but even so, his arrival in a battered old pickup and wearing clothes to match took them by surprise. Clearly, they were not the only ones going through hard times. Even the personalised number plate had gone.

There was no shortage of willing volunteers when George explained that he was looking for help in finding a friend's daughter and grandchildren in an area near the docks. They knew the street he was looking for, but they had to be prepared for a rough ride in getting there. Law and order had not returned to the dockland's streets, and the only security was in numbers. Three of them would travel in the lorry and two in the pickup with George and Bill. They would stick close together and leave George to do the talking.

The wisdom of travelling in a group was soon evident. Once clear of the suburban housing areas and into the densely populated city streets, the sense of peace and calm Bill and George had encountered on their now-familiar run between the Welford road and the Avenue gave way to open intimidation and harassment with scarcely disguised violent undertones. The exchange of friendly greetings and well-wishings at the barriers and barricades was replaced with muted hostility and sometimes worse.

Finding the street they were looking for was not difficult; finding the family was more of a problem. None of the surrounding streets could be described as salubrious, but this one was at the bottom end of the desirability scale. Growling dogs, fighting children, and belligerent adults had to be avoided or confronted as they worked their way along the street asking for information on the family's whereabouts. Even if the family had not left voluntary, they were better away from this place. They abandoned their door-to-door enquiries and began to tour the neighbouring streets looking buildings that might be serving as refuges.

They found the family in a church hall along with a dozen other families who had either feared of staying alone or had been pressurised to leave their homes. George would have liked to have taken the lot out of the city with him, but the most he could do was to promise them that things would get better and that his friends with the lorry would not forget their plight.

Sally could hardly believe her eyes. The wealthy Mr Butler from the best apartment in Carlton Towers, someone her father spoke of as a true gent and someone she had known from childhood as a generous provider of ice cream and other treats, was there in person asking if she would like to go and stay with her parents at Barton. She'd prayed often enough in the church, but she hadn't expected this.

Mr Butler was telling her quietly that one part of the journey was not very pleasant and the children might find it frightening. Who cared about that? Life here was frightening. They could handle a bit more.

With Sally and the two children in the backseats of the pickup and the two previous backseat passengers now standing on the back of the lorry, they returned to the Old Hall for a quick snack and look-around.

Sally could not make it out. What were these ordinary families doing in such posh houses, and how was it that they were on such good terms with Mr Butler who was obviously the real owner of the grandest of them all? She could hardly ask them, but they seemed nice people, so perhaps they deserved a bit of good luck.

And Mr Butler had still not told her how they were going to get out of the city, which everyone knew was sealed off. No one even mentioned it. Everybody, it seemed, had secrets, and everybody knew better than to pry.

But it worked, everyone was happy, and the children would have stayed there forever. Mr Butler was so kind to them, showing them how to drive a little tractor, given to him when he was only ten. His parents must have been very rich. Some people had it all.

What an odd journey it was after that. They went through lots of barricades, but instead of having to argue with the guards, they were allowed to pass with cheers and hand-clapping. All it took was for Mr Butler to wind his window down and wave.

And then, when they got to the place with horses, there was this funny little man who insisted on calling Mr Butler, George, and a strange little boy named, Billy, who was very good with the children. He had a game he told them. They would all dress up as spacemen, and he would pull them through a secret tunnel on a magic boat to another world. But it was important that they kept their eyes closed all the way, otherwise the magic would not work. The children loved the game and wanted more, but she was happy to do the trip once.

What a surprise it was when they all got to the other side. There was Mr Butler's wife, Frances, waiting for them with bottles of lemonade. Such a nice lady. She hugged both the children and Billy, who blushed like a beetroot when she gave him a kiss.

Then she led them through the woods to a really nice white car and sat with them on the backseat all the way to Barton. It was a bit tight for space for the four of them, but no one minded. And when they got to the apartment, my Mum and Dad nearly fainted with shock when they saw us standing there at the door. They didn't seem to be expecting us, but they were overjoyed anyway.

It had not been the best of days for Colonel Millar. The news coming in on Mr Butler's whereabouts and what he was up to varied by the hour. Somehow or other, he had managed to get into the city and managed to get hold of a vehicle to drive round in. Someone was travelling with him, and from the description, it was Mr Rigby.

Surely, the two of them were not up to their old tricks again, taking away without the owner's consent. Any more hints of criminality would be disastrous. But that's what it seemed they had in mind. Why would they have been heading for the docks with a lorry close behind if they were not intent on theft, and grand theft at that?

He had begun to worry about his instruction that Mr Butler should not be arrested under any circumstances. Wrongly interpreted, it might look as though he himself was part of some illicit plot or organisation.

And then the news that he was heading back towards the Old Hall with nothing more than a human cargo of a woman and two children. Relief at first, but soon followed by near panic. George must have a secret family, and now he was going to install them in the house he had shared for years with his wife. How was he going to break that news to the general? Fortunately, he had not arrived at an answer too quickly. The whole lot of them were travelling south towards Barton in the Range Rover, and the women and children in the back seemed to be in holiday mood, not at war.

Captain Jacobs deserved a good kicking for putting him through all this stress. He still didn't know how they'd slipped in and out of the city with apparent ease; he still didn't know who they had brought back with them; and he still didn't know what they'd done with the canoe.

When Frances and George returned to their apartment, they found a white envelope pushed under the door. The note inside was brief. 'Mr Millar requests Mr Butler to join him for a drink in the lounge of the Pines Hotel on his return from Norburgh.'

'Cryptic', said George, 'now what is he after?'

'He's after you, George, and I can guess why. He wants you back on active service in the city.'

'We'll see about that but not before I've had a good wash and shower. There were things in that tunnel you wouldn't want to talk about. I gave Eric and little Billy a good pay off, enough to cover their losses if it turns out that we've unintentionally exposed their secret money earner. They did us proud today. When times are better, I may even get a racehorse as an interest for us all. But whatever it is the colonel wants to talk about, he's not going to get long to do it. I have an ambulance to collect later this evening, and I'm not going to risk them shutting up shop before I get there.'

CHAPTER 21

Dinner with the Colonel

Colonel Millar had carefully selected his place in the hotel lounge. It took George some time to spot him, tucked into a seat in the furthermost corner well away from the bar and casually dressed. The colonel obviously had plans for a discreet meeting although his arrival in the town in a military helicopter had attracted more than a few interested glances. But the colonel saw that as a small price to pay for the certainty of catching George before he disappeared once more on some new adventure. He stood and waved across the lounge, concerned that George might overlook him and make a quick getaway.

'So nice to see you again, Mr Butler, and how kind of you to see me at such short notice. Did your trip to the city go well today?'

'Very well, thank you, colonel; we got just what we wanted.'

'I hear you went by boat.'

'Yes, the tide was with us.'

'Better than by ambulance, I imagine, and by the way, have you any plans yet for getting your party to Bowland?'

'Probably by ambulance, colonel, it's a tried and tested method.'

The banter could have continued for some time but mention of the ambulances reminded George that he had business to attend to that evening. He needed to get on with things.

'So what brings you to Barton this evening, colonel? Nothing serious, I hope.'

Such hope did not last for long. The colonel's explanation was not merely serious, it was positively alarming. He began by reminding George of their meeting four days earlier when they had talked about the breakdown of law and order in the city and by thanking him for so generously agreeing to lead a convoy of aid trucks in a bid to avert the possibility of the aid donors terminating their support. That operation, he assured George, had been a great success, and he could not be thanked enough for what he had done. It had resulted in a mass return to work by the police and emergency services across three quarters of the city's housing areas, and they were now in receipt of daily aid deliveries.

Unfortunately, efforts to extend the improved conditions into the inner-city areas were not working, and the situation there was becoming critical, a state of affairs which George had no doubt seen on his trip that day to the docklands.

It might be possible, the colonel suggested, to bring about gradual improvement, but time was rapidly running out. General Aspel had been summoned to attend a meeting in Geneva with the donors within the week, and unless he could assure them that their aid was reaching all parts of the city and that the return to law and order was complete, the indications were that the nation would be left to fend for itself, something presently still well beyond its capabilities. Regretfully, therefore, George's participation in one final push was requested.

George sank back in his chair, his head back, his eyes closed. They were right. They were all right, Frances, Bill, and the rest. There was more to come. Probably much more. Would he ever be able to retire to that peaceful valley?

He needed time to think. And he needed the thoughts of others. He slumped back to the table, arms crossed, resting on his elbows. 'Can you stay for dinner this evening, colonel? Just the two of us, plus Bill Rigby if

I can find him. We need to go through this very carefully, but right now, I have to dash off to see a man about a dog. I'll be back in less than an hour.'

The colonel was more than happy to extend his stay in the lounge. He had George on board; that was the main thing. As George left, he couldn't resist a parting shot, 'Make sure it's a good runner, Mr Butler. We don't want someone selling you a pup."

The cheek of it, thought George as he rose from his chair, he's brazenly following my every move, but he still has the nerve to beg for favours. 'Don't you worry, colonel, it's coming from one good home, and it's going to another down in Bowland.'

Once more, George found himself dashing around to get things organised. After a quick word with Frances to tell her that, once again, she had got it right and that it was unlikely that he would be leaving in the morning for Bowland, and after tracking down Bill to ask for his help in collecting the ambulance and in discussing with the colonel yet more ideas for saving the city, he set off with Bill for the Barton ambulance depot.

On the forecourt stood an old but well—polished ambulance obviously on display for the evening's business. Bill and George strolled round the ambulance with the air of men familiar with the routines of purchasing second-hand vehicles. Mr Gerrard and his two colleagues appeared from the garage to greet them.

As soon as they were in earshot, Bill, with obvious intent that they should be overheard, remarked loudly, 'It's not quite what we were expecting, but it might do.' George muttered an inaudible reply and strode briskly to shake hands with the would-be vendors.

'This is my transport manager, Mr Rigby, he declared introducing Bill with a flourish, He knows about vehicles.' The vendors paled, sensing disappointment, but relief soon returned as George drew from the Range Rover a sizeable hold-all and suggested they should all retire to the office to complete the deal.

The deal was done as George had agreed. He handed over the thirty thousand dollars for counting and received his receipt made out to the Valley Farm Community Group. In a matter of minutes, there were more handshakes; then with thanks from George for the two sets of uniforms left in the ambulance, Bill and George were back on the forecourt.

'You could have driven a harder bargain,' said Bill. 'I'll bet that they would have accepted twenty thousand, perhaps less. They were in no position to hold out for the best price.'

George smiled. 'Bill, there's a time for bargaining and a time for getting things done. This evening was a time for getting things done. And that's why we are off now for dinner with the colonel. There's more for us to do that we never bargained for and that we'll do whatever the price. Mind you, I am beginning to wonder whether our involvement in the army's affairs is entirely coincidental. I have a feeling that we are being watched all the time, but I can't figure out why. Do you feel that, Bill?'

'Feel it. I know it. Why else did they fit a tracker to the Range Rover. But it's still a mystery. Unless it's our cash they're after. They couldn't be planning to rob us, could they? Worse still, supposing we never come back from the colonel's latest task for us, killed in action and not even soldiers. What would that look like on our gravestones, always assuming they leave our widows with enough money to buy a pair?'

'Bill, at times, your imagination is far too vivid for your own good. Anyway, if we snuff it serving our country, what's the loss? We've both had a good innings. But I trust the colonel, so let's be going.'

The head waiter at The Pines restaurant was more than happy to seat George and his two guests at a much-sought-after secluded table in a small corner alcove even though that meant disappointment for the two lovebirds waiting hopefully in the bar. Frances and George were renowned for generous tipping and with their wealth; one day, if the hotel ever came on the market, they might even end up as owners.

The colonel was impressed. His position in the army counted for little when he dined out in civilian clothes. It was all so different than dining in the officer's mess. There, rank was everything; here, it was money.

The colonel had heard much about Bill from Captain Jacobs, but this was the first time he had met him face to face. He had been expecting another giant of a man and found it slightly incongruous that such a diminutive figure was effectively George's second in command. Together, he thought, they looked like David and Goliath acting as a team. The more the implications of this preyed on his mind, the more attentive he became to every word Bill uttered. If Bill was the brains of the team and George was the brawn, what might that lead to?

They ordered drinks, studied the menu, and talked about the weather. The starters came, the main courses came, but still, the small talk continued. It was not easy to discuss food for the starving whilst tucking into smoked salmon and lamb cutlets. But whether out of decorum or courtesy, it was left to George to raise the subject of a return to the city.

'Colonel, I've only had the briefest of discussions with Bill about whether we can help in 'one last push', as you put it to me earlier, to restore law and order in the city, but we are not unwilling to talk it over with you. We will, however, need a small favour from you if we do agree to go back in.

'Tomorrow, we were planning to move to our farm at Lostock all those in our party who want to go there. That's twenty people in total. Mr and Mrs Robinson and Mr and Mrs Pritchard have decided to stay here in Barton, at least for the time being. To get there, most of the party will be travelling in an ambulance purchased by the Valley Farm Community Group for charity work in Bowland. It will take two or three trips, and Bill here was going to do the driving. Now, if we are going to spend the next day or so preparing for and carrying out another mission in the city, can you provide army drivers for the ambulance? We do have, by the way, two sets of ambulance drivers uniforms just in case we are required to stop at any barriers or barricades along the way.'

'No problem', said the colonel, greatly relieved at the modesty of the requested favour, 'and we'll do it tomorrow. We don't want your ambulance parked up at Carlton Towers any longer than necessary; it's already attracting attention.'

After that, they got down to the hard work of deciding a plan of action for the colonel's proposed mission. The colonel had in mind a repeat of the previous mission involving a preparatory run through selected areas in the Range Rover followed a day later by a relief convoy led by the Range Rover.

Both Bill and George were adamant that would not work for the inner city areas. The level of fear and unrest they had encountered trying to travel through the areas was on a different scale to that encountered in the suburbs. Bill made the point that, if they got out of the Range Rover to try to address people, they would be more likely to be pelted with stones than heard in silence. George commented that they had received a better reception in a pickup truck and lorry than in their Range Rover.

They all eventually agreed that, somehow or other, the advances they had made in the suburbs needed to be utilised to inspire confidence in the inner city population.

All sorts of ideas were put on the table, putting soldiers into police uniforms to mingle with the crowds, trailing banners behind aeroplanes, arranging a rally of cars bearing national flags, and flooding the areas with relief trucks were just a few. But as they talked, bit by bit, some of the ideas started to develop into a plan.

They would stage a people's march. Volunteers from the suburbs would assemble at the national football stadium near the docks and would lead a huge convoy of relief trucks to the city's central square. George would head the convoy and address the crowds in the square. It seemed a good plan in principle, but what if it got no further than the first barricade and the leading marchers were brought to a halt?

More thought was needed, and so was more coffee. It was getting late, and the restaurant was emptying. George beckoned the head waiter to inform him that they would be staying at the table for another hour or so, that they would need a few jugs of coffee to keep them going, and that Mr Millar would need a room for the night. It was all arranged without a murmur.

'Colonel', said Bill when they were able to settle down to talking again, 'I've heard you military types talking about shock and awe tactics. That's what we need, something to startle the people into standing back, letting us pass, and then joining in to swell the march. We could do with a couple of elephants, an open-top bus with a jazz band, and George in front on a set of stilts. Add on the army band in full regalia led by the general riding a camel, and it would be perfect.'

George and the colonel were in full agreement with the concept but less than happy with the details. As George pointed out, the national zoo was in Bowland. But Bill's comic idea got them thinking. They did need something spectacular. The question was how to contrive something spectacular on the most modest of means and in next-to-no time. What they needed was a few more drinks, a brainstorming session, and an achievable plan.

Gradually, an ambitious drink-fuelled plan emerged covering two days of hectic activity. On day one, which was to be the next day,

Bill and George would tour the suburbs in the Range Rover seeking volunteers to leave the following morning by bus for the people's march. Additionally, on day one, Bill and George would visit the paddocks at Kentford to put certain proposals to Eric and little Billy and would also visit the Old Hall to seek the support of the dockworkers living there.

On day one, the army would arrange for assembly of a fleet of buses at the airport and would arrange for a fleet of twenty relief trucks to be loaded up and ready for the following morning. The army would also arrange for a public address system to be set up in the city's central square and would guard it overnight. Three of the army's stoutest and calmest ceremonial parade horses would be boxed up and taken to the airport with their keepers. Four army helicopters would be put on standby at the airport as would two hundred soldiers in plain clothes.

On day two, following assembly at the football stadium at 10.00 hours, the people's march would commence with fifty of the plain-clothes soldiers mingling with the civilian volunteers at the front end, fifty at the back end, and two by either side of each relief truck. The precise details on how the march would be led would be fixed when the turn-out of volunteers could be better assessed as would the deployment of the horses and the helicopters. Draft proposals for George's address at the central square would be prepared by the army's public relations department, and a film crew would be present in the square. The colonel hinted that, if things went well on the march and in the square, it might even be possible to resume television services to screen the events to the nation.

Finally, it was agreed that the participation of informal groups of musicians would be encouraged to lift the mood of the marchers and the bystanders. Bill and George had argued for the attendance of the army band, but the colonel explained that would require approvals from above, which he preferred not to seek. It was still too early in his opinion for the army to be seen to be playing any significant role in efforts to restore law and order or to be seen to have recognisable presence in the city.

As midnight approached, the tired trio called it a day.

CHAPTER 22

Back in the City

Bill and George still had a lot of explaining to do to their respective spouses before the night was out. But Carol and Frances took it all in their stride. They would happily organise the group's departure for Bowland, making sure no one was left behind and everything was fully packed. They were relieved to hear that soldiers would be driving the ambulance. If anything did go wrong, they would be in good hands.

There was no need for Bill and George to worry about them; their worries would be about Bill and George, back again in the city without them. They were beginning to wonder if there was more to these near-daily city trips than they had been told. There had better not be.

It was another bright morning when Bill and George set off in the Range Rover for their first port of call, the service area army base at Greenfields where they were to refuel and pick up two plain-clothes soldiers who would be travelling with them for the day as security guards. Captain Jacobs, it seemed, would be tied up for the day organising the colonel's list of things to do.

'I can't help thinking', said Bill, as they cruised along the motorway, 'that the army has far more control over what's going on in the city than the colonel cares to admit. For all we know, this red brigade lot could be an army unit in disguise. Supposing General Aspel and Colonel Millar have turned traitor and are now running the army under the control of some foreign power, the ordinary soldiers wouldn't know;

they just do as they are told. And what about us, who are we really working for?'

'Bill, you're a great one for conspiracy theories, but I'll tell you who we are working for; we are working for the people. You are quite right though; there is something fishy about the relationship between the army and the red brigade. But they cannot be one and the same. Our army is too small and too poorly equipped to be mounting, or even running, a relief effort. My guess is that they are doing what we are doing, the best that we can in the circumstances.

'Look at it this way, Bill, today and tomorrow, you and I will be prominently trying to achieve something worthwhile, not for ourselves but for others. And there will be those who think we are in it for our own gain. But they will be wrong. We just have to keep faith in the army. There is nothing else.'

'Sorry for mentioning it, George. I was just testing your resolve. And in all honesty, I'd trust Colonel Millar with my shirt.'

The journey plan for the day was that, on reaching the city, they would drive anticlockwise round the ring road to the Eastcote interchange north of the airport and then, taking an anti-clockwise route through the Eastcote suburbs, on to the Keston suburbs, the Kentford paddocks, the Welford Road, and Glebe Pastures suburbs, finishing at the Avenue and the Old Hall. With the soldiers in the back of the car, they had no difficulties getting onto and off the ring road, and they were soon at Eastcote. The change in ambience since their last visit a mere four days ago dumbfounded both Bill and George. The barricades were still there but were now manned by polite and helpful policemen. All-around shops and businesses seemed to be reopening, and instead of surly and bewildered crowds standing on street corners, people everywhere were getting on with life almost as though not much had happened.

Bill and George were instantly recognised and applauded for what they had done to help the area get back on its feet. When George explained the purpose of the present visit, the support was overwhelming. These people were going to turn out in force for tomorrow's march. And so it was at the other barricades they visited at Eastcote and Keston.

By the time they got onto the dual carriage towards Kentford, Bill was becoming quite agitated at the prospect that the number of buses laid on to take marchers to the stadium would be woefully inadequate, and George, less obviously, was becoming concerned that an oversupported march might become uncontrollable.

As soon as they reached the next officially manned barrier on the road, George asked to be put in touch with Captain Jacobs. It was an unsuccessful attempt at communication. All George wanted to say was that early indications were that they might have underestimated support for the march, and it would be wise to have additional standby resources. There was nothing for it but to drive back down to the airport to get the message conveyed from there. They didn't know whether to laugh or to cry.

Delayed by the best part of an hour, they eventually reached the Kentford paddocks in midafternoon. Eric had seen them coming from a mile away and was waiting for them in the stable yard.

'If you want the boat back, you can't have it; the deal was done.'

'Eric, it's your boat to keep, but don't rely on it for a permanent income. Times are changing.'

'Well, what do you want then?'

'I'd like you to turn up at the airport early in the morning and give me a lesson on how to ride a big black horse.'

'I charge you know. But if you fall off, it's none of my business. And what madness are you up to now?'

'I have in mind a life-changing career as a jockey. Will you be there?'

'Who would miss that? People would pay good money to see you on a horse.'

'I'll take that as a yes then. Now where is little Billy?'

Little Billy appeared like magic from behind a stable door. Never one to miss an opportunity, he knew that, if Mr Butler was on the premises, something might come his way.

'Billy', said George, standing well back from the lad to avoid any impression of towering menace, 'would you like to join me tomorrow in a parade through the city centre? Me and my friends have been thinking about who should be at the front end of the marchers, and the idea we've come up with is that it should be a group of young people. We would like you to drive a little tractor I own at the head of the group. What do you say? But let me first tell you that we'll be going through some rough areas, and it's not completely free of risk.'

Little Billy was not averse to taking risks. That's what jockeys did for a living, and a few bruises and broken bones came with the job. 'Yes, Mr Butler, but how will I get there?'

'Eric will take you in his pickup to the airport. You need to be there at nine. Make sure he gets up in time. When you get there, I will be waiting with the tractor to show you the controls. After that, a bus will take you to the football stadium, and after that, you'll be in the driving seat of the tractor.

'If anything goes wrong, I'll be right behind you, possibly on a big horse. But that won't frighten you, will it? You are going to be a star, I just know it.'

'What about our expenses?' chimed in Eric. 'We should get something for the day.'

'Eric, you'll be walking behind the horse, and if that isn't rewarding enough, I'll buy you a new paddle for your boat. Now before we go, let's have a look at Frances' horses, just to make sure that you're still feeding them or that you haven't sold them off as prime beefsteak.'

With the stable tour over, they took down the registration number of the pickup truck for airport security clearance, waved good-bye and headed for the Welford road and the adjacent suburbs spreading down to Glebe Pastures. Once again, Bill and George could only marvel at the improved feel of the area. Many of the barricades had been removed, and those that remained were manned by uniformed guards.

Like Eastcote and Keston, people were going about everyday business and without fear and suspicion of everyone not immediately known to them. The white Range Rover was welcomed at every stop and much as George was delighted to be among friends, the degree of adulation with which he was greeted was something of an embarrassment. But it all helped to ensure that the news of a people's march the following day received a rapturous reception.

Confident in the knowledge that they would not be short of support on the day, they headed for The Avenue and the Old Hall. The frequency of Bill and George's returns to their old homestead was beginning to unnerve the dockers and their families. This was the second visitation in successive days, and as they unlocked the estate gates for the Range Rover, they wondered what was in store for them this time.

The last thing they expected was a request that they should all take part in a march the following day with their teenage children, all twelve of them, playing a lead role. The added request that they should load George's tractor on to the lorry and take it to the airport early in the morning added more mystery to mystery. But when George explained what it was all about and why they, as inner—city folk, were the people best suited to restoring the confidence of their erstwhile friends and neighbours in the docklands, they could hardly wait to get started.

'Would it be possible', they asked, 'for them to travel in the march as a group on the back of the lorry, waving national flags if they could lay their hands on some?'

George had not thought of that, but why not? It would add a bit of variety. 'No problem', replied George 'except that you might have to share the lorry with a jazz band. We're encouraging everyone who can play a musical instrument to join the parade.'

With the day's work done, or nearly done since they still had to report back to the colonel, they made their way back to the ring road and to the service area hotel where they would stay for the night. The colonel and Captain Jacobs were waiting for them, anxious as to whether they would be bringing good news or bad news. It was a bit of both; good, that the march would probably be well supported; bad, that there was no way of telling how well it would be supported.

A very worried look crossed the colonel's face as the realisation of potential disaster came home to him. They had made no plans for big numbers. If thousands instead of a few hundred turned out, they would need first aid, refreshment, and toilet facilities at intervals along the way. They would need a heavy presence of marshalls and security personnel, and they would need miles of barrier rails. And even if all these could be arranged at such a late stage, the very fact that they had been laid on would destroy the informal and spontaneous image the march was intended to convey.

'It's too late now to worry about everything,' said Bill, after they had passed their worries around for the best part of an hour. 'What we need to do is focus on the pressure points, the first being if the marchers get stopped and crushes occur, the second being if more people try to get into the central square than it can hold.'

Captain Jacobs brightened up. 'We can manage that. I'll post tough men, incognito of course, near to each barricade to make sure that the marchers can keep moving, and I'll post more men around all the entrances to the square to close it off if it looks like overflowing.'

'Good man', said the colonel, 'and I think we can risk doing a bit more at the square without blowing our cover. I know its late captain, but I want you to get as many temporary facilities into the square as you can muster; I doubt that anyone will question how and why they came to be there. It's more likely that the marchers will take their presence for granted.'

CHAPTER 23

The People's March

Bill and George were ready for more than one drink by the time they were released from their deliberations with the colonel and were able to book a table for dinner to try to relax. It had been an exciting day, almost exhilarating at times, but tomorrow could be something else. It might be triumph, it might be disaster, but whatever it was going to be, it did not bode well for a good night's sleep. They were not going to get one anyway, but they did not know it at the time.

They might just as well have tried sleeping through a heavy metal rock concert. Throughout the night, the service area resounded to the sounds of men and vehicles coming and going, loading and unloading, and repetitive flashes from turning headlights pierced the thin curtains of the hotel's single-storey bedrooms. Dawn, when it came, was a blessing. At last they, and all the hotel's other occupants stealthily drawing back the curtains, could see what was going on. The car park had become a marshalling yard.

It was an impressive sight and an even more impressive display of effort. Every available unit of mobile facilities apparatus in the country must have been commandeered and transported. Whatever shortages might befall the marchers in the city's central square, it would not be shortages of refreshment stalls and toilets.

As Bill and George surveyed the scene all thoughts of self-pity for their broken sleep soon gave way to recognition that to achieve all this a great many people, the captain and the colonel included, cannot have had any sleep at all. What a dreadful let-down it would be for them if they did not get a good turnout.

The level of activity they encountered on the road from the ring-road interchange down to the airport was a good sign that they would not be let down. Groups of people, many with children, were already on the move, and it was not yet nine o'clock. Could they possibly be thinking of walking all the way to the stadium and then taking part in the march to the city centre? It looked as though they could. George slowed the car to a modest pace while Bill, leaning out of the passenger window, shouted to each group that there would be buses at the airport. They got a lot of friendly waves in return. A carnival atmosphere was not far away.

On arrival at the airport, more evidence of the organisational effort that had been made was everywhere. Signs directing marchers to the car parks and the buses had been erected. Red brigade personnel were handing out flags and banners, bottles of water and direction sheets. Convoys of loaded trucks were lined up ready to move. Fleets of emergency service vehicles had been assembled. Thankfully, it was not going to be wasted effort. The stream of arrivals, mostly on foot, coming through the gates, would see to that. Bill set off to look for the dockers and the lorry; George set off to look for Eric and little Billy.

All were found without much difficulty, and it was no time at all before little Billy was confidently driving the tractor. That was easy enough, thought, George but what about me and the horse? He set off with Eric to examine the contents of a large horsebox clearly visible above the cars on the far side of the car park. The two attendants were expecting him and readily led from the box his intended mount. It was a huge horse, one of three, all black as ebony and as proud as emperors. Even Eric was impressed. 'You're going to need a ladder to get on this one', he chortled, 'and it's a long way down if you fall off. You might need a parachute.'

'Thanks, Eric', retorted George, 'but don't forget that I'm a dab hand with animals, and this one, like the rest, will know who's the boss. Just show me how to work the controls.' George patted the horse on its neck in preparation for mounting and received a hard stare, not unlike that of the colonel's. Any argument as to who was the boss was settled, and George knew that it was not him. After that, they got on very well together.

The riders for the other horses arrived, and they went through some simple training exercises. George's horse moved on cue with its two fellow horses; it stopped when they stopped, and all George had to do was to sit tight and look as though it was something he had been doing all his life. He did it very well. He was still doing it well when Captain Jacobs appeared.

'I can see that you're an accomplished cavalryman, Mr Butler, and that you need no introductions to your co-riders. Now, here's the plan. The three of you will be ride line abreast behind the children following the tractor. Should there be any sign of trouble, you all stop instantly. The trouble will be dealt with by soldiers in civilian attire who will be close by at all times.

'When you get to the square, dismount at the steps to the city hall, and your horse will be led away. If at any time you feel uncomfortable during the march, stay put on the horse, tug on the reins, and your coriders will help you off. Now, if you are happy with that, we'll box up the horses, get them down to the stadium, and meet you there in half an hour.'

George was happy.

The road to the stadium was already filling up with chattering groups of walkers, some carrying placards, others carrying flags and banners. It was a slow drive, but there was still one hour to the intended start time of twelve noon, and there was no need to panic about late arrival. But both Bill and George were beginning to panic about crowd control at the stadium. They hadn't put much thought into that, and as it became increasingly obvious that thousands rather than hundreds were going to turn up, it occurred to them that, in their enthusiasm to drum up support for the march, they had failed to consider the management of it. It could be chaos when they reached the stadium.

But it was not. Half a mile from the stadium, they were under control of the red brigade acting as stewards, and inside the stadium, the red brigade was already forming the assembly into marching groups. A rough estimate suggested two or three thousand already there, but more were arriving by the minute, and by the time they were all on the move, it was likely to be double that number.

Controlling it all was the casually dressed Captain Jacobs, striding around, giving instructions, and directing how the various groups should be placed in the line. Little Billy, grinning from ear to ear, was at the front on the tractor, now sporting a pair of national flags on poles attached to the bonnet. Behind the tractor, the dockers' children, together with another fifty or so teenagers directed to join them, were in place, all equipped with national flags.

George and his co-horsemen would come next but would not join the line until it was ready to move. Behind the horses would come the white Range Rover, which, the captain declared, had become a signal of hope to the people of the city. Bill would be the driver. Eric, the emergency horseman, should one be required, would be his passenger.

The first of four jazz bands already entertaining the crowd would be next in line, followed by the dockers on the lorry. After that would come groups of about one hundred marchers interspersed with groups of wheelchair participants, jazz bands, and other musical groups, and then the unexpected but much-welcomed parade floats, which were turning up outside the stadium in good numbers. At the rear of the line would be the sizeable fleet of ambulances, which had arrived from across the city.

Exactly on twelve noon, to a blast of trumpets and cheers from the crowds, the march commenced. Captain Jacobs counted them out, group by group. Forty-six of them, about five thousand marchers in total, he calculated. If a similar number joined the march in progress, it was going to be tight. The capacity of the central square was ten thousand at the most.

The plan for getting all newcomers to join the march at the back would have to be implemented. It was essential that all those who had formed up in the stadium were able to get into the square. The ambulance drivers had already been instructed to drop back as the length of the column increased; now, they would need the help of the red brigade to police the behaviour of the newcomers.

Timing was also on the captain's mind. By his calculations, it was going to take over an hour to clear the stadium, and assuming two hours for the marchers to cover, at a modest pace, the five miles to the stadium, the front end would be entering the square at 14.00 hours and the back end at 15.00 hours. Newcomers could still be entering at 16.00 hours. Something clearly needed to be done to keep the early arrivals in the square occupied. It was time to call the colonel.

Few of the people living in the streets around the route of the march knew that it was going to take place. For the great majority, including the self-appointed guards at the barricades, it came as a great surprise to hear the advancing sound of jazz bands and then to see a vast column of flag-waving people led by a group of children proceeding towards the city centre. At first, the bystanders stood and stared, caught between awe and admiration, but as their numbers grew and the clapping began, more and more of the bystanders abandoned their inhibitions and joined the march. Whatever it was all about, it was fun, and fun had been in very short supply for the last few weeks.

So powerful was the march's impact that, even in the roughest of areas, the barricades were willingly removed to allow it unimpeded passage. By the time the march reached the central square, it had collected many more thousand followers than anyone had expected.

As the march had progressed the calls between Captain Jacobs and the colonel had become ever-more frequent, and both had been working flat out to avert the potential twin disasters of a crush in the square and disorder due to boredom in the square. To avert the crush, the captain had arranged the immediate mobilisation of all available manpower at the airport and deployment to the square and its surrounding streets so that they could safely be used to hold overflow crowds. The colonel, meanwhile, had extracted permission from General Aspel for George to make some promises to the assembled crowds, and this had been conveyed to George enabling him to inform the early arrivals that he had important news to tell them when they were all together. And to keep the crowds happy while they waited in the square, the colonel had an idea. The musicians should be allowed to stage a concert.

At four thirty in the afternoon, George got the message that it was time for him to make his speech. Seizing the opportunity as soon as it came, he drew the concert to a close and nervously ascended the full flight of steps fronting the burnt-out city hall. Microphone in hand, he looked down on the massed ranks of eagerly up-turned faces and immediately wished he was somewhere else. A golf course would be ideal. The seventh hole at Barton, looking down the pine-edged fairway to the sea, would be perfect. What was he doing here? How had it come about? What was he going to say?

He remembered that Captain Jacobs had handed him a script. Which pocket was it in? Had he lost it? Oh, forget it, something will come to mind.

'Marchers, musicians, fellow citizens, I think we now have a full house. Thank you, thank you all for your efforts in getting here today and for making our march not only a peaceful march, but also a joyous occasion. And thank you for waiting so patiently for everyone to arrive. We've been wonderfully entertained over the last two hours by an entirely spontaneous and unrehearsed concert given by some fabulous musicians. A round of applause please for the musicians.'

The thunderous roar from the crowd was close to deafening. Not a person for miles around could have failed to realise that something special was going on. George was warming to his task and momentary thoughts of telling a few jokes crossed his mind before the enormity of his task came back to him. He was in danger of forgetting why they were all here. Thank goodness he had some pre-prepared notes, or did have.

'Thank you, thank you, thank you all for that. Now what I invite you to do is to look around you, all around you. Now what do you see? You see one of the most represented assemblies of citizens ever to fill this historic square in its five-hundred-year history. You've come from all areas of the city, you've come from all walks of life, and you've come from all parts of our community.

'And, most importantly, you've come with a message. A message to all that we will not be defeated by the events of the past few weeks, and we will not be defeated by thoughts of more difficult times ahead. We will emerge from these times of hardships stronger than ever. And we have the will to get this city back on its feet and restore it to its rightful place as one of the best cities in the world in which to work and live.'

George paused, conscious that his oratory was beginning to run away with him. He needed to take a reality check. They hadn't come here to listen to him preach. Since when was he known for his sermons? They must have come for something else. Of course! How could he forget? They had come to help restore law and order. What good people they were.

'So let us show that we have that will. And let us start by restoring law and order across the city. We need a return to normality. We need to get people back to work. So tomorrow, do your best to do just that, and if you are in the police or emergency services, don't be shy of taking the lead. We all want to see you out and about on the streets. You are our rock and our future is in your hands. Be brave.'

George paused again. There was something else. Ah yes, the stick and the carrot bit. Best to go easy on the stick though, it could spoil the day. Concentrate on the carrot.

'And if these last few weeks, you have felt that we have been deserted and betrayed, put those thoughts behind you. We are not alone in our struggle. We have supporters who will see us through this crisis of national insolvency. You've seen them in the streets, you've seen them here today. I call them the red brigade, and I can tell you this, as long as we do our bit, the red brigade and whoever is behind them will do theirs. Already, with their financial help, power supplies have been restored, and I can tell you that, tomorrow at noon, television and landline telephone services will be restored.'

A mighty cheer went up from the crowd. 'Good old George," some were shouting, but George had more to say.

'And if you tune in to our national news programme at noon, guess what you are going to see. You are going to see yourselves on television. Wave to the cameras everyone.'

When the furious frenzy of waving had worn down, George, once again, thanked everyone for attending, wished them a pleasant journey home, and said how much he looked forward to meeting them all again in the future. Once again, the square rocked with cheers and extended handclapping.

Chapter 24

Back to Bowland

Bill took the steering wheel on the drive back to the service area. George slumped in the passenger seat trying to relax. With the two soldiers in the back, little could be said about the day's events, and for some miles, they travelled in uncomfortable silence. Bill broke the tension by commencing discussion on the unlikely possibility of the nation's rugby team achieving full international status, a subject with limited time-consuming potential until Bill let it be known that both he and George had, in their time, played for the national team. After that, the miles flew by.

On arrival at the service area hotel, Bill and George made straight for the bar to mull over the most extraordinary day of their lives. It had been eventful, exhilarating, and at times, exhausting, but had they achieved anything of lasting value? Supposing nothing had changed, and they had to do it all over again.

They had planned to stay at the hotel that night and to travel to the farm early in the morning, but now they were thinking of making a quick run for it in case the captain or the colonel turned up with plans for a repeat performance. Their fears abated when a waiter brought a letter for George.

It was from the colonel, thanking them for their stalwart efforts and apologising that he and Captain Jacobs would not be able to join them for dinner as they had hoped; they had been summoned to an important meeting with General Aspel. He wished them a pleasant journey to Bowland, and he wanted them to know that transportation of the Barton party had been achieved successfully and without incident. In the fullness of time, he hoped to visit them at the farm. The letter justified a few more drinks, after which all thoughts of driving on to Bowland were abandoned.

An early morning check revealed that all telephones were still out of action, so if they were to get to the farm in time for the promised television replay of the march at noon, there was no time to waste with long-winded good-byes. They were into the car and off straight after breakfast. By eleven they were at Stourmouth, arguing once more with the officious self-appointed border guards. It was no more a short hold-up, and without too much regard for speed limits, they reached the farm with a good quarter of an hour to spare.

Their reception on arrival was something to remember. The cheers rang up the valley long and loud as the farm yard filled with the full roll call of the newly formed community. 'All this', said Bill, 'and they haven't yet seen us on the television.'

They stood packed, all twenty-four of them, in the farmhouse's spacious living room awaiting with eager anticipation some flicker of life on the giant television screen that graced the end wall. A roar of approval went up as a fluttering national flag came into view accompanied by the familiar sounds of the national anthem. Around the room, the occasional sob of relief could be heard. Normality was returning.

A news report came on confirming just that. It started with scenes from around the city, the towns, and the countryside of people going to work, of children going to school, and of smiling policemen directing traffic. Both Bill and George had private doubts about how much of it was staged and how much was reality, but who were they to spoil the occasion? Even if it was propaganda, it was in a good cause.

Then came a special tribute to the character of the nation and there it was, little Billy on the tractor followed by a joyous procession being cheered with flag-waving crowds lining the route. And was that George astride a giant black horse? Surely not, he doesn't even ride. But it must be. There's the white Range Rover with Bill waving from the window. And there's George, yes that's George all right, standing on the city hall steps addressing the crowds. Who wrote that speech for him, and what on earth have Bill and George been up to these last few days? And why Bill and George?

If ever George had been embarrassed in all his life, it was now. He must have been on drugs or something. He could not have done that for love nor money if it had been rehearsed; it just came over him. No more of that, thank goodness. Once in a lifetime was enough.

And then he realised that the room had gone quiet, very quiet. They were all waiting for something, looking at him with amazement from all directions. Drinks all round, he declared, both arms in the air, bring out the bubbly. He wasn't going to make another speech. Ever.

When the excitement had died down, George suggested that they should all check their phones to see if any were working. It was a good way of getting them to disperse, and all George wanted was a quiet stroll up the valley with Frances. They walked slowly along the stony track towards the small wood at the edge of the moors with Frances doing most of the talking. Everyone, she said, was loving it there, the children in particular.

The transfer from the hotel to the farm had gone without a hitch. The drivers had been wonderful in helping them load and unload and had not minded that it took three trips to transport everyone. Not once had the ambulance been called to a halt at any of the barriers. It was now in the barn, but she had already let it be known in the village that it was for community use. A request had already been put for it to be used to tomorrow to take some of the less-mobile villagers to a public meeting in St Jude called by the organisers of the Freedom for Bowland movement.

'And how's that going,' asked George. 'Do you sense any local support for it?'

'Not really', replied Frances 'but there again, there's not much obvious resentment of it. These country people keep a lot to themselves, and they don't like to be thought of as sheep easily led this way or that. They've taken the collapse of the economy very well, but unless a new national government takes office soon, they might be swayed to set up one of their own. They are very confident in their own capabilities, and they haven't been through the terrors suffered in the city.

'The army quickly took control here and saved them from that. But things can change very quickly and perhaps they are. Things today, with the restoration of power supplies, telephones, and television, are already looking a lot better than they were a few days ago. And I have a feeling, George, that we have to thank you for much of that. What a performance that was in the city. And what a surprise. Not just you and Bill, but Eric and little Billy. How did you ever manage to rope those two in?'

'Frances, a man has to do what a man has to do, except that, in our case, even now, I'm not quite sure what we were doing. Some good I hope. And as for Eric and little Billy, they were fully compliant, after I had threatened them with eviction unless they took part.'

'You didn't, George.'

'Well, not exactly, but I would have done if they hadn't jumped at my offer of fame and fortune. We'll buy another horse or two for them to look after. That will be just reward for their efforts. But about this meeting in St Jude tomorrow, do you think we should go? Just to show solidarity.'

'Solidarity, George, solidarity with what? I haven't a clue where I stand. What about you?'

'Well, you know what I mean. Just to show solidarity with the villagers. And anyway, we might want to participate in the debate.'

'George, what are you up to now? Has Colonel Millar put you up to something?'

'Of course not. Colonel Millar does not rule my life. I'm up to nothing, absolutely nothing.'

'George, Colonel Millar has you well and truly hooked. But still, I think we should go to the meeting. All of us if you can arrange the transport.'

'I'll have a word with John about that. He's been here long enough to know what's available for hire. A bus would be best then we can take some of the villagers.'

John came up with the goods. A double-decker bus hired from Stourport Transport. They used the ambulance as well, and after house to house calls throughout the village, a complement of more than one hundred was raised. No one was going to miss a free day out. It took on all the appearances and character of a holiday trip to the seaside. More than a few had no intention of wasting the day listening to talk of independence, but who cared? It was a jolly get-together. Perhaps those nice people at the Valley Farm could be persuaded to do it more often.

The organisers of the meeting, which was being held under the grand title of 'The Future of Bowland, Let the People Have Their Say' had managed to hire for the day St Jude's theatre hall, a modest entertainment venue with seating for three hundred. All but a few seats were taken, much to the delight of the chairman who solemnly scanned the hall as though looking for troublemakers before anyone had spoken.

His delight would have been severely dented had he known that a third of the seats were occupied by the residents of one small village.

He began by introducing himself as Leader of BIP, the Bowland Independence Party, and by thanking them all for attending on such a fine day and at such short notice. He then went on to introduce the four speakers sitting with him on the platform. Mrs Barry, the deputy leader of BIP, who would be covering the history of Bowland and the ancestry of its people. Mr Morris, the treasurer of BIP, who would be covering the cultures and traditions of Bowland. Mr Paterson, the secretary of BIP, who would outline the commercial benefits of independence. And Mrs Reynolds, the legal adviser to BIP, who would explain how independence would be implemented.

The chairman concluded saying that he would be summing up, following which there would be an open question session and then a hand vote on the question 'Do you support independence for Bowland?'

'Not exactly a balanced platform,' George whispered to Frances. 'He's going to be disappointed and surprised if he doesn't get a hundred per cent vote in his favour.'

'He's not going to, is he?' whispered Frances in return. 'I can sense that there is at least one person here who is determined to spoil his day.'

'Good gracious,' replied George, with exaggerated swivelling of his head. 'I wonder who that could be.'

Mrs Barry took to the floor and explained that she intended to show them that the people of Bowland had a distinct identity, which was quite different from other parts of Borovia. There was, she said, incontrovertible anthropological and archaeological evidence that, historically, they had been different peoples. They had arrived from different directions and settled as two communities separated by the river. Only in comparatively recent times, no more than two centuries ago, had Bowland been incorporated into Borovia, and that was by military conquest. At no time had the people of Bowland been asked if they wished to be part of Borovia.

Mr Morris commenced his talk by saying that Bowland was, and always had been a rural community. Its people were people of the land and always would be. They had no natural affinity with urbanisation, and that was reflected in their lifestyles, and although they had long welcomed tourists and holidaymakers and would continue to do so, they were not driven by commercial desires. At heart they were village people, and the few towns they had in Bowland were either market towns or seaside resorts.

At one time, they had their own language, but sadly, usage had declined after their assimilation into Borovia. Fortunately, they had managed to retain their artistic traditions and their reputation for unique painting and pottery. But even that was threatened by the tide of cheap copy products flowing in from the rest of Borovia. The only hope of the people of Bowland if they wished to retain their cultures and traditions was to press for independence.

Mr Paterson rose to describe the commercial benefits of independence. The position, he said, was clear. Bowland was a self-sufficient community. It could feed itself, and it could pay its way in the world. It was iniquitous that the people of Bowland should be paying for the mistakes of the Borovian government and brought to ruin by the profligacy of its overcrowded capital city. Left to itself, Bowland would be a financially viable nation. The longer they remained attached to Borovia and its mountain of debt, the more difficult it would become to break free. Now was the time for action.

Mrs Reynolds was brief and businesslike. They were not pushing for independence with their eyes closed. They had done their homework on the legalities of leaving the union. They were confident of gaining international recognition and confident of retaining the benefits of international treaties. They would honour and maintain the employment contracts of all health service workers, police, and emergency service personnel. They had plans in place for early democratic elections.

The chairman stood and thanked the speakers. They had, he declared, made an irrefutable case for independence and for pursuing that case without delay. There was, he said, time for a few questions before he took a vote, but he hoped that the excellent speeches they had already heard would be enough for all to give independence a ringing and unequivocal endorsement.

A few hands were nervously raised. What about pensions? What about passports? What would be the national currency? All were easily batted away by Mrs Reynolds. The chairman raised his arm and pointed to the giant of a man who was already on his feet, 'Last question please, I'm afraid time is running out.'

'Mr Chairman, thank you for that, and a thank you to your four speakers for their well-delivered presentations. It has been more than worthwhile coming here today to hear what they had to say. Now, I do have a question, and I ask it as person who has business interests here in Bowland, as a person who owns farmland in Bowland, and as a person who has a home in Bowland. My question which is somewhat rhetorical, and is a question to which I am not expecting an answer from the platform since it is addressed to everyone here around me, is this. Is it right to take a vote at this public meeting when only one set of arguments has been heard? Would it be right if such a vote was to be taken as representing the considered views of the people?'

The chairman, stony faced and evidently very unhappy, shuffled in his chair and attempted to intervene. But George was not for stopping. 'I could, Mr Chairman, argue that independence was not in the best interests of the people of Bowland. I could make the point that access into Bowland is very restricted, and without the viaduct at the estuary crossing, it would be all but inaccessible. I could make the point that Bowland has no higher education facilities of its own. I could make the point that the Borovian army is one of the biggest employers in Bowland. I could make many more similar points, but I am not seeking to argue a case for or against independence. All I am suggesting is that there should not be a vote today. And all I am proposing is that, if there is a vote, then everyone should abstain. Thank you, Mr Chairman.'

The chairman scowled. 'I've said there would be a vote, and there will be a vote. All in favour of independence raise your hands.' Only twenty or so obliged. The chairman pushed back his chair and, without a word or a call for the vote against independence, stamped out of the hall.

Back in the bus, Frances turned to George. 'You've done it again, haven't you George?'

'Done what?'

'You know perfectly well what. You and Colonel Millar. And by the way, did you spot the plain-clothes army people in the hall? The officer who supervised the ambulance moves from Barton was there, and I think he was recording it all. But perhaps he was just there to make sure you came to no harm. The army's trying to look after you for some reason or another, George, but I can't think why. You seem determined to make life difficult for them. Anyway, I hope they look after us all now that you've angered the independence people. Let's hope they post some guards at the end of the lane.'

Frances was on the mark once again. For the next two weeks, there was always an army jeep somewhere in the village. The independence people, if they were bent on revenge, kept their distance. And down on the farm, the recently arrived city dwellers were beginning to settle into the ways of country life.

All of the children would have been happy to stay there forever, roaming the lanes, climbing trees, and gathering bluebells. Not all of the adults were quite so content. John and Mary were delighted with it; Robert and Janet Harvey found it most relaxing as did Amanda and Mark Brooks, but for the remainder the needs of getting back to the businesses they had left behind and of progressing the education of their children, were never far from their minds. And then there was the problem of boredom. How long could they sit around doing next to nothing?

For Frances and George, life at the farm was never going to be boring and certainly not when they had around them a group of friends to play host to. Circumstances required their dinner menus to be less varied than they would have wished, but there was no shortage of good local produce. Frances had taken up painting, and George had joined the golf club at St Jude and was adding yet more friends to his collection. The Sunseeker, ferried over from Barton and now berthed at St Jude, was in near daily use for pleasure trips, fishing, and occasional hire to trusted acquaintances for purposes best left unexplained. It was not exactly paying for itself, but for once, it was worth every cent of its eye-watering purchase price.

But as the days passed and the good news that life in the city was returning to something like normal, even if the people were still relying on food aid. A cloud of worry began to gather over all the adults at the farm. How and when could they return to their city homes? The fears which had driven them away were evaporating leaving the never expressed, less still discussed, question of 'What are we doing here?'.

It probably worried George more than most. For the Old Hall residents, he was the one who had persuaded them to allow their houses to be occupied by agreement; now, it was up to him to arrange their lawful return. He needed to build some houses for the dockers and to do it quickly.

He had the land, he had the plans, and he even had the planning permissions. But what he did not have was a functioning building company. And until travel restrictions in and out of the city were lifted, he never would have. The prospect of travelling daily to work by canoe had no appeal, and somehow or other, bulk materials had to be transported.

The colonel had given him a telephone number to ring in case of need. He was in need now, so he rang the colonel. He had an idea, he said, an idea of how to get the city back to work with some vigour. Remove the blockade of the city and Butler Developments would be hiring labour the following day.

The colonel was wholeheartedly in favour. He would discuss the matter immediately with General Aspel. 'And how are you getting on at your farm?' he asked. 'I had hoped to pay you a courtesy call, but as you probably know from the television news coverage, the army is gradually taking over distribution of food aid in the city, and we have all been kept very busy.'

'Life here', George replied, 'is as it should be. All play and no work. But even that cannot go on forever. And some of us down here are beginning to miss the buzz. Believe it or not, there are some here who want to go back home to the city.'

CHAPTER 25

Donor Relief

Once again, the men in sharp suits were arriving in Geneva. High on their agenda was the situation in Borovia. Mostly, they were high flying financiers representing some of the world's wealthiest businesses and investment funds, but some were men more used to wearing the uniforms of commanders in chief of national armies. Others were the anonymous and deliberately inconspicuous heads of national intelligence agencies. None were conviction-led philanthropists, but like it or not, philanthropy was the name of their game.

It was not the tiny nation of Borovia that had brought them all together in the first instance. Borovia's troubles had come to a head years later. The origins of their assembly lay in covert meetings of discussion groups set up to consider the potential consequences of a domino-style collapse of overborrowed nations. The financiers feared that such a collapse could threaten not only the sources of the vast wealth they were accumulating, but also their rights to ownership of it. Confiscation on a grand scale might well become a rallying cry, powerful enough to secure the support of desperate governments.

The generals feared that they could become the last-resort guardians of law and order of demoralised and distressed societies or even worse, that they could become the last-standing pillars of government of such societies. Pillars without any democratic mandate, pillars without any financial resources, and pillars without any experience in the art of government. The soldiers would be the fall guys left to pick up the pieces of the devastating consequences of national bankruptcy. That was not their role.

The intelligence agencies feared that national bankruptcies could threaten the very concept of western-style democracy. How many politicians could be trusted to put the long-term interests of their countries before their own short-term interests of winning votes? How many politicians would be prepared to tell the people that the good times were over if that meant losing votes? National destruction by democratic vote would not be intended. But could it be avoided if the majority of the people found more appeal in deeper debt than in facing reality?

The discussion groups never included politicians, and every effort was made to ensure that they knew as little about them as possible. And no politician was ever included in the organisations that were the fruit of the discussion groups. These were to be privately funded organisations, entirely free from political control or influence. These were to be organisations that emerge from the shadows only as a last resort and that are operated only on their own strict terms. Whatever else they would be, they would not be gullible aid donors adding more plasters to the self-inflicted wounds of reckless nations.

As more and more previously solvent nations slid deeper and deeper into debt, unable or unwilling to that accept they were no longer the world's productive hubs of prosperity, the fears of the discussion groups intensified. It was apparent that the sophisticated financial rescue packages put together by regional and world banks were no more than holding measures designed to postpone the inevitable day of reckoning. They might be painful measures to adopt, but like measures adopted to ward off the impact of the advance of old age, they were treatments for the condition not cures. For the malaise of debt addiction, there was no known cure that the patient would, or could, willingly adopt.

But what if, the discussion groups debated, the increasing number of overdebted patients knocking on the doors of the international financial relief clinics generated overdemand on the available services. Or what if weariness that the demand was never ending generated an enough approach to finding solutions to other people's problems such that the clinics effectively shut up shop? In either scenario, would it be the case that, sooner or later, one of the weaker patients with an advanced form of the ailment would simply be left to die? And if that happened, what then would be consequences, particularly if one collapse led to others?

The consequences, they concluded, could potentially be too serious to ignore. Left unchecked, the collapse of nations could eventually bring them all down. They might own half the wealth of nations, but what value would that be without nations? Something would have to be done, and they were the ones who would have to do it. Payback time would have arrived, and it would be best if they commenced preparations for its arrival.

The last thing they had in mind was simply handing over money to those who had led their nations to ruin. Nor would they hand their money over to governments too incompetent to use it productively. If they were to be involved in the salvation of failed states, it would be on their terms and under their management. In preparation for that, they developed a three-pronged plan involving identifying and monitoring nations heading for collapse, developing useful contacts with individuals within those nations, and setting up a relief organisation under the innocuous and untraceable title of Donor Relief Effort or DRE as it came to be known.

The small nation of Borovia rapidly came into view as a prime candidate for inevitable, if not imminent, collapse. Once a prosperous trading nation with a well-earned reputation for the manufacture of high quality goods and for the provision of world-rated financial services, it had lived for too long on its past glories, and it now found itself with a population it could not afford to feed; welfare, and pensions commitments it could not afford to pay; and businesses unable to compete on world markets.

To add to its woes, it had a long history, bordering on tradition and supported by an institutionalised raft of ever increasing complex tax allowances, that, for the wealthy, taxation should be optional. The net result was a nation whose people lived well, particularly at the upper end of the scale but whose government was permanently in debt. Borovia was a nation that lived in denial of reality and apparently enjoyed the experience.

But reality was catching up and doing so rapidly. Paying the interest on the accumulated debt was becoming unsustainable, and even to the most optimistic of lenders, it was becoming evident that Borovia could never repay its debts. A crash was coming, and this was going to be a crash that had all the makings of a crash where the institutionalised bystanders would remain as bystanders. No World Bank ambulances would be attending this scene to pick up the pieces. There had been too many warnings of impending disaster for aid or sympathy.

General Aspel had been flattered when first invited to attend a small gathering in Hong Kong on international security matters. He was not accustomed to such attention, and he was far from certain what contribution he could make to what was described in the invitation as a meeting on 'Strategic Vision'. Still, he had always wanted to visit Hong Kong, and he could never be accused of overdoing attendance at worldwide symposiums of dubious purpose. He struggled to remember the last occasion. So, but not without some trepidation, since the acronym DRE on the invitation meant nothing to him, he confirmed his intention to attend and that he looked forward to meeting the hosts.

He found it a curious meeting. It was far more informal than he had expected and no one in particular seemed to be in charge. There were no formal presentations, there were no formal introductions even. The agenda seemed to develop with the flow of discussions and so did the timetabling. Mostly, they talked about the state of the world's economy and international security matters, drifting from time-to-time to doomsday scenarios and the difficulties of small nations.

He had an uncomfortable feeling that, when the subject did turn to the problems of small nations, they were all waiting to see his reaction. It was always a guarded reaction. He still had not worked out what DRE stood for, and he could not face the embarrassment of asking. He flew home wondering what it had all been about.

At much the same time that the DRE started to take an interest in Borovia and the commander-in-chief of its army it was also starting the process of establishing secret bases around the world for the storage of emergency food supplies and the transportation equipment needed to distribute them. They were looking for disused airfields in remote locations and they found them in the faraway steppes of Central Asia, dilapidated and neglected. Once small cogs in the military might of the united states of the Soviet Republic, they now stood derelict and empty, surplus to the requirements of the new rulers of the steppes. And the new states were open for business.

It took some time to build the bases up to operational capacity. Buildings had to be constructed and fitted out with refrigerated storage bays, runways had to be repaired, staff had to be recruited and management systems installed. Then came the tasks of acquiring the aeroplanes, the trucks, the food supplies, and of training the personnel who would be charged with delivering the relief aid. The whole operation rivalled anything that national governments, acting alone or in concert, were prepared to undertake.

But as the paymasters of the DRE often reminded themselves, the money they were spending could, and perhaps should, have provided revenues for national governments. But what would they have done with it except squander it? They, in contrast, had a meritorious mission.

CHAPTER 26

The Borovian Experiment

Bit by bit, General Aspel was beginning to learn of the DRE's mission. He was invited to attend more and more discussion groups, and he did not have to be told that, bit by bit, he was effectively being drawn into an organisation with secretive aims. And as the organisation developed confidence that the general was supportive of the aims and confident that he understood why they must remain secretive, he became more and more involved with development of the mission. The fact that he was in good company, a fact that he only gradually came to realise, gave him great encouragement. At last, after a career in the backwoods, he was playing with the big boys and playing in a very big league.

Nevertheless, despite his new found self-assurance, a characteristic that concerned his wife, alarmed his governing politicians, and frightened his staff, General Aspel was shocked to learn that his own beloved nation of Borovia was high on the list, if not top of the list, of nations adjudged by the DRE to be heading for inevitable and imminent financial self-destruction. The news, when it was conveyed to him, was unexpected and alarming, but viewed in retrospect, he was most embarrassed that he had not seen it coming.

He had been sleepwalking and daydreaming at the same time. It was all too obvious now why he had been drawn into the fringes of the DRE network. And it was all too obvious now that the informal visit to Borovia by the most senior of the military commanders he had come to know was not a sightseeing trip as he had been led to believe. It was a visit to inspect the situation on the ground and to warn him that the DRE would provide aid only so long as it could be distributed peacefully and properly.

It was some time before the implications of the warning struck home to the general. Borovia was a peaceful country, always had been, and hopefully always would be, even in hard times. But what if financial collapse of the nation brought with it wholescale desperation and despair beyond anything in its previous history? How long then would it remain peaceful?

And one thing the general knew was that, if law and order was to be maintained in Borovia as it fell to pieces, his small, six-thousand-strong army was neither equipped nor manned to do it. Some very hard decisions would have to be made as to how it could be done, and he would have the task of making those decisions.

And so throughout the months leading up to Borovia's crash, the general was spending more and more of his time planning for the inevitable financial collapse with his trusted subordinate, Colonel Millar, and clearing his plans with the DRE. The finally agreed plan was drastic but nothing else was left on the table. The twin problems were how to put the army's limited resources to best use and how to ensure that all food aid supplies went to those most in need. Underlying everything were two inescapable but controlling factors, one that half of Borovia's population of eight million people was concentrated in its capital city, Norburgh, and the other that the army was based entirely in the countryside.

Recognition that the city relied entirely on food supplies brought in from the countryside or from overseas and that the countryside could more or less look after itself required that the DRE food aid should be directed to the city and distributed under the control of the civilian law enforcement agencies, the army would control food distribution in the countryside and ensure that the countryside was not overrun by food seekers from the city. That might mean temporary restrictions on freedom of movement between the city and the countryside, but that was unavoidable.

Had the general realised in the early days of planning that he had been placed at the sharp end of a very risky experiment in the provision of relief aid and that, if things went wrong, all the blame would fall on him, he would have doubted that he had the courage or the confidence to put in place the drastic measure of completely separating the city and the countryside. But when the realisation dawned, it was too late for change. Too late to try to use the army in restoring law and order in the city and too late for the army to devise a new plan to hold back any tidal wave of people flowing from the city into the countryside. It was too late for anything other than to sweat about the risks he had taken in fencing off the city.

When the long-anticipated crash in Borovia eventually came, it came with a ferocity that no one had foreseen, less still planned for. The button was pressed activating the DRE's city-based action plans, but within days, it was clear that implementation was at a standstill.

A top level emergency meeting was held in Geneva to consider whether to cancel the DRE's first actual experiment in relief aid and to withdraw immediately from Borovia or to accept the assurances received from General Aspel that, given more time, the aid distribution problems could be resolved. The vote on that occasion was to allow more time.

Then, four weeks later, the time came for a second meeting in Geneva but, this time, to take a long term view of the Borovia experiment. The latest reports from General Aspel were encouraging, and he would be present in person to report on the progress being made to restore law and order.

The chairman opened the meeting by reminding the twenty financiers gathered round the table of the background to the formation of the DRE, its aims, and the decision made at the highest level to embark on experimental intervention in the bankrupt country of Borovia. The chairman reminded them of the predicament they faced at their earlier meeting when it became apparent that the relief aid they were supplying was not being distributed. He reminded them of the decision they had taken at that time to continue the aid on an interim basis. The present meeting, he informed them, had been called to review the situation on the ground in Borovia and to decide whether or not it was in their best interest to offer long-term support to continue with the experiment notwithstanding that Borovia was a nation whose political and financial problems might take years to resolve. He then called in General Aspel to give his progress report.

The general was nervous but well prepared. The initial problems, he explained, arose from the highly visible collapse of government brought about by a wave of arson and looting, which in turn led to a near total breakdown of law and order across the city. One serious consequence of that was that relief food aid could not be safely distributed. It had taken some weeks to bring the situation under control, but all city-based police and emergency services were now operating satisfactorily. The aid was now being distributed safely throughout the city. He thanked the DRE for its assistance in bringing about the change, mentioning in particular facilitating the restoration of power supplies, television, and landline telephone services, and for undertaking payment of public service staff salaries, an act that was instrumental in getting people back to work.

The chairman murmured his approval and asked what more could be done to speed the return to normality. 'Two things', the general replied, 'removal of the blockade of the capital city, Norburgh, and restoration of mobile phone services.' Both, he explained, had served their purpose in controlling disorder, but they were now having unintended adverse effects on the community. They were hampering the return to work, and for some industries, they were preventing it all together. The chairman indicated that the requests would be considered.

'Now I would like you to stay a little longer,' said the chairman. 'We are about to move on to discussing who is to lead Borovia back to good health, and we would like to hear you view on who is the best candidate. You will recall that, originally, you provided us with a list of twenty names and that, with some changes, we cut that down to ten as a result of our own investigations into the financial affairs of the named individuals.

'Getting the right person is for us of the greatest importance. We need someone who commands the respect of the people. Someone they will follow. Someone not motivated by political ambition. And someone who will explain to the people of Borovia the awful mess they are in, how they got there, and how difficult and painful it is going to be to get out. If the DRE is to maintain its support of Borovia, the nation must have such a leader. Who would be your selection?'

'In my view', relied the general, 'there is only one person who fits the bill, and that is Mr George Butler. That may surprise you as Mr Butler was not on my list of twenty, and he is number ten on your list of ten. Would it be an impertinence to ask why you put him on your list?'

'Not at all. In conducting our own researches, he came to our attention as the highest payer of personal taxation in Borovia. The only wealthy person, it appears, who pays his dues in full. You may wish to know that most of the names we deleted from your list contrive not to pay any tax at all. But please continue.'

'Thank you. Had that information been known to us, he would, I think, have been on our original list. It goes some way to explaining why Mr Butler is so at ease with people of ordinary means. He shares the burdens of the state with them.

'But the reason he is my choice is the extraordinary influence he has had in restoring law and order in our capital city and the reception he has received from the people in doing so. With your permission, I would like to show you a video recording of the people's march he organised. When you kindly agreed to restoration of television services, this piece of film took pride of place. As you can see, he has become something of a folk hero and, in my opinion, rightly so.

'More recently, and you will see this also on the video, he has defused the emerging movement for independence in the rural province of Bowland. And, of course, apart from all that, he has national standing as president of the country's rugby federation and as chairman of the country's largest house-building company. And I can tell you, in respect of house-building, that we expect it to play a big part in aiding the recovery. Perhaps, in concluding, I should add that, so far as we can determine, Mr Butler is the only one of the ten people on the final list who has remained in Borovia throughout its recent troubles. The rest, sad to say, appear to have fled abroad.'

'Thank you, general, Mr Butler looks like an excellent choice. How did you come across him? Did you find him, or did he find you?'

'It was a chance encounter with one of my subordinates that brought us together. I don't know Mr Butler personally. We last met on a rugby field about thirty years ago.'

'Do you think he is aware of our interest in him? And more to the point, do you think he would take on the burdens of leadership?'

'I doubt that it has ever occurred to Mr Butler that he might be asked to lead the country, and we have gone out of our way to keep our interest out of sight. As to whether he would take on the leadership, my view is that, with persuasion, he would. Everything we have seen suggests that, in a crisis, he would put national interest before personal interest.'

The general was thanked and then asked to retire while the chairman discussed the matter with his colleagues. He was soon recalled. Yes, he should approach Mr Butler as soon as possible.

Chapter 27

Golf with the General

The response to George's suggestion to Colonel Millar that the blockade of the city should be lifted was not slow in coming. It came in the form of a personal letter from General Aspel delivered by an army courier whilst George and Bill were happily engaged on the village sports field teaching a group of local youngsters the finer arts of passing a rugby ball and taking goal kicks. George took the envelope, but the courier, a smart, young soldier on a motorbike stood by saying that the general had told him to ask Mr Butler if he was able to give an immediate reply. 'Don't open it', said Bill jokingly, 'it may be a summons.'

It was a summons, of a sort. It read:

Dear Mr Butler,

Regarding your recent discussions with Colonel Millar, I am pleased to inform you that your ideas have been well received. There are, however, a few details that still need to be resolved. Would it be possible for us to meet tomorrow at the St Jude Golf Club? I have provisionally booked a ten-o'clock tee time.

Yours Sincerely, General Aspel

'It's worse than I thought,' said Bill. 'They're not even giving you time to prepare your defence. Still, I'd like to be there at the death. Can I come and caddy for you?'

'Not likely', replied George, giving the courier an affirmative yes for the general, 'this is a one to one encounter.'

Frances read a lot more into the general's letter than either Bill or George. 'If you think, George, that this is just about chatting over a few details, you've got a shock coming. Generals don't do details. No, they're lining you up for something big here, George. What this letter says to me is 'We need more help from you but we cannot have anything on record about it.'

'I hope you enjoy your game tomorrow because I have a feeling that it may be some time before you can fit in another one. Still, a man has to do what a man has to do, as you keep telling me. So stop worrying. Have no fear, we'll all be behind you, whatever it is you have to do. Anyway, what is it that you are worrying about?'

'It's my handicap,' replied George. 'I'm still on scratch, and I have only played twice in the last month. If the general's on twenty-eight, I'm in for a good hiding.'

'Oh dear', said Frances, 'how sad.'

George arrived early at the course for his game with the general. Being a new member of the club, he did not recognise many faces, which was something of a relief since he was keener to get to the driving range than to spend time discussing the state of the nation in the bar. His driving was not up to scratch.

The chap next to him was hitting the ball further with a three wood. Thankfully, he didn't stay for long, allowing George to step up his concentration levels. When a reasonable degree of confidence in his hitting was achieved, George headed for the practice putting green. Yet again, he struggled to find his usual skills, not like that chap again who was now single putting everything.

'Sorry', said George as a particularly bad putt overran his target and crossed the chap's line, 'I'm having a bad day. You seem to be doing better. My name's George Butler by the way; I am a new member here. I don't believe we've met.'

George's self-introduction was greeted with a smile and a firm handshake. 'Mr Butler, I'm so pleased you could make it. I'm Tim Aspel. I should have recognised you, but it's many years since our paths last crossed. You won't remember it, but there I was, just about to score a winning try for the army against our old adversary, the university team, when I was flattened by a flying tackle. I remember it well. In fact, I think I may still have the bruises to prove it. It's a pleasure to meet you again after all this time.

'But of course, I have been hearing a lot about you from Colonel Millar. He's been keeping me fully informed of all the good work you've been doing in the city and down here in Bowland. The army cannot thank you enough and that is one of the reasons I wished to meet you. To thank you in person, not just from the army, but also from the nation. We all owe you a debt of gratitude, and I owe you an explanation of how you came to be drawn into all this. But shall we head for the first tee, we're due off very shortly.'

They collected their trolleys and strolled to the tee, quickly slipping into the standard routine for such occasions of discussing handicaps and how badly and how infrequently they were each playing. George was privately horrified to find that he had to give the general ten shots. He was going to have to pay for his misspent years of relentless practising. Oh, to be a twenty-eight handicapper on days like this.

But he soon found that things were not as bad as they first seemed. For a medium-sized man, the general could hit the ball a colossal distance but not always in the right direction. And to add to the general's woes, he had an unfortunate knack of landing in bunker after bunker, an occurrence repeated so often that George began to wonder if he was doing it on purpose.

For the first six holes, the pair engaged in little but small talk about the weather, their careers, and their families, as they advanced down the fairways. But on the seventh tee, all square and waiting for the players in front to clear, the general started a move towards the real business of the day 'So what led you to buy the farm at Lostock, George?'

'It was about three years ago', said George, 'when a group of us decided that it was time to purchase a bolt-hole in the countryside. For years, we had been talking about the inability of our politicians to cure the government's addiction to debt and the consequences we might suffer when the day of reckoning came. We all knew that, as a nation, we were living well beyond our means and that political talk of borrowing for the future was no more than a ruse to avoid facing the facts. We seemed to be caught like passengers on a runaway train where the drivers instead of applying the brakes were shovelling more coal into the engine. When we bought the farm, we were simply getting ready to jump off the train.'

The General smiled. 'It's no coincidence', he said, 'that your story matches mine. About three years ago, you were not alone in starting to plan for the future. That's about the time that I became involved with a group debating the international implications of national bankruptcies. The probability that they would occur was becoming obvious. There were serious concerns of a domino effect if nations started to fall one after another.

Out of those debates came an organisation called DRE; you know it as the red brigade. The initials stand for Donor Relief Effort. The best way I can describe it is that it is a non-political organisation financed from the offshore wealth of billionaires and mega-international companies.

You can make your own judgment as to whether it's a charity or a form of sophisticated insurance. I think it all depends on whether you see it from the receivers' end or the givers' end. But anyway, what this organisation wanted to do, and still wants to do, is to provide life support for financially stricken nations that have no other avenues of support.'

They played on towards the seventh green, their discussion halted by George's progress up one side of the fairway and the general's progress through the bunkers on the other side.

'I was saying', said the general as he eyed up and sank a thirty-foot putt, 'that, about three years ago, I got drawn into this DRE organisation, but what I did not know at the time that the country they were watching most closely was Borovia. That, I was to discover later on, was why they had roped me in. They needed the army's co-operation in making their plans work.'

George set himself up for his short four-foot putt and watched with dismay as the ball slid round the edge of the hole leaving him with a three-foot return putt. 'Oh, bad luck,' said the general. 'I'll give you that one. Still all square. Now where was I, yes, the Borovia plan. Now, I've an apology to make here, George. The Borovia plan was an experiment. An experiment that went wrong from the start and an experiment into which you and your friends were quite unintentionally drawn.

'The DRE, you see, had set themselves very strict operational rules. The first of which was that they would be, and always would be, non-combatants. They would provide aid, but they would not get involved in the maintenance of law and order. The second one, and the one which I think must have caused you a lot of headache, is that they would only give support to countries where the army avoided becoming openly involved in maintaining law and order.

'What they feared, and quite rightly I think, is that, if the army was seen on the streets trying to control disorder, that could easily slip into the use of firearms and a slide into civil war. And their third rule, which I think you can see coming, is that they would never support one side or the other in the event of civil war.'

They had reached the eighth tee and a difficult par three where the green perched precariously close to the cliff edge. The general was still in full flow.

'Those are the rules, and in the case of Borovia, they might, at first sight, have seemed easy enough to apply. For a start, it has a long history as a peaceful nation, and although half of its population lives in the capital city, it has never been seen as a problem that the army has no troops stationed in the city. Add to that the reality that Borovia's army is far too small to take on nationwide maintenance of law and order, it was never in anyone's mind that it might be expected to do so. When it became apparent that Borovia was going to collapse, and the promise of aid from the DRE was the only visible lifeline; it was not immediately obvious that the DE's terms would present any problem.

When maintenance of law and order in the capital collapsed, there was, as you can imagine, a major problem. What we have been doing since then is to conduct our operations under the DRE rules. It has not been a comfortable time for us, trying to hold the nation together but not being seen in the capital. But whatever else, we couldn't let the people in the capital starve.'

They both played safety-first iron shots from the tee to avoid the cliff edge, and both were on the green in two, Both holed out with two putts, but now the general was ahead by one on handicap. George needed a birdie on the long par five ninth hole if he was to get back on level terms at the halfway mark.

It was time to put some pressure on the general. 'So who then is in charge of the country at the present time? Is it the army or the DRE? And I still don't understand why you needed to impose the blockade of the city and why it is still in force?'

'I'll tell you when we have played our drives at the ninth', said the general, 'but you remember the old saying that he who pays the piper calls the tune? Well, the DRE are the only ones with the money to keep us afloat, and like it or not, we must dance to their tune.'

The general drove into yet another bunker; George hit a cracker down the middle of the fairway. The hole was as good as won, but it was still a long way to the green. The general resumed his explanation when he was back on the fairway.

'Things went wrong, George, even before the start of the relief operation. The original plan was that the DRE would provide food for the city under the control of the civilian authorities, and the remainder of the country would look after itself under control of the army. We planned for that and for an emergency blockade of the capital if that was necessary to keep the two apart.

'When the government lost control of the capital, the DRE were all for abandoning the entire relief experiment before a plane had landed. They were persuaded not to. I promised that half of the army's troops would operate in the capital ostensibly as part of the red-clad relief force.'

'That explains a lot', said George as he sank another winning putt to even the score again, 'but where are we now? Is the DRE still pulling most of the strings?'

'Yes they are, but thanks to the efforts of yourself and Mr Rigby in the capital, they are beginning to release their grip a little. You'll be pleased to know, George, that removal of the blockade is now only a telephone call away, and restoration of mobile phone services will not be far behind.'

'Will those be your decisions, Tim, or the DRE's?'

'I make recommendations, but although the DRE never had any intention of getting involved with the running of the country, they are now in the thick of it. They hold the purse strings, and it's their money that is being spent on running essential services. They can turn off the power supplies and the taps as and when they see fit.'

'That's not a good situation for us to be in for long. So how did the power, telephone, and television shutdowns come about then? We all thought they were part of some master plan to keep everyone in the dark.'

'To some extent, they were, George, but not entirely. They were never pre-planned, but once in force, we could see some security benefits in keeping them in place as control measures. In the first place though, neither the DRE nor the army ordered the shutdowns. You might say that they were switched off by suppliers unwilling to provide services for nothing. The DRE has worked hard behind the scenes giving reassurances on payments to get them restored.'

By now, they had reached the fourteenth tee, and George's mind was reeling. His thoughts that things were getting better were starting to dissolve. Far from the nation being off its life support machine, it was still firmly hooked on to it.

He hit a very bad drive into the trees. The general took his opportunity to go on and win the hole, which he did. He was two up with four to play. And he was still biding his time in getting to the point of the friendly encounter he had arranged. George sensed that there was more to come from the general. They were not just playing golf, they were playing a waiting game.

Finding themselves held up again at the fifteenth tee, the pair sat for a while on a well-placed bench looking out to sea. 'How do you see this all ending?' George asked. 'We can't go on forever living off the DRE. That would be worse than living in debt. Is there any plan to get us out of all this mess?'

'There's a lot to be done,' replied the general after a thoughtful silence. 'It's going to take a bagful of plans; getting people back to work, installing a new government, dealing with our accumulated debt, and probably most difficult of all, shaping a whole new vision of where this country stands in this modern and rapidly changing world.

'We have to shed all talk of punching above our weight and face the fact that it's a tough world out there with billions striving for a standard of living no better than we had fifty years ago. It's all so different from the world we grew up in. We were amongst the top dogs then, making everything the world needed and raking in the proceeds. How things have changed.

'They're after our jobs now, George, and they're after our food. And who can say that they are not entitled to either? We've had our turn in the sun, but will our people want to hear that?'

'It's your honour', said George noticing that the fairway had cleared, 'but just tell me this before you aim for that bunker up there, what do you think will happen if we just get another vote-seeking bunch of politicians promising the earth? Where would we go from there?'

'Who knows', replied the general taking his shot, 'but we're not there yet; we're here, and that's all we can deal with. And right now, I have to deal with that bunker you so kindly drew my attention to. I might just have missed it otherwise. But on the other hand, I might have been in those big clumps of gorse up there; they look really wicked. You did me a good turn there, George. Oh bad luck, but you should be able to find the ball.' It was another shared hole.

On the sixteenth hole, their conversation dropped down to the more mundane matter of George's plans to resume housebuilding as soon as possible. The general declared that it was just what the nation needed, a return to work through a mass housebuilding programme. That would get the full support of the DRE, and for George's site at Kentford, with its two thousand potential plots, they might even assist with development funding. The brightening tone of the discussion brightened up George's game, and he won the hole leaving him one down with two to play.

The seventeenth hole was another long par five, and with tiring legs, they eased their way along the fairway avoiding the rough and the bunkers by playing a series of safety shots. They had plenty of time for conversation, and they still had plenty to talk about.

They talked about debt; would it be better to default or to attempt to pay off as much as they could by taking a hard line with people who had avoided payment of taxes or with people who had abandoned the nation in its hour of need? The total value of their abandoned houses would be worth billions.

They talked about a new style of government, which would be precluded by law from borrowing to fund its routine expenditure. And they talked about inspiring the people to take responsibility for themselves and their families and leaving behind the belief and expectation that the government should provide everything they needed and wanted.

George was quite exhausted by it all, particularly as he had been doing most of the talking. Still, the hole was shared, leaving George one down with one to play.

As they stood on the eighteenth tee, again waiting for the fairway to clear, the general again thanked George in the warmest of terms for his inspirational work in the city, for his valuable contribution in promoting unity of the nation rather than breakup, and for putting forward ideas that could serve as a blueprint for the nation's future. George almost blushed with embarrassment. It was beginning to sound as if the general thought he had saved the nation single-handed. They took their shots and strode together down the fairway, rejuvenated as the final green came into sight.

'George, have you ever asked yourself why the army has been keeping a close watch on you these last few weeks? You must have noticed.'

'We did indeed. We discovered the car tracker within days of you fitting it, and there were many other signs. We thought that you suspected us of being involved in some criminal activities or that whatever it was we were doing might interfere with your operations.'

'Well yes, it was both of those at times, particularly when you turned up at Greenfields in stolen ambulances and later when you were seen driving round the docks' areas in a battered old pickup truck. But all that was secondary to our real interest in you.

'Some time ago, a list of names was put together on the instructions of the DRE with the aim of identifying someone they could work with in holding the nation together until a new way forward for Borovia was found. They were looking for a civilian because, as you will already have gathered, they will not provide relief aid to any nation where there is even a hint of a military takeover. Would it surprise you, George, to know that your name was on that list?'

George gave no immediate reply. He moved forward and took his shot onto the green. He watched it land then turned to the general, 'I'm no politician, Tim, never was, never will be.'

'The DRE don't want a politician, George, they didn't even want politicians on the list. They want someone who commands the respect of the nation, someone the people will trust. Someone of stature who has shown himself to be a man of the people and someone who can lead the nation in its hour of need. And, if they are to maintain their relief aid to Borovia, they want someone who will take on the task of appearing very shortly on television to give an address to the nation that will ring in its ears for years to come. They have asked me to inform you, George, that they want you.'

George looked down at his ball, putter in hand. It seemed like eternity to the general as George stood fixed to the spot without making a move. Then came a few practice swings of the putter before George paused, took a backward step, and then, with head still down, muttered to the turf, 'Well, Tim, this is it. I either make this putt, or you win the match. But if you were to give me this putt, it would be a draw. A fair result I think for a hard-fought game. I could live with that. Now, what am I going to tell Frances when I get back to the farm?'

THE END

Edwards Brothers Malloy
Oxnard, CA USA
December 27, 2013